JACKPOT
A ROAD TRIP LITERARY FICTION NOVEL

ANITA RENAGHAN

This book is for Jennie and DD. You have been constant friends and voices in my ear for most of my life, and you are a big part of my jackpot.

1
SCAVENGERS

Tom watched her on stage. She was giving him breath and taking it in the same instant. Her sweet voice was baptizing his ears, her brown eyes hiding themselves in the words, her smile and her frown melting into one movement. She had looked directly at him seven times. She had stared at him, alone at his table. The first two times, Tom had thought that she was looking through him, into the story of her own song, into her mind. But by the third time she looked his way, he thought that he'd caught her wondering. Tom doubted he would ever be lucky enough to really catch her eye. He came and went from the bar each Tuesday, as that was when she was there playing her guitar. That was when he was at peace with the world. It was remarkable to Tom that someone could express the same feelings he had; feelings he wouldn't dare admit to having. And now it was 10:30 P.M. He knew that this would probably be her last song of the night, and that he would board his bus home soon after, never brave enough to break his silence.

The cheap bar was hideous, with its low hanging medieval style lamps and the squares of tile that were slowly peeling into nothing. The heavy wooden chairs and tables were a poor man's artwork, having been carved into by a thousand hands. Low, orange lighting finished the bar with a rancid, desperate glow that made Sarah squint as she looked at the plastic beer placard on her table.

Sarah sat in the hole in the wall pub across from an empty chair, a far cry from valet parking and pink champagne. She was North Shore Chicago. She was money. She had no idea how her boyfriend had heard of this bar or why he really wanted to bring her here. But here they had been, seated at a small round table lost in the smoke. Baker's Tap must have been the cheapest place that Sarah had ever seen. She gazed at the people, the regulars, all huddled in their little groups holding conferences on worthless topics. Some threw plastic darts at electronic game boards, some played a lottery game, and others played video golf. Sarah's family belonged to an exclusive North Shore country club, and she sneered, doubting that any of these patrons had ever seen a golf course, much less played on one.

Sarah had looked around the room, verbally judging each person until the argument. That was when Randy told her she was a shallow, opinionated bitch. He laughed when he said opinionated, and then further explained to Sarah that she never had an opinion of her own about anything he had ever asked her. He told her she had spent her entire existence degrading others to feel better about her own worthless life. That was when he had stormed from the bar, leaving Sarah alone in a neighborhood that she had never been to in front of a basket filled with balls of fried grease that made her want to vomit. It was at this moment she realized she might as well have been her mother; devoid and tipsy, a thin, beautiful picture, a pretty smile on a tiny body, but maybe nothing more.

There was a girl on stage playing her guitar well, singing even better, the crowd occasionally offering a spattering of cheer. Sarah had paid little attention to the songs until Randy had left. Then she had to pay attention, had to pay attention to herself. She was worried about her appearance and how it might have looked when Randy left. Sarah knew she had to save face. It never dawned on her she would never see another person in this bar again, or that none of these people had even noticed he had left. They didn't care where she was from or what her last name was or how much money she was worth. Sarah knew that the girl on stage was watching. She was seeing little dramas being played out all over the bar.

Sarah didn't want to touch the table for fear that it wasn't cleaned properly. She crossed her legs, her tiny mini skirt even a little baggy on her meager frame. She was the quintessential picture of who would not be in Baker's Tap on a Tuesday night, and all she had to do was turn her nose up at the crowd and keep her mouth shut to appease Randy. If she had, at this moment, she would be in the front seat of his Jaguar on her way home. Or in the back seat and on his way home.

Some voice told Sarah that Randy had brought her there to test her. He wanted to see her lighter sensibilities, how she reacted around common people. He wanted to see her out of her normal surroundings, away from her family and friends. He wanted to see if they could share a proper moment together or if she was just a product of her parents. Sarah had failed Randy's test miserably and had failed herself again.

Over and over, she dated catalog models. She liked how she felt on the arm of a handsome man. They all ended up walking away, though. It was her fault. It must have been. But maybe it was the food. All the fat and calories that had stuck to her bones over the years they were ruining her, causing men to run away. She tried to sort it out any other way, but Sarah knew she must not have been pretty enough or pleasing enough. She watched all the eyes that were pretending to watch the girl on stage, all the eyes that must have been noticing her, sitting there alone.

———

William sat at the bar watching Tony serve drinks and waited patiently for his second and last beer for the night. He had been coming to Baker's Tap for a few years now, and Tony's antics did not surprise him. The round, Italian bartender had been giving one of the lonely regular's free drinks for two hours. Tony could do that. He owned Baker's Tap. The funny thing about the middle-aged man was that he would give out the drinks and say that they were from some other regular to introduce strangers. Tony was an ear for the sad ones, a friend for the partying ones, and a match-maker in his own right. The girl at the end of the bar sipped her fresh beer and smiled at William. William smiled back before he realized Tony had told the girl that the beer was on him.

"I think she digs you, William," Tony said as he brought William's draft and took his cash from the bar.

"I'm not interested, Tony, and you know it."

"She's pretty, William." Tony flashed a smile as his eyebrows took a ride up and down his forehead.

"You get these people drunk until they'll talk to anybody. Now, how can you consider that romance?"

"Come on, Bill, it's human nature." When William didn't budge, Tony tried an insult. "At least they talk to somebody. You, you're always alone. How about it?" Tony gestured toward the pretty girl.

"You sweet talker, you," William answered with a smile, but something in his dreams, or maybe his nightmares, pushed William away from the beauty and the wanting. He turned his back on Tony and looked up at Vi. She was playing for a nearly attentive crowd tonight. William wondered where the girl got her inspiration to sit on a stool in front of people who didn't care and who wouldn't remember. She was the background noise that allowed the patrons to confess their sins to each other through beer-stained lips. But Vi stood out. She always had some bar song, something for people to sing along with. She would sit up there and look down at them, seemingly oblivious to whether anyone was watching.

William turned back to Tony who had made his match for the night. One of the other regulars was down at the end of the bar, chatting with Tony's victim of charity for the evening. She seemed to enjoy the company; anything to fill up the time on a lonely Tuesday night in the big city of Chicago. William allowed himself to notice her. She was pretty with long, wavy, reddish-brown hair, high cheekbones, eyes dark with mystery. He pulled the bottom of his gray and blue sweater down over his dark gray slacks, measuring himself against the young stud that was making his move on the girl. William dressed nicely for Baker's Tap on any night, but he always dressed nicely after a hard day's work because it made him feel human again. The girl's smile was like a gift, but he shrugged it off and took a drink of his beer. He didn't want her for her hair or her dimples, nor for her innocent laughter. William was a bachelor and wanted to stay single. Sitting alone at the bar and turning away from the girls who tickled his fancy was the only way he knew to do that.

———

Vi's brown eyes scanned the bar as she played through the chords of her last song for the night. It was the same old type of crowd, if thirty people justified that title for a hole in the wall bar lost on the northwest side of Chicago. At Baker's Tap, it was unfamiliar faces each Tuesday except the loyal few that came and drank, and ignored Vi just the same. Here, with the cheap beer and jukebox ambience, there was at least one typically loud drunk representative present, and the dart crowd was also present and accounted for. There were some couples in the bar but mostly single men looking for a night of romance and girls looking for "the one". Vi knew that there was only one person in the bar who was there to see her.

He sat in the back to her left and watched her tirelessly

every week. He looked to be about twenty-five, his black hair matted to his forehead, redefining the depth of his eyes that looked like glass from the stage. Tonight, he wore a flannel shirt with a T-shirt underneath. This fan of hers never cheered after her songs. He would just sit and smile at her and wait for the next one. Vi did not know who he was and didn't have time for him in her life as she was working toward a career in music. She wanted no baggage when she decided it was time to make the move to Nashville. Still, she looked at him, wondered who he was, and even found a little stir in her stomach at the prospect.

Vi thought about the chorus of her song as she sang it, the words bringing back memories when she cared to listen. It brought her a smile of nostalgia, and sometimes it brought tears. Tonight, it made her wonder about the friends who used to come see her play. They had all gotten married and disappeared from the nightlife. Vi thought about marriage, but only because it was only months before the new millennium and talk of the year 2000 and the Y2K computer bug and all the havoc it might reek made her anxious. Mostly because the changing of time to the new millennium made Vi realize that time was fleeting.

The guitar rang with the final chord until Vi hushed the strings with her palm and lifted off her stool. "Thank you." A few clapping hands followed her well-built frame off stage. Vi tucked her guitar in its case and made her way to the bar where Tony had placed a Diet Coke in a short glass. Vi stirred the soft drink as if it were mixed with whiskey and then removed the straw and sipped. She lit a cigarette from a pack she had set on the bar. Her stool swung around effortlessly, and Vi scanned the room from a different angle now.

She saw a few of the regulars at a corner table eating their late suppers. They waved, and Vi waved back. She saw the girl at the end of the bar, now swaying from Tony's generosity, another shot in front of her and her new suitor. At a table near the front door, Vi saw a girl sitting alone. She had come in with a well-dressed man two hours earlier. Vi had noticed the couple from the stage, their clothes, their money; it was as obvious from the bar as it was from up front. Vi also saw the guy leave in a hurry, displeased with the girl. Vi couldn't hear their conversation as she played, but she could see that the man hadn't kissed the girl, and he left her sitting there alone and never came back.

The girl looked harmless from the stage, but from this angle, Vi could see the look on the girl's face as she scoffed at the others in the bar while one of the young, drunk locals took his chance. He was at her table now, gushing masculinity all over for his own benefit, overshooting any chance he might have had with the girl. Vi wondered if anything had ever changed in all of humanity: the same people through generations feeling the same emotions, losing the same battles, fighting for the same dreams, Vi following the same path to meet the same end others had found before her. She lived freely in a world of choice but couldn't help but wonder which ones she controlled and which ones controlled her.

She watched the boy's antics until she noticed her silent fan moving toward her, his steps quick and sure, his deep eyes pits of darkness caused by the overhead lights. For a minute she thought that four months of Tuesdays had finally given him the courage to approach, but he moved toward the door and sat down at the table where the rich girl was being harassed by the large, Irish looking punk. Vi didn't care about the disappointment she was feeling. She would not form an attachment to her black-haired fan. She wouldn't allow it. Vi pulled on her cigarette and shook her head at the obvious secret, the one that everyone knew, but no one would admit out loud. Everyone is always looking for someone better.

The Irish guy was a local Vi recognized. His name was Sean, and he usually sat at the bar and argued with anyone who cared to bring up any topic. None of the others minded his attitude because Sean kept them occupied, and that's what they were in the bar for in the first place. Vi crushed her cigarette out in the ashtray behind her.

"You inspired me with your last song, kiddo."

"Hey, William." Vi greeted the man who sat two stools from her. William was always dressed too nicely for his surroundings, his pullover sweater unfair competition to the other boys in T-shirts, his unshined loafers the only thing that gave him away to the working class. Vi smiled at him quickly and then returned her eyes to the table near the door where three characters, like everyone else in the bar and throughout the city, played out their scene. "What's up with you tonight?" she asked over her shoulder.

"I'm going to hit the jackpot." William said with the enthusiasm of a race announcer.

"I know, William, like every other Tuesday night, right?" Vi laughed as she lit another cigarette and breathed the smoke in deeply, the capillaries in her lungs closing faster than a virgin's thighs. "I should thank you, though. You inspired the hook line of my song, 'I'm Waiting to Hit the Jackpot'." Vi sounded sincere enough, although her sarcasm was usually too quick for William. "Are you going for tickets tonight?"

"You bet he is," Tony intruded on the conversation as he threw a five on the scarred wood bar in front of William. "It's up to twenty-eight million now." Tony's bulbous belly pressed into the bar as he leaned forward and slammed his hand on the five-dollar bill next to William. Tony's faded T-shirt was so worn and thin that Vi thought she could see his hairy chest underneath.

"Don't tell me he's suckered you into playing, too. You're too old to be that dumb."

"And you're too young to be that cynical." Tony retreated to the other thirsty customers as Vi puffed away, keeping her attention aimed at her glass-eyed fan. He hadn't said a word since he sat at the table with Sean and the girl, but he sat there still. Vi could hear Sean coming on to the girl. He wasn't the smoothest, overbearing, hormone-driven boy she had ever heard speak, but close. The girl kept insisting that she wanted to be left alone, and then she insisted she was in the bar with Vi's nameless fan. And would Sean please go away?

"What'cha watching?" William swigged the last of his Bud and pocketed the five that Tony had left for him.

"I can't tell if it would make a better drama or a sitcom." Vi pointed to the table near the front as Sean's pickup lines were being shot down as swiftly as he could deliver them.

"He's relentless," Vi said to William.

"Poor girl," William agreed. "I can't decide if he was born that fired up, or if it's all the drinks talking."

"I think he's just like that. A traditional Irish Catholic

boy," Vi speculated. "I also think that the booze accentuates just how unappealing he really is."

————

Sean's tight frame hunched over, one foot on the floor, the other on a chair, his faded jeans and denim jacket a sad mix with the girl's expensive attire. He tucked his medium length, fiery red hair behind his ears and took Sarah's hand in his oversized, callous palm, only to lose that battle as well. "Let me buy you a drink."

"I told you I'm with him." Sarah pointed at Tom and moved her eyebrows in his direction, hoping for some help, but the black-haired boy continued to sit at the table in silence. When she'd heard the pretty Irish lilt in Sean's voice, she'd let down her guard for a second and it was a big mistake.

"You and this guy? I don't think so." Sean was too smug for his own good, but he'd heard enough lies to tell them from the truth. "Anyway, he's not doing a wonderful job at it, is he? You have nothing to drink in front of you. He doesn't seem to mind me being here, and he's been sitting across the room staring at the stage since I got here. I'm more attentive than anyone you have ever known. Now what will you have?" Sean's crooked nose curled up. He apparently broke it in a fight, one most likely started by his mouth. He whisked his medium length red hair from his face with the grace of a vain woman, and his narcissism couldn't have become any clearer to the four others who watched him.

"Well, if you were really that attentive, you wouldn't have to ask what I am drinking," she snapped at him. "Anyway, I need to get home. It's late." Sarah stood halfway before Sean took her elbow and sat her back in the chair. Now the black-haired statue sat forward, ready to spring.

In a half whisper under the noise of the crowd and the booming jukebox, Sean pushed forward. "I'll take you home, baby. I'll take you anywhere you want to go, and then to a place that you've never been." Sean smiled, pleased with himself. No one else was.

Sarah stood, making her way toward Vi and William who still sat and watched from the bar.

"Come back, honey," Sean called, watching her go, her frame slipping back and forth underneath her skirt, underneath her panties. He let the rest of his vodka-rocks slide through the ice cubes into his mouth. He was fashionable in his choice of beverage as swing dancing and martinis straight up had made a remarkable return to Chicago, and Sean had continued to suck them down on the rocks. But Sean didn't pick his drinks to fit in like the yuppies he worked for. He wanted to get drunk. He wanted to forget. He wanted to order another. Sean laughed in the face of the black-haired man who remained standing on his right.

Tony approached behind the bar and offered his bartending expertise to the rich girl, but she wanted a cab instead. "This fine specimen of a man will take you home," Tony offered as he gestured to William.

"I can't drive her home. I've got to go get our lottery tickets."

The stranded girl tried to ignore William, but she could see Sean approaching. "That's okay, thanks. I'd rather take a cab. You know, talking to strangers and all."

Vi smiled. "They don't get any stranger than in this bar,

that's for sure." Sarah tried to smile back, but she was having a rough night and couldn't find the strength to pull the twenty-six muscles in her face up in a curve. Vi pointed at William with her cigarette butt before stamping it out in the ashtray. "You can trust this bird, though. His name is William, and the only thing that he's interested in picking up on Tuesday nights is his lottery tickets."

Sarah eyed William who was already standing, keys in hand. He looked like a decent man, dressed better than all the other clowns she had seen in the place, but then again, she had thought that of Randy before he had left her there. Tony cleaned a few glasses as everyone waited for Sarah to decide. "You're the singer," she answered.

"Name's Vi. But you can call me Vi." Sarah at least attempted to smile this time. She looked back toward Sean who was still watching for her next move, and the loner who was watching Sean. "I'm the singer, but you have a bigger fan club in here than me tonight."

"Yeah, well. I'd hate to wait in here for a cab with that jerk around. I'm Sarah." The girl introduced herself, shaking hands with Vi and offering her hand to William who held up his car keys.

"If I don't leave now, I'll be late."

"They don't draw the winning ticket until Wednesday night," Vi pressed. She knew William was methodical about buying his tickets on Tuesdays, but like everyone else in the bar that knew this, she mocked him.

"Don't ask." Tony wiped the bar in front of the three. Tony made it his business to know everyone who came into his place, as he liked people to be happy. That's why he was always introducing people and making them sit together. He wanted everyone to have company. It made life so much more bearable. "William, take the girl home."

Sarah wanted to spit. This place was so disgusting. She wanted to turn away from these people who did not know how she was used to being treated, but her bubble had burst when Randy left, and all she could do was pick up the pieces. "I couldn't..."

"You will," Tony told the girl. "Besides, Vi here is going with."

"I am?" Vi asked herself as she thought about her Wednesday and the plans she didn't have. "Why the hell not?" She turned to her right. "Let me pack up my guitar, William."

William huffed as he weighed his options and searched for the answer on the floor, but Tony provided it when William looked up at him and saw his stern face. "Fine, fine," he conceded. "But I've got to get my lottery tickets first."

"That's fine with me," Vi said over her shoulder as she walked toward the stage to grab her guitar. The dark-haired statue followed Vi's movements with his eyes as he stood next to Sean who was gearing up to make his next move on Sarah. But before Sean could build himself back up, Sarah had followed William out the door with Vi and her guitar. Sean didn't hesitate as he made his way out to the parking lot, Vi's dark-haired fan right on his tail; silent like a puppy dog, yet not there to befriend or to protect.

———

William approached his 1994 Lincoln Towncar. It was a boat, a yacht among the tugs sailing through Chicago streets, in port now shining under the streetlamps that lit the tiny parking lot next to Baker's Tap. The baby blue paint looked fresh, and anyone could tell that this man cared for his toys. It was a warm fall night in Chi-town. The low percentage of October humidity was bearable, unlike in the summer when Chicagoans would swim through the thick air in a constant battle with lethargy. A cool breeze swept over Lake Michigan and through the streets before retiring to the suburbs. Storefronts beckoned passersby with neon signs, and the flat buildings lined up together for miles as if waiting at a starting line. The neighborhood would have been quiet but for the remaining sounds of the city: the ever-present whooshing generated from the thousands of tires on the expressways, the Latin music blaring from a nearby apartment, and the crinkling of the littered paper and plastic as the wind rolled it over battered pavement and sparse grass before it attached itself to a fence like a flea to its host.

William took Vi's guitar and opened the passenger door.

"Shotgun," Vi called. Sarah waited for Vi to get in the car so William could close the front door and open the back door for her. Like a true gentleman, he did. Neither of them minded, as his three older sisters had unwittingly trained William in the art of being polite. Sarah's perceptions of men were jaded after two years of dating, looking for "the one", and what had become an attempt at husband hunting. As tired as she was of the game, she always enjoyed the courtesies of a gentleman. They made her feel feminine and proper. She smiled up at William as he closed the door behind her.

William walked to the trunk and opened it, placing Vi's guitar inside.

"You getting lottery tickets for real?" Sean asked from

across the parking lot. "I haven't gotten mine yet either." Sean didn't normally play the lottery, but everyone at Baker's Tap had heard about William's addiction to the game. Sean knew that this was his ticket inside the car, his path to this beautiful girl with the light blue eyes and short black skirt.

William closed the trunk and stretched to his fullest height for the benefit of the two men who approached. He recognized Sean and the other joker as the ones who had been sitting at Sarah's table earlier. "You play?"

"You bet," Sean said as he closed the distance, the other in tow. "I heard you talking to Tony about the lottery. You're the one that always goes for tickets, right?"

"Yes," William replied, offering nothing more.

"Well, can I have a lift too, then? I'd like to get some." Sean smiled outwardly at William, his double entendre unraveling Sarah's clothes, making him want to burst into laughter.

"We," the other one said, pulling his shoulders up to his ears as he looked everywhere but at William.

William studied the two strangers for a second. He knew Sean was a loudmouth, but he didn't recognize the quiet one. William thought for a moment, ready to complain, but in the end consented to two more stowaways. He shrugged. "Hurry up," William answered as he slid into the driver's seat and closed the door.

Sean smiled as he looked at Sarah in the back seat. He opened the door, but before he could sit down next to her, his new stalker slid into the car and placed himself in the middle.

"What's going on?" Vi asked protectively. "You know these guys, William?"

"No, not really," William answered.

Annoyed, Sarah moved over behind Vi, whose silent fan sat quietly in the middle as Sean closed the door and William started the car. No one spoke for a minute as William handled his Towncar out of the small space and onto Halsted Avenue. He adjusted the rearview mirror so that he could see into the back, an unnecessary gesture as Vi had already turned around and was watching the two new passengers.

"I'm Sean," the drunken pest said, offering his hand to Sarah. She ignored the introduction as Vi took Sean's hand.

"Hello, Sean," Vi said condescendingly as she eyed Sarah. "What on earth brings you here?"

"Stow it, Vi." Sean knew the singer from the bar, and he was in no mood for her sarcasm tonight.

"Who's your friend?"

"We're not friends," the dark-haired boy answered. The four waited for him to introduce himself, but he remained quiet, averting his eyes from William's in the mirror. He kept his line of sight clear of Vi who was moving over in the front seat to gain his attention.

"I'm Vi. This is William, Sarah, and Sean. You got a name?"

The answer was on the tip of his tongue, but Tom held out for a moment. There was something personal about telling another his name. They would feel free to call him by it. They would feel familiar, like they knew him when really they had only the first piece given to him by his parents. Ten seconds passed as if it was an hour. William rolled down the windows, taking in the cool October air as he drove north over one of the steel bridges that conquered the Chicago

River when down and submitted to her boat traffic when raised.

"I'm Tom Darby." His eyes caught Vi and then let her go, but she felt their presence lingering over her. She could not distinguish their color clearly as Tom was in the center of the back seat, which remained in shadows. From the brightness of the lights on stage to the dark of night, Vi could tell that this man's eyes were something to behold. Perhaps she would sneak up on him during the daylight sometime and catch their beauty. Perhaps they would inspire a hundred songs.

"It's good to know you, Tom Darby," Sarah added, still ignoring Sean. Tom kept his eyes forward but nodded in recognition of Sarah's appreciation. He didn't get to know Sarah; he didn't try to know anyone. Tom could keep to himself, even in the back seat of a crowded car. It was as though he was uncomfortable in his physical body, wanting to remain a spirit to keep invisible to everything.

Vi turned and sat face forward, not really caring where William was taking them. Everyone looked outside at the night, trying to project themselves beyond the car. William drove safely as a thirty-seven-year-old man would. Past his crash causing days, he sped mildly and drove calmly enjoying the silence that invoked a concentration surely to be broken if he ever settled down to have a family. He smiled at memories of, "Don't make me pull over and come back there!"

William imagined himself as the road, going everywhere, leading humans to their destinations all over creation, the atoms in the concrete bouncing around in a frenzy, yet each piece of concrete ironically remaining still. Going nowhere.

Sean sat behind William fidgeting with the ashtray that was built into the door, pulling its shiny lid up, causing the small squeak easily recognizable to those that had spent long journeys in a car, then letting the springs snap the lid closed a millisecond before grasping it again. The tiny sound was almost lost in the air that was rushing over the car and forcing its way into the open windows. Sean tired of the ashtray and moved on to a gum wrapper he had produced as the sole occupant of his T-shirt pocket. He tore it slowly into small strips, the dull side pulled toward him, the shiny side lost underneath. He didn't like silence, especially when he had been drinking. It made him think of the small flask of vodka he had tucked into his denim jacket. He wanted some, just a little, but Sean wasn't willing to chance the others' reactions, whether negative or positive. If the others didn't mind him drinking in the car, they'd probably want some for themselves. So, he kept his mind busy until he shredded the gum wrapper into mere bits of dust.

"Can we get some music back here?" he complained.

William turned on the radio to an easy listening station and an uncomfortably slow love song serenaded them. Sean rolled his eyes. He imagined sound waves traveling through the city, through his apartment, through his own body, searching for someone to hear, someone to listen, lost in the night in this exciting city, finally crossing the finish line in William's car only to bore the crowd to death with its own triumph. "Forget I asked."

"You can turn right up here on Addison." Sarah leaned forward in anticipation of leading William to her neighborhood on the north side. She then realized that her new position made her more accessible to Sean's line of sight and slipped back into the leather seat. Tom remained still, blocking Sarah from Sean's view. Tom felt relief, finally aware of a use for this awkward cage that was his body. He stole a glance to his right and found Sarah smiling at him.

William drove straight through the yellow light. "I have to get my lottery tickets first, Sarah. You agreed that was okay." William said this both matter of fact and sternly in the same sentence. Sarah knew she had agreed to this, and she knew from his tone there was no changing his mind. She sighed quietly and conceded as William pulled the Towncar into one of the hundreds of cloned gas stations in Chicago. He stopped the car and recorded the mileage as Vi and Sean watched in disbelief.

"How old *are* you?" Sean mocked. "My grandpa used to do that when he gassed up old Betsy. That's what he called his car."

"What kind of car was it?" Vi asked.

"I don't remember. Any kind," Sean responded. "He called all of his cars Betsy. I never understood that." Sean opened the heavy door and stepped out. Vi had opened her door but waited in the car. She turned toward the back to learn the color of Tom's eyes, the ones on the boy she wasn't supposed to allow herself to have interest in, but he was squinting underneath the interior light.

"Maybe he liked the Beach Boys." Tom stopped talking as abruptly as he had started and looked at the floor as if embarrassed by his own comment.

Sean ducked his head in the car, his mouth open wide. "He does talk, after all. We should get this on tape."

"Stow it," William responded as he cleaned the windows, careful to wipe every droplet of dirty water off. "So he's shy. You do enough talking for the both of you, don't you think?"

Sean was still as he digested William's comment. For a second, Sean appeared as though he was debating whether to argue with William and whether he should start a skirmish on this lot. The alcohol in his blood outlined his face in red and the anger colored it in. Sean was ready to push into William, ready to fight him to the ground. It was his natural reaction, as he had inherited the fast, scrappy movements and the fiery Irish temperament from his father. The uncounted drinks he had consumed since he had gotten off work five hours earlier didn't help. Sean was still for a moment as the adrenaline rushed out of him, his expression turning agreeable as he shifted his attention back to Tom. "What did you say?"

Tom remained seated in the back seat next to Sarah, his eyes forward as if he was a Marine in boot camp, frozen at attention. Vi came to Tom's defense. "He said that maybe your grandfather liked the Beach Boys."

"Of course he didn't like them. They were after his time."

"It was a joke," Vi said, rolling her eyes as if speaking to an imbecile. "Tom was referring to the fact that the Beach Boys wrote songs about their car, Betsy. That's all. You don't have to be so particular." Vi smiled at Tom and exited the passenger side.

"Particular? Who even uses that word? And what do you know about the Beach Boys? Playing your country or folk or whatever the hell it is." Sean threw the crumpled gum wrapper on the ground and Vi picked it up, held it out to

Sean, and then threw it in the garbage as William returned the squeegee to its dirty, water filled receptacle.

"There's enough trash in the city with guys like you walking around. We don't need to litter." Sean laughed as Vi leaned back in the car to talk to Sarah and Tom. "You guys don't want anything from the food mart?"

At the mention of food, the candy and cakes, the sandwiches and pastas, the poison, Sarah changed the subject. "You shouldn't let him put your music down," Sarah said with conviction before calming herself. "I mean, do what you want, but I liked what I heard." Tom smiled at Sarah.

"Thanks," Vi nodded as she stood up and stepped away from the car. "I need to hear that once in a while."

2
GOING

Vi held her chest still for a minute as if she was reminding herself that she had been breathing, alive and kicking, making herself happen. It takes time, this music thing, more time than anyone ever liked to admit. And usually it passed poor fools up, those left getting ready, getting their name outside their kitchens, and getting left behind by the newer, younger sound just when they had perfected what was once the newer, younger sound. But Vi had been writing for six years and knew that her music was close to ready, ready to stand up to the professionals on Music Row, ready to take her to the next level of her life. She had dreamed, prayed, cried, laughed, and had almost become who she had been trying to create over the years.

Four-hundred ninety miles south and east of where Vi stood in this gas station, they told her that songs would stand on their own if they were truly *great* songs. Everyone has good songs, you see. She drove back and forth every three months and played in pits and coffee shops for others who were just like her, only exactly different. They were just dreamers to Vi. She was the real thing. She transformed herself into the round at The Bluebird Cafe in Nashville as she sat on a stool in Baker's Tap, Chicago. Upon that wooden stool, she spewed the words written in confidence between her heart and her pen. The paper kept her secrets. Secrets until she whispered the words like a nightingale through the microphone and out into no one, well maybe into this guy Tom. In either case, she would play for herself as every musician has to in order to survive. No one understood her music like she did, as no one understood Vi as Vi did. When she let her songs out, she left them hanging in the air for anyone to critique and to like or dislike. Trash, beer, and whiskey make for interesting interpretation.

Vi smiled and looked up from the sidewalk, unconsciously smoking her cigarette. There were no stars to be had in the clear night sky. The glowing bulbs from millions of watts of electricity left their light to linger in the atmosphere and removed any hope for city residents of wishing upon a star. Vi needed no more wishes, she just needed the last ounce of guts it took to pick up and move. But for now, she would have to be happy riding around in William's car, and perhaps tomorrow would be the day that Interstate 57 South would beckon her for good.

Across the parking lot, Sean headed for the door of the gas station behind William who, after finishing pumping the gas, closed the gas cap and practically buffed the paint from the side of the car below it. Sean attempted to strike up a conversation with the older, wiser fool. "I play the quick pick. How about you?"

William entered the small building after Sean. There was one attendant on duty behind a Plexiglas wall. William placed a twenty in the small metal opening, waited for his thirty cents change and turned to leave. Sean lingered over a bag of Cool Ranch Doritos before deciding against them. He wanted another drink. He wanted to sneak a swig from his little carry along. He wasn't ready to give in to the late night munchies yet.

"You ready?" William asked as he held the door open.

"What about the lottery tickets?"

"I don't buy them here." William left Sean inside the chilly store. The heat should have been turned on this late in the year, but the city still had a few warm days left of fall, and anyone trying to save a buck left the heat off until they became uncomfortably cold. Sean stopped and debated a quick drink before leaving it alone and stepping outside.

"Ready to go, Vi?" William called.

"Yep." Vi climbed back into the car where Tom and Sarah waited in silence.

Sean trotted toward the car. "What do you mean you don't buy your tickets here? What the hell's the difference? They've got a machine. It's the same game all over."

William looked at Sean for a second before responding in a tone reserved for nagging children. "It's not the same game all over. I play at Phil's Breakfast and 7UP. It's good luck."

"You buy your lottery tickets at a place called Phil's Breakfast and 7UP because you think that it's good luck? I never heard of such an asinine thing in my life." Sean's drunken tone was loud and his forehead folded into five small wrinkles as he attempted to understand William's motives. "And I never heard of this place. If it's so famous, then how come I've never heard of it?"

"Are you doing anything tonight?" William calmly waited for an answer.

"I'd like to be, but Sarah and I are stuck with you yokels right now."

Sarah shook her head and looked down into her lap.

"Let's go, I'm aging here. Menopause is just around the corner," Vi yelled from the car.

William smiled and shook his head. "You're not doing anything tonight, so what do you care if you have to go a little farther for your lottery tickets?"

Sean thought about this before shrugging his wide shoulders as William sat in the driver's seat and wrote the amount of gallons of gas he had added in a column next to the mileage. He reset the trip odometer and started the Towncar as Sean opened Sarah's door.

"Scoot over, Sarah." Sean smiled right into her like the devil, and Sarah felt herself cower a bit, but she didn't move.

Vi turned around in her seat. "Come on, let's not start this again."

"What? I know she's not with this guy Betsy over here." Sean pointed at Tom who remained in the middle of the back seat with no intention of moving over to make room. "I just want to sit next to her and get to know her before William drops her off at home and she's out of my life forever." Sarah didn't move, she just sat and looked at Sean who was holding the door ready to sit down in the back seat.

"Enough, Sean." Vi shook her head in disgust.

"Are you getting in the car?" William pulled the gearshift down three notches ready to pull away.

Sean looked at Sarah expectantly, and she looked at William for an escape. There the five froze, waiting with the car in drive, going through the seconds of their lives at a standstill. Finally, in the last instant of sanity, right before voices would be raised, Tom leaned forward over Sarah and looked up directly into Sean's eyes as if he could see clear through to the apartment building across the street. "She's not interested. Give it up or walk home from here." Tom leaned back into his seat and sat as still as the wax statue he was before. The others hesitated in amazement as Sean weighed his odds against Tom. Finally, Sean smiled.

"All right! Wait for me." Sean closed Sarah's door and ran around the back of the car to get in behind William who used the three seconds to internally debate the ethics on pulling away and leaving Sean stranded at the gas station. Sean jumped in the back seat, and it was too late to ditch him. All smiles as he pulled the rear driver's side door shut, Sean's arm swung forward between Vi and William, gesturing for the car to move onward.

"I like you," Sean said to Tom. "No one ever says anything to me, except yes." Sean felt camaraderie toward Tom. He rarely liked to say what he felt, only how disgusted he was with the world, but his last martini was kicking in, so he smiled wider. Tom continued to ride in his trance. "I know that I usually intimidate people, and I don't take 'no' for an answer. But hell, I don't get 'no' for an answer."

"If you'd stop and listen clearly to people and what they're really saying to you instead of worrying about your pretty boy attitude like you could get anyone that you wanted, maybe you would understand better that girls like Sarah really aren't interested," Vi stated.

"And girls like you?" Sean remarked.

"Please," William added. "Girls like Vi are smarter than to

waste their time on anyone. She pursues her music, and that's it."

Vi sat still, everyone expecting her to comment as she always did, each of her comebacks seemingly prepared before the conversation to fit humorously or callously at the perfect instant. Now her eyes squinted, and she was puzzled about what to say, wondering if it was necessary to defend her practices or decisions to four strangers. "How do you know what I want, William? I've seen you about five times in the last four months, and the deepest discussion that we have had is the ethics of putting ketchup on a hot dog."

"No way." Sean answered, leaving the topic of Vi's personal life and shifting gears. "No ketchup."

Sarah said, finally entering the conversation, "I have to agree with Sean, but probably just this once. There is no ketchup on a hot dog. It's just not done."

"William would disagree with both of you," Vi added, happy about the change of attention. "Several of us had this insane discussion just two weeks ago at Baker's."

"If I want to put steak sauce on my hot dog, it's my business." William drove on, both of his hands on the wheel ready for a verbal battle on the subject.

Sean looked at Tom. "Care to comment?" Everyone looked at Tom.

Tom looked out the window.

"Ethics of hot dog toppings are not of interest." Sean sat forward on the seat behind William. "I don't care if you put steak sauce on your hot dog. I don't care if you put Tabasco on your hot diggitty dog. But everyone in Chicago knows that there is no place for ketchup in or around the bun. Poppy seed or plain? I don't care. You like tomatoes? Then have a few fresh, juicy slices on top. But ketchup? No!" Sarah and Vi nodded in agreement, allowing Sean to fight this battle for them.

"Where does it say, 'Thou shalt not put ketchup on a hot dog'? Show me one place." William waited as the three others shook their heads. "And if this is true, then why is there ketchup at every hot dog stand in Chicago?"

"It's for the fries," Vi retaliated.

"I think when they built the new Comiskey Park, they had a plaque installed over each vendor that said 'Thou shalt not destroy hot dogs with ketchup'. It was a big thing." Sean smiled at the back of William's head. "I think it actually delayed the opening of the stadium by a couple weeks because they had to screw these plaques into cement walls."

"He's right," Sarah played along.

"Hilarious. You're both insane, thank you." William rolled his eyes.

Vi interrupted. "You guys, William's right." William huffed before Vi finished, knowing that a smart-aleck remark was close to follow. "There were no such plaques installed at Comiskey. How I remember it, when Harry Caray died, and they had the big tribute for him at Wrigley Field, they actually carved it on a plaque dedicated to *his* memory."

William reached over and unhooked Vi's seatbelt with the press of a finger. As the belt slid up, pulled by its automatic retracting system, William smiled. "Jump light's green."

Vi reattached the buckle with a sarcastic laugh as Sarah corrected all of them. "No, Vi, I believe the plaque at Wrigley Field read 'Thou shalt not eat hot dogs at all when there is still room for beer'." Tom even had to smile as the rest of them laughed out loud. Sarah sat back smiling as she was feeling comfortable, of all places, in the back seat of this blue Towncar among four strangers. She could stay calm as long as Tom stayed between her and Sean, although even he seemed to mellow out. Sarah looked at the four others in the car and wondered how they were so different from her. Less than an hour earlier, she had been judging them, looking down at their meager lives. Sarah knew why she laughed, why she sneered at those around her as if they were lepers. She knew exactly why Randy had left her at Baker's Tap. Her mother had taught her that those without money didn't count in this world.

Sarah hadn't felt this carefree, without the help of alcohol that is, since she returned from college a year earlier and moved back in with her parents. They lived in a large house in the northern suburbs along the lake with the perfect cars, the perfect job, the perfect country club. Sarah was, of course, intended as an offering to the gods as the perfect daughter. She had one older brother who was twenty-seven, married to a delicate housewife who kept everything spic and span and had already given him a son.

Sarah pulled the lever for the electric windows and sucked in more air lest she lose control of her stomach and regurgitate all over the upholstery in reaction to the nausea brought on by her thoughts. Her brother had married who she was supposed to be, who her mother had been creating these years. No one could resist the influence of twenty-two years of training, and whether it was what Sarah had wanted never mattered. It's who she had become.

Sarah was almost glad that Randy had dumped her in the bar tonight, or she would probably be lost somewhere right now among his countless thrusts, wondering if this was what love was. Sarah always mistook lust for love. It wasn't her fault, really. She had heard the word love most times over the past six years, passing swiftly over boy's lips, spoken in haste and mixed with adrenaline, like a cop reading Miranda Rights to his latest collar. *I love you, Sarah. You know I do.*

It began when she was a child with her parents and moved through the years to this very night when Randy had left her at the table in the bar. It was all mislead guidance, their loving her, creating her, telling her what she needed, in the end screwing her over.

Why did Randy leave? Like most of them, it was because he needed space. He could have all the space that he wanted, it was his for the taking. Sarah had never called on a boy, not even once, because her mother acted as if she were born in the 1800s and would fall down clear through the carpet and smash her head on the floor underneath, adding a concussion to the original heart attack that would be caused if Sarah ever did something so forbidden a lady. *How ridiculous,* she thought; that her mother's ancient concepts of what a woman should be had kept the only smile on Sarah's face that she could form until tonight. It had been artificial her entire life until William had the audacity to defend ketchup being put on a hot dog.

"Where the hell are we going?" Sean yelled as William pulled the car onto Elston Avenue. They were riding northwest now, out of Chicago and toward the suburbs.

"He's going to take me home, Sean," Sarah said.

"I'm going to get my lottery tickets first. Would you like me to repeat this announcement every fifteen minutes?"

"Please do. I often forget that they are so hard to acquire. Phil's 7UP Breakfast, was it?" Sean mocked.

William huffed as he changed lanes. "It's Phil's Breakfast and 7UP. And I'm telling you it's good luck for me."

"Have you ever won anything?" Sarah asked.

"There's actually a place called Phil's Breakfast and 7UP?" Vi was smiling. "That almost sounds like a song."

William ignored Sean and Vi. "No, Sarah, I haven't won anything yet."

"Then why do you think that it's good luck for you if you've never won?" Sarah didn't intend to razz William, she was just interested in the art of polite conversation, knowing not to say anything if it was not positive.

"Because I like it at Phil's. It's like the one place on earth that I feel completely comfortable, like I belong there. Have you ever felt that way about a place?"

"No," Sarah answered after taking a moment to think. "I guess not. I mean, once I hid from my mother in a cleaning closet, and by pure luck realized that she'd never find me there, ever. It's like she's too good to clean so she doesn't have to know that it's even there."

"Who cleans your house?"

"The maids."

"Maids, plural? Ah, to dream," Vi sang whimsically. "Just give me that number one song."

"You can have it," Sarah said. She was relaxing in front of these strangers, becoming part of their conversation. Sarah had heard some of the house staff talk so freely, and she wondered what it would feel like to always be so open, to always let go of the words on the tip of her tongue. "That closet was the only place in my existence as a child that I could be free because I knew there was no way my mom would sneak up and correct me."

"That's why you're the way you are," Vi said.

"What way am I?"

"You know, prim and proper. All done up, sitting up straight. Like a model."

"I'll say like a model," Sean added. "Va-voom."

"Va-voom?" Vi mocked him. "Who talks like that?"

Sean got defensive and sat back. "Guys like me talk like that."

"I thought we weren't going to talk about guys like you anymore."

"Okay," William interrupted, before they took their views to another level. "Sarah, I don't think that your closet is quite the same as what I mean. I'm talking about a single place on the earth, like you're pulled there. What I'm saying is that no matter what was on this piece of land..."

"Where is this piece of land?" Sean interjected.

William continued, thoroughly convinced by his own explanation. "No matter what was there, I would always like it in that spot. I'm drawn to it like the tip of the arrow on a compass pulls north. There's nowhere else in the world that I have ever felt that." Tom sat in the back slowly nodding his head in agreement. "Thank you, Tom. See, he agrees with me."

"Why don't you move there? Buy Phil's diner or something?" Vi asked.

"I don't know." William looked in his side mirror. "I guess that I'm afraid it would wear off, and then I wouldn't feel that way anymore about anything. Then where would I be?"

"I know what you mean," Vi added. "Sometimes I think I will lose my creativity if I move because I have always lived here and written here and found my inspiration here. Like, Chicago might be what's giving me these songs." Vi looked out her window at the passing apartments and townhouses.

Sean shook his head. "I do not know what you're talking about."

"Sometimes I have no idea what I'm talking about either," William admitted. "But this feeling is unmistakable, and it's worth the ride to me." Elston Avenue melted into Milwaukee Avenue, and a minute later William turned the Towncar left onto Touhy Avenue, letting it crawl further from the city.

Sean leaned back. "Well, you're way in the deep end of the pool, as far as I'm concerned."

Vi turned around and smiled, conniving. "Drowning?"

3
THE LONG HAUL

Tom sat in the back seat between Sarah and Sean, nodding his head in agreement with William, though not speaking a word of his thoughts. He had something in his life like what William was talking about, something that made him feel right, as though he was meant to be there. His was not a place, it was a person. Tom was at home whenever he was in her presence or when she was in his thoughts. At these moments, he could breathe. The words that poured from her mouth were like a cool spring to him. He could bathe in her thoughts, and somehow he knew she would understand who he was without him ever saying a word. There was a way, like in a dream, that she would look into his eyes and recall his life story, and in her understanding of him, she too would fall in love as he had. She would know in one look he had kept to himself these years for reasons dark, deep, and painful. This secret would reveal itself to her alone, and she would not be afraid. She would save him from it.

Tom went through years being the quiet one that people

like Sean would never understand. They mocked him, tried to beat him up, and eventually left him alone. And Tom was happy being left alone. Unless he thought of holding his savior in his arms and telling her she kept his soul safe. His dreams played out in his head, but Tom knew he would never bring himself to tell her. He was afraid of the adage, "Like father, like son", and although he would kill himself before ever hurting her, he knew that the demon that his father had been was planted within himself. It was in his DNA or in his upbringing. It was this unthinkable fear that had kept him mute.

The way his father would turn the music so loud it would drown out his mother's screaming, to the neighbors anyway. The way Tom and his brother would be sent to buy oranges and cigarettes for their father, knowing that he would be beat them hours later; the pillowcase barely holding together as its seams pulled against the force of the fruit impaling against the stomach flesh, insulting the body underneath but never telling, never showing much of a bruise or a scratch. The sweet smell of the juice pouring over Tom and his brother causing them to wretch. The way his father would joke that this was truly the only way to make a drink, a freshly squeezed screwdriver, although the old man rarely mixed anything with his vodka anymore.

The way the juice would sometimes seep out of the pillowcase onto the floor and, ribcages battered and bruised, Tom and his brother lying next to each other in the juice, bodies aching, muscles throbbing, yet somehow their skin left unharmed, silent to the punishment. Tom's brother had become his father over the years. He was angry, full of adrenaline, uncontrollable. He spent his life in a scummy shack of a house, a case of beer as an appetizer, bottle of whiskey for the main course, and a pretty little blonde for dessert. Tom knew his brother turned the music up a couple times a week, blaring, nothing comprehensible, accompanied by the sound of the wincing that she made which sang his brother to sleep as his mother's cries had.

Tom remained still, holding back the bile in his throat and looking out the windshield of this William's car, controlling the temper he no longer had. He had digressed into himself over the years, the complete yin to his brother's yang, silent protector tonight for this girl Sarah. He could be for her the man he wished he could have been for his mother. Tom walked the streets of his days, barely alive, keeping himself inside lest he unleash his fury on the world. And as William had spoken of a place where he felt perfect, where he was home, Tom sat here, silently basking in his perfect place. Her brown eyes drew him back into the car and calmed his heart while the curly strands of her brown hair gave way to its lingering light summer highlights and flew wildly and freely around her face, trapping the air and then letting it go, and trapping his soul for keeps.

Tom hadn't listened to music in years because it drew him into his horrible memories. All music had done this until hers. He lived in Bloomingdale, forty-five minutes west of the city, and it was nothing less than fate that had driven him out of his apartment and down the street, onto a train and then a bus. This same fate drove that bus passed Baker's Tap on a Tuesday night where his savior was walking, guitar in hand, falling into the darkness of the club and into the light of his life. That bar had been his church for four months of Tuesdays since. And on this night, fate had put his history to use. His need to protect Sarah from Sean had pulled him into these stranger's lives and into the same car with her.

"Where exactly are we?" Vi asked as she let the window roll up to its stop before pulling her untamed hair from her eyes.

"Niles." Everyone was quiet, moving through maps of the city in their minds, noticing the buildings spreading out before them. "It's in the burbs, northwest of the city," William said in anticipation of the inevitable, "Where the hell is Niles?"

"Exactly how far are we going for these tickets?" Sean asked.

"It should only take us about forty-five minutes to get there," William answered calmly, as if it would make perfect sense to his passengers.

"Forty-five minutes!" Vi, Sean, and Sarah blurted simultaneously.

"Tony wasn't kidding. You are fanatical about the lottery. I can't believe you didn't tell any of us this before we agreed to come with you!" It agitated Vi at first, but then she let out a laugh. She had nowhere else to be at the moment, and she always enjoyed an adventure, as she never knew where her next musical story would strike. She also liked the country-side, although it would be difficult to see at night.

No one noticed Tom smile in the back seat. Two more hours of peace for him and then it would probably be back to his apartment, back to another week of insanity doing the job, and waiting for Tuesday to come the way most longed for Friday.

"I can let anyone out that wants to go," William stated matter of fact. "Just say the word. But I didn't ask you to come with me, and you all knew that I was going to get my lottery tickets first."

Sean shook his head, trying to find humor in a situation that disgusted him. Not that he wanted to be sitting at home alone, but he preferred somewhere with an icebox and an eighty proof nightcap. He reached up to feel his flask that was still tucked neatly into his pocket. Sean wondered if there was enough vodka left to carry his buzz through the rest of the night. "Man, I can't believe you. Normal people go down to the local convenience store for their tickets, but not you. You drive an hour out of the city to some Hicksville. You're whacked, my friend."

Sarah remained silent in the seat behind Vi. She was close enough to her house that she could find a cab and be there within twenty minutes. But something inside of her didn't want to let her out of the car and out of these people's lives. She was changing, opening up, learning the humility Randy had been trying to teach her. She hadn't cared to listen to him and was now spending her night with four strangers. But that was better than sitting at home with the constant distraction of food calling to her. Sarah would take a long ride instead of a shorter one. Either way, she knew she would remember this night. Its lessons would be written in her pages of time as one of the best or worst decisions she had ever made.

"What if this guy's like Jeffrey Dahmer? You know?" Sean looked around the car for agreement. "What if he's some psychopath taking us out into the middle of nowhere to cannibalize us?"

Sarah leaned forward into Sean's line of sight and raised her eyebrows as if to say 'please'.

"I'm serious," Sean continued. "Did you hear about that guy who made furniture out of skin and bones? We're talking human flesh here."

William shook his head and chuckled to himself but didn't waste his breath in denial of Sean's wild accusations.

Tom leaned forward and turned his head to his left, and the others took notice as the mysterious boy rarely gestured. He paused, ready to speak like a ringmaster with the first spotlight. Only Tom was not waiting for the suspense to build. He was looking for the quickest path between two points. He was waiting for the perfect words to find his tongue and let them hang as all four strained to hear him against the wind that continued to pour into the car, "If William is what you're saying, and he's luring us out somewhere to kill us all, then you and your pecker aren't as smart as you think you are." At that, Tom looked suggestively between Sean and Sarah and then ahead again, noticing the way Vi's eyes crinkled, almost closed, as she laughed. Tom heard only her joy.

Sean shook his head and smiled in defeat. Sarah tried to hold her laughter back and to hold her legs crossed tightly together. "William, you've got to pull over somewhere. I need to use the facilities." William looked at his watch as his lips clasped together in disapproval. But without a word, he pulled into an Amoco gas station and stopped the car for Sarah.

"Gotta go to Amoco!" Sean sang repetitively as he bounced on the leather cushion behind William. "Gotta go to Amoco!"

William turned in his seat without putting the car in

park. "Are you going to act like a three-year-old for the rest of the night?"

"What's your problem?" Sean retorted as he ceased the flopping motion. "It's just something that my brothers and sisters and I would chant when we were on a road trip and we had to stop for a pee break. Lighten up." Vi followed Sarah, and Sean opened the door.

"Give me a minute William, I gotta go to Amoco, too."

"Hurry, Vi. Times'a'wasting." William put the car in park and looked back at Tom who sat alone in the back seat like a child afraid to leave the room for fear of missing something. "If you need something, now's the time, because I am not stopping again." William didn't wait for Tom to respond as he was sure that the boy wouldn't utter a word. He watched through the store window as Sarah entered the washroom in back followed by, what William guessed, must have been one of Sean's Olympic medal winning tactless remarks.

————

Vi walked around the food pantry and was soon joined by Sean who picked random items from the shelf and offered them to her. Vi didn't mind Sean. He was sometimes a pretty funny guy, but it was that vulgar, unfiltered humor that sometimes rode her nerves. Vi was sure that through the course of her twenty-seven years, she'd heard just about everything, and she could handle a guy like Sean. But she didn't have to handle him because she wasn't the kind that he would hit on, either. It was girls like Sarah who had to fend off the clumsy forwardness of his comments.

"Are you in here, Sarah?" Vi called as the restroom door closed behind her.

"Yes," Sarah answered. "William didn't leave without us, did he?" Sarah wasn't worried because she knew that a man like William wouldn't leave her. On the other hand, Randy had.

Vi was in and out of her stall in no time. Sarah was still in the larger stall, mentally arguing about the difference in levels of importance between sanitary practices in a gas station washroom and the necessity of emptying the bladder before it emptied itself. After cleaning the toilet seat and laying three lengths of paper over it before hovering uncomfortably, Sarah realized the level of snobbery that had been engrained in her.

"If we take too long, William will leave without us. He's really weird about his lottery tickets. Is everything okay in there?" Vi attempted to fix her hair, but the knotted curls looked as in place as they were going to get. Sarah finally exited the stall and, after scrubbing her hands like a doctor before surgery, primped her already perfect looks. "What is there to fix?" Vi asked.

"I hate when people say that to me." Sarah stopped her fidgeting. She stared in the mirror for a moment, almost seeing herself. She continued primping after a pause that might have been mistaken as thought, if she hadn't been so beautiful.

Vi shrugged as though she were almost sorry. But she wasn't. She had struggled with her image for years, being the tomboy, the cute one, the cool girl who fit in with the guys. She had been told that she was beautiful and hadn't believed a word of it until recently. Vi spent her years watching her sister as she now watched Sarah. Out of the corner of her eye in the mirror, she noticed the ease at which certain women could fix themselves. Vi didn't actually admire this. She was more in awe, as these same women were in awe when Vi would strike up a conversation about chocolate pudding with a complete stranger. It was ironic, really. Vi was at home among these men, some of whom she held affection for. And these same men liked to spend time with her, to pick her brain and get the inside scoop on women. Later, these men would laugh at Vi's perception of the current topic of conversation, praise her analogies, and then walk out into the night with her sister or one of the Sarahs of the world.

Vi had thought for years that she was witty and her sister was beautiful until she realized she looked just like her sister. She too had the face, a mixture of her parents' faces. She finally saw in herself the same trademarks that her sister had: the curled up button nose, the perfect eyebrows, the high cheekbones. Everything except the natural way the hair was to fall when brushed, or the gliding of the lipstick over already stained lips. All but the endless and relentless hours in a lifetime wasted powdering and re-powdering and plastering and painting. Vi wanted none of that. She was learning to accept her beauty as truly unique, and it was there, on her, to be worn at all times instead of brushed on and washed off, and yet only noticed occasionally. Vi admired Sarah in the mirror. Sarah made it look so simple to keep up with coloring in the lines, and at the same time, completely impossible.

"What do you think of William?" Sarah asked as she zipped her purse closed.

Vi caught herself staring and moved to the bathroom door. "I hardly know him."

"I thought you did. That's why I agreed to take a ride home from him." Sarah stopped herself from panicking as rolls of news footage about rape and kidnapping spun through her head along with her mother's countless warnings.

"I know him from the bar," Vi reassured Sarah. "We're both regulars at Baker's Tap. I see him when I play there, and sometimes Tony will introduce the locals to get some interesting conversations going. William's cool, but a little strange. He goes for his lottery tickets like clockwork. Every Tuesday night when I finish my set, he's out the door."

"Oh," Sarah calmed herself. "So he likes you? He's there to see you?"

"No, no." Vi laughed. "William's not my type, that's for sure. I think Sean is right. William is a little loopy."

"I think he's sweet," Sarah said defensively.

"You're one of those people that can't be alone for five seconds, aren't you?" Vi's rhetorical question was followed by a moment of silence as Sarah's jaw hung in midair. "Was that out loud?" the singer asked, leaving the washroom with a smile.

"What are you girls doing in there?" Sean asked, hovering in the food mart, his arms filled with junk food. "Anything that I need to know about?"

"Geometry. We were doing geometry. There's a wonderful poster on the wall in there," Vi led Sean on. "It's a man, a model. He's got to be the perfect size; height, length, and width, circumference even." Vi walked directly past Sean and out of the store as Sarah came running from the washroom.

"I can be single for five seconds!" Sarah shouted to Vi before she realized Sean was in the food mart, gawking out the door.

Sean dropped his groceries on the floor right there in the aisle and pulled his left arm up to his right hand and pointed at his wristwatch. He smiled at Sarah and winked hard. "Four seconds left," Sarah walked out before Sean could finish. Sean looked around like a child preparing to make a break for the cookie jar and before retrieving his groceries, he snuck to the women's washroom door and peaked inside. Seeing no poster like Vi had described, he retrieved his chips and candy. "Liar," he said to himself.

4
CHIPS

"Get a move on, Sean. I thought that women were supposed to be the slow ones."

Sean ignored William who had started the car rolling before the rear door was even closed. "Liar, Vi. There was no poster in there."

"You went into the women's water closet?" Vi feigned in her best shocked English accent. "On my honor, I never."

"I'll get on your honor." Sean smiled long enough to let everyone know he was joking, but his humor died quickly under Tom's piercing stare.

William pulled onto Touhy Avenue and headed west. Everyone kept quiet as they read the street signs and store logos. There was a martial arts academy next to a deli, then a small furniture store, then a butcher shop, and then the rest of the world. The Towncar glided smoothly past Harlem Avenue and into the twilight hours. The wind drowned out the radio that William had left on at a barely audible level.

Each one thought this was an odd adventure, going only William knew where, yet going and not looking back, sharing a ride with four strangers and letting the driver drop you at a location of his choosing. In any instance, it should have been more awkward than it was turning out to be.

Sean thought about the trip. This was turning into a Tuesday night from out of the Bermuda Triangle. He wanted to stay home and relax, maybe watch some television and have a couple of beers like every other guy lost and single in the great city of Chicago. He'd had a beer, and the television was on for a while, and it was probably still on because when Sean decided to leave, he left. There were pictures all over Sean's tiny studio apartment: brothers and sisters, parents, friends new and long lost. They held his attention on nights when Sean felt like an animal trapped in a cage during a full moon. He would travel to the refrigerator, open another cold one, and go into the hallway or by the window where the memories were, the photographs, the people who knew him when and still hung on. Sean clung to the shared memories, although he was changing every day as they were, changing and growing apart. There were no arguments or disagreements tearing at their relationships, just time doing to them as it did to everyone. Sean walked around his apartment, these images staring back at him, making him remember those he missed, those he loved, those that were gone. He couldn't look away, couldn't break his desperate concentration.

So Sean stepped out, ran out. The problem was where to run among the millions of people moving frantically about each other like little lead balls in a Plinko machine; falling, turning, trapped inside. They droned by each other in the hallways and on the streets, looking for someone else to take away the madness and to fill the void. But as distrustful as urbanites could be, they were all looking everywhere madly without really seeing anyone. It was amazing how two could pass on the street without a nod or even eye contact, passing and looking and not acknowledging the other people within arm's length. Where were they all running? Some knew the secret, others took years to learn it. There was nowhere far enough. There was no escape, no drug that would last long enough, no company that would distract someone forever. There was not one single place to escape the self, not on this earth. Yet he still ran.

When he left his apartment, Sean had walked a few blocks and turned back toward home. *On a Tuesday night? To be worthless for the rest of the week?* If he went out, he would end up hung over and tired and he had tried to reason with himself, but Sean couldn't see past tonight. There had been hundreds of Tuesdays up to this point in his life, and there was no reason this one should matter any more than the others he had wasted. He needed to go out lest he sit insanely in his apartment and stare back into eyes that were possibly fixed on his picture hundreds of miles away feeling the same madness, the same need to run, and the same impossible escape ahead. Was the backseat of this Towncar where Sean was supposed to be? On this insane lottery ticket run behind a lunatic at the wheel with three other unsuspecting passengers? Sean could no better account for this night than any other. No better than he could account for a Wednesday or a Thursday or an inebriated weekend. And no better than he could account for the things he had thought or said an hour ago, or what he would think and say in the coming hour. Sean had run from his apartment and into these people's lives. He knew he should pull his manners together and be thankful that he wasn't back at Baker's Tap halfway through a bottle of Southern Comfort, and halfway through a week that he would be left to survive alone after a night like that. Just the same, he licked his lips at the thought.

Sean tried to be quiet and enjoy the night, but that wasn't what life was for a guy like Sean. He didn't recognize the night for the darkness or the stars. Guys like him needed distractions like Sarah to calm them down and take their minds off their worth and what the hell they would accomplish in the next second. Accomplishments were the ticket to a fulfilled life; list of things done, tests conquered. That's what made the desperation go away. That's what he had heard from those older and wiser than him. And somehow the odd mixture of company in this car dissolved the constant pressure for success. They took a desolate soul lost within itself and tested it. This wasn't a test to be completed, though. It was like training. Sean was learning to live with the minutes and the seconds as himself, a lesson that came hard only thirty minutes since he had chased Sarah from Baker's Tap.

He sat back, allowing a moment more of silence as they traveled by the Pickwick Theatre in Park Ridge, one of the 1920s historical landmarks that had been beautifully preserved by its owner. Sean knew that the effort had been worthless, as someday it would be crumble like everything else. Sean looked down at the bags of chips he had purchased. He thought that maybe if he munched on something, he would get his mind off the drink that he so desperately wanted. "Okay, who wants Cheetos and who wants Doritos?"

"That's a lot of cheese," Vi chimed in, glad that someone had pulled her from her own internal battle before she began to really question what it was she thought she was doing with her life. When she noticed the blue bag in Sean's hands, Vi reached over the seat and took the bag. "I love Cool Ranch Doritos!"

"Oh no," William yelled. "There will be no bags of food opened in this car!"

Vi and Sean ripped into the two bags of chips simultaneously, the crackling of the plastic overpowering William's complaint. Tom also dug into the chips, but Sarah declined as she was always watching what she ate lest she become something she disliked. Her mother had continually explained to her over the years that Sarah was what she ate.

"Put those away," William whined. "I've never had food in this car, and I'm not about to start now." William tried to grab the bag of chips from Vi, but she pulled her arm away before he could reach it. "I don't want to be cleaning until Christmas after you slobs." William reached over to the passenger side again, but Vi was too quick for him.

She laughed at William's disgruntled expression. "You'd better just concentrate on driving and let us have a snack. If you keep trying to grab this bag, you're the one who's going to get the car all messy." Sean leaned forward and crunched a mouthful of Cheetos in William's ear, making a child's chewing and humming noise. This earned a smile from Tom.

"Don't make me come back there. If I have to pull over, you're in real trouble!" William was serious, his eyes set on the road, his fists clenched on the steering wheel. The air in the car stifled for three seconds as everyone held their breath, but even William burst out laughing when he realized what he had said.

"Jesus, William, you sounded just like my father." Sean laughed so hard that he almost choked on the chips in his mouth, and even Sarah laughed at what every parent in America must have said at least once, even hers. "Do you want a chip or what?" Sean offered the bag to William who declined. Tom gladly accepted the offer and ate the chips quickly in succession, one at a time. He rolled them into his mouth as if he hadn't eaten in days. "Easy there, Tom. Chew your food."

Vi turned to Sean in defense. "He is chewing, Sean. He's a growing boy. Leave him alone."

"You guys better not get crumbs all over the upholstery," William added.

"We'll vacuum the car when we get back. How's that?" Vi offered. "Of course, we can't get back until we get there."

William rolled his eyes in the mirror as he watched Tom's arm moving from the bag to his mouth like a machine, the same motion every time shoveling the chips in. "Are you going to complain about the drive again? I have to work in the morning too. Why do you care so badly about the time? It doesn't really mean anything, anyway."

Vi spit a Dorito on the dashboard in response to William's remark. "Time doesn't mean anything? What the hell's that supposed to mean?" Vi leaned forward and shined the dash with her sleeve, throwing the wet chip out the window. William waited to respond until she cleaned the vinyl to his satisfaction. Sean and Sarah leaned forward in anticipation of the impending argument.

"It means nothing anymore. It's just a marketing ploy

these days." William stopped, happy with his answer, but one look at the faces on the passengers in the car told him he'd have to defend himself again. He hadn't decided if Vi, Sean, Sarah, and Tom were suitable tools for an interesting conversation or if they simply annoyed him. "What does time mean in our society? Back in the day, men were like ants. They'd count on the seasons to collect the food and things that they'd need to get through the winter, and then they'd hunker down for winter. They needed the crops and the animals, and the time to take care of business. We don't need this now; we have artificial everything. Time isn't that important."

"What about crops? We still need food to live." Sarah felt justified with her answer. It surprised her she had just defended food, her reigning enemy for ten years running. It took William less than a second to respond.

"I could grow a cornstalk or a tomato plant, anything I want. I could live in a house in Alaska, and in the dead of winter. With a little man made heating equipment, light, and seeds, I'd be all set."

"You're not serious about this, are you?" Vi asked, certain that William was.

"I am. What does time mean to man these days? Not a thing. Tonight the newspapers already say that it's tomorrow, magazines say that it's next month, car manufacturers say that it's next year. I could be sitting in a 2000 Towncar with a November magazine and a Wednesday paper right now. Think about it. It's not Wednesday, yet the papers say that it is. It's not 2000 yet, but all the new cars on the lot? You betcha, 2000. It's ridiculous to me. Why can't we just call these things what they are? Why are we in such a rush?" No one answered

William, and he sat satisfied that he had proven his point and he would win this argument, ketchup on a hot dog or not.

Tom stopped eating the Cheetos and cleared his throat, handing the bag back to Sean. Tom didn't talk, he didn't converse, so when it seemed that he might want to, everyone sat patiently like a waitress waiting for a table to order. Tom stopped chewing on the Cheetos, stopped chewing on his thoughts, the ones that the rest hoped he would share. He wiped the cheese from his hands onto his pants before speaking. "It's like payday. This time thing is like payday. You work for two weeks and then they give you money for it. They date the check today though, not two weeks ago."

"Thank you!" William chimed.

"That's ridiculous," Sean said. "You are using an example that makes no sense to defend William, and he makes no sense."

"It makes sense," William defended Tom, if not himself.

"They release a magazine issue with next month on the cover because we're going to be reading it next month, after we find it in the store on the rack. It takes time to print and ship, you know." Sean was sure that everyone else had lost their heads, and Tom shrugged before sitting back, now with the bag of Cool Ranch Doritos to himself.

"But they wrote the articles and printed it last month, so why not just call it what it is?" William asked.

"Still makes no sense," Sean said defiantly.

"It makes sense," Vi agreed, watching Tom devour the yellow chips. "You're not one-year-old when you're born. You have to wait a year. You live a year, then you're one."

Sarah laughed as Sean shook his head ferociously and

covered his ears. "No, no, no! That makes even less sense. It's almost the complete opposite point William is trying to make. In fact, now I agree that he's the only one who is making any sense to me. What's in the air you guys are breathing over there?" Sean leaned over Tom and sarcastically sucked in a lungful of air. "William is right. The media has changed everyone and everything. Time means less and less for us as we grow older, that is, unless it's October of '00."

"Why next October?" Sarah asked, pulled into the joke.

"Because that's when these chips expire, and I don't want anything to happen to our friend Tom here." Tom smiled, pausing his feast, as he read the expiration date on the blue bag. He nodded and grabbed another chip.

"So if it's 11:38, is it the minute building up to 11:38, or is it 11:38 and some seconds?" Sarah asked inquisitively.

"It's 11:38 already?" William seemed frantic. "We'll never get there on time!"

"I'm sure that they'll still have tickets when we get there, William." Sean leaned forward to address Sarah's question. "It depends on whose theory you want to accept. I guess it could work either way."

Vi turned around and pulled the top of the seatbelt over her head so that she could sit comfortably. "That reminds me of the millennium, like 20th Century Fox. It's 1999 now, but for the past ninety-nine years it has been the 20th century. That never made sense to me."

William responded before anyone else could. "That's because the first hundred years until ninety-nine was the first century."

"Was man even around in the year ninety-nine?" Sean asked.

"We must have been or no one would have been here to keep track," Tom said unexpectedly. "You guys are so worried about our future, and we know nothing about our history. It's borderline pathetic." Tom sat motionless, waiting for the verbal abuse that was sure to follow, but everyone remained silent, looking in his direction. His father had taught him to keep quiet at all costs, but these four, Vi especially, had drawn him out. He prepared to retreat like a turtle hiding inside its shell until the fury outside subsided.

"We can't change the past, so what's the point of knowing it?" Sarah asked. She didn't care about her ancestors, only who she was and where she was going. She was still trying to break free of where she was, unsuccessful yet still hopeful in a hopeless sort of way.

History accounted for powerful people's decisions and mistakes. Sarah couldn't have cared less about Abraham Lincoln and George Washington or when and where they had meant something, much less their road to greatness. They didn't affect the outcome of what she had become. Sarah was sure that as an English girl, her mother would still control Sarah's life, and her father would still have no interest in who she was or wanted to be.

And the slavery issue? Well, that just wouldn't have affected her as a Yankee, would it? She smiled at the thought of herself on a scorching hot and humid summer day, done up in a corset and huge dress that covered every piece of skin but her face. Even in those times, her mother would have been doting over her to "sit up" and "don't eat that" because it would change her figure for the worse, and she didn't want to "look like those other girls who couldn't get husbands". Sarah's smile turned down, her daydream giving in to a tight-lipped sternness created by her anger and the hatred she felt toward her tyrant mother. These moments came and went; Sarah blaming her flaws on the training her mother had imposed, the insane lessons taught over and over until they were beaten into her subconscious. In this moment, Sarah blamed her mother instead of the food.

"Do you have any of those chips left, Vi?" Sarah asked politely, holding back a tone filled with the defiance that she felt in that moment. Sean handed over the remaining Doritos, and Sarah thanked him without opening the bag. She sat still, the wind filling her ears, trying not to crinkle the bag too loudly. Sarah reached in and pulled out a chip. She felt its rough texture between her thumb and forefinger. She knew that the Cool Ranch coating would leave a stain on her fingers, one that she would have to wipe on a tissue lest she lick her fingers in a second gesture of defiance against her mother.

Sarah held the chip up, still apprehensive of the consequences. If Sarah ate the chip, she might feel better, but in fact she would feel worse because she would have put something into her body that might leave a trace of unfit around her waist, something that might make men overlook her or turn away in disgust. That and it would make her breath stink. Sarah fought the battle alone, each blow crashing silently in her head. She played both sides, herself and her mother, arguing over a damned potato chip.

"Is something wrong with the Doritos?" Sean asked, wondering why Sarah stared down at the chips instead of eating them.

Caught off guard, Sarah lied. "No, I was just thinking about the whole history thing." Sean waited for Sarah to continue, but she kept quiet. Sarah bit into the Dorito and crunched half of it into her mouth. For a second, she felt victory stirring through her body. All the years of not wanting any food poured out of her. The tears and hatred that she squelched in her gut were all at once lost and then found again faster than a lighting bolt could strike. Her moment in the spotlight lasted exactly a second, and then Sarah thought about spitting the chip out.

She had images in her head of obese women, the images that her mother had planted there methodically over the years. Thoughts of being fat had made Sarah very sick for a couple of years, her tiny, pale frame working toward extinction. The effects still rode with her these years later, although she allowed herself enough nutrition to live. She was not ill, not sick to her stomach. She was bulimic, and she had been anorexic. Usually Sarah wasn't hungry, or that's what she had told herself. Other times, she would eat the foods her mother forbade. She would shove them down her throat in a moment of passion only a bulimic would know, the passion mixed with shame and guilt and the eventual purge. Sarah cringed as she imagined herself hovered over the toilet bowl like a heroine addict unable to keep her stomach. She was more disgusted with herself than an addict would have been because this was a habit that she chose, not the result of a drug. More guilt, more need for the potato chip, more need to sit still and never want for food again. Sarah hated her mother at this moment. She hated Frito Lay for making the chips and Sean for bringing them into this car. But mostly Sarah hated herself.

Sarah didn't want her mother to have a hand on her life tonight. This car, these people, they were her saviors. They would somehow help to change her. Sarah knew that, yet she hadn't known a thing for herself her whole life. She hoped that this one night was going to dictate her actions from here on out. Maybe Randy had been right to say that she was a snob and a bitch. Maybe he was right to leave her at the bar, and maybe Vi was right in the bathroom at the Amoco when she'd said that Sarah couldn't be single. Was that was her problem all along? The eternal quest for the perfect husband? If her parents were living proof, Sarah knew that money didn't guarantee love and happiness.

She forced herself to swallow the mushy Dorito and threw the other half out the window. Tom noticed and said nothing, but he looked into Sarah's eyes long enough to be saying something. She concentrated on the bag as she folded it carefully, still tasting the Ranch flavoring that would stay with her through the entire night. Tom took the bag from Sarah, her eyes moving up into his half-smile. He took the shame from her and brought back everything wonderful about this random drive with four strangers. Tom knew somehow. He had read her actions. Sarah wondered for a moment if Tom didn't talk much because he could read minds.

"The Rosemont Horizon!" Vi yelled. "Now I know where we are. I'm gonna play there someday."

"No way," Sean countered. "That's gotta seat over twenty-five thousand people. That's just a few more than Baker's Tap."

"I said someday, not tomorrow."

"She'll play there." Tom was still smiling at Sarah, but he turned his head to look at Sean quickly and decisively.

William stopped the car at a red light before the tracks at Mannheim Road. "Can I have free tickets? I'll come see you in concert."

"Sure," Vi smiled. "You can all have free tickets and back-stage passes. And after the concert, we'll drive out to the middle of nowhere to buy lottery tickets."

William waited for the laughter to subside before he defended his actions. "Phil's Breakfast and 7UP is not in the middle of nowhere. It's east of nowhere by about five miles."

5
PLANE NUMBERS

"Billions and Billions Served," William recited in amazement. "That's ridiculous." McDonald's, the best moneymaker of them all in the twentieth century, or whatever century this really was by Father Time's watch. William was thirty-seven, and he remembered when the red and yellow signs were still touting sales in the low millions. He wondered how many hamburgers they would sell before he was dead. He imagined himself ninety-three, walking the street with a cane and a hat, and as he dropped from a stroke, the last thing that he would see before fading into oblivion or heaven or hell would be the McDonald's sign. 'Over A Quadrillion Served', he imagined.

William smiled at the thought, figuring that there would be more people served at Mickey D's than there would be seconds in his life. "Remember going with your parents and getting the little toys in the illustrious Happy Meals?"

"We used to go to Burger King," Vi volunteered. "I'd walk around the house with that little crown on my head pretending that I was the queen of the green shag castle. I wonder if they still have those cardboard hats."

"They do." Sean was definite, and Vi turned in wonder at how he might know this. "What?" Sean said defensively. "I went to a toga party a few weeks ago and my friend had on a toga and a Burger King crown. It was actually one of the coolest outfits there."

"I don't know that I've ever been to a McDonald's," Sarah admitted. She remembered seeing a few commercials as a child when the nanny would allow her to watch television, and she remembered passing by McDonald's and Burger King in her mother's Jaguar, but she couldn't ever remember a time when her mother would answer her pleas with more than a, "That food is no good for you. You don't need it. Do you want to grow up to be fat? You are what you eat, you know."

Sarah commented once that it was called fast food, not fat food, and she'd like to be fast, so she wouldn't mind in this instance being what she ate.

Her mother had looked over at Sarah with an intense scowl. "Don't get smart with me," was the response, one that had taken Sarah years to appreciate. It dawned on Sarah when she was in high school that this was one of the sillier things for a parent to say, especially one who spent a sizable chunk of money on her education. This reaction was, of course, before Sarah realized that her mother didn't want her to get smart at all. She wanted Sarah to be a proper, beautiful, petite girl covered in gold and displayed like a trophy.

Sarah watched the yellow McDonald's arches slip behind the Towncar and realized too late that admitting she had never been to McDonald's was the wrong thing to say in a car full of fast food eaters.

"You are kidding me." Vi turned all the way around in her seat again so she could see Sarah. "William, we have to go back."

"They're closed. She'll have to go another day."

"They're closed? It's after midnight?" Sean asked.

"It's after midnight!" William yelled frantically, looking to the clock. "No way, it can't be."

"Well, I read it off your clock, so it must at least be 12:15 in the WORLD, OF, WILLIAM!" Sean's words rolled loudly from his tongue like a carnival announcer's.

"I can't believe this!" William huffed and hit the steering wheel, causing everyone in the car to freeze. "I've missed it!"

"We passed Phil's?" Sean asked, curious how angry the person in control of the vehicle was.

"I missed 12:12. 12:12 a.m. came and went and that's that." William was exasperated, and he shook his head as he drove on.

"Is Phil's in some sort of other dimension that you're taking us to?" Tom asked. Unable to decide whether the usually silent man was serious, no one commented. "We have to pass over the threshold at 12:12 or we can't get there?"

"Forget it." William drove on, clutching the wheel.

"What?" V prodded.

"Never mind. You guys will think that it's another stupid thing that I do, and I will not give you fuel for another discussion on my defects."

"We haven't been doing that, William. We're not trying to make fun of you. We're just trying to make conversation."

Vi reached over and touched William's arm. "Come on, tell us what's so important about 12:12?"

"Forget it," William yelled. "Just leave it alone!" At the instant William was defending himself, a loud pop sounded from outside the car and the steering wheel pulled to the right. "Not now!" William pulled the car over as everyone else braced for the impact that never came.

"What the hell was that?" Sean hollered from the back seat.

"More soothing sounds from my night in hell," William answered as he stopped the Towncar on the shoulder. "Flat tire."

———

William reached into the glove compartment to pop the trunk open. He exited without a word, and the others followed him out into the cool night air. The stretch of Route 72 was like that of a highway, four lanes divided by a median with no extra lighting. It was pitch black out and difficult to see, but that left room for the stars to shine. William removed Vi's guitar from the trunk, and Tom helped to remove the jack and the spare tire.

"It's beautiful out here." Vi and Sarah moved away from the car as the men worked the jack. Vi looked up at the sky and noticed the moon, a giant yellow ball shining down like a flashlight, whispering 'I see you' simultaneously to the world and to Vi alone. "This is what I miss living in the city. I can never see the stars. I think that's why so many people get lost. You have no perspective but your own world, and it's like there's nothing outside of it. Like Chicago is in some sort of self contained biosphere."

Sarah nodded in agreement, as her mother had taught her. Always be polite and agree, even if you really don't know what someone is talking about.

"What about you, Sarah?" Vi asked. "Do you like the city?" Vi lit a cigarette as she waited for Sarah's answer.

Sarah looked around for the line marking where the horizon met the ground, but it wasn't visible in the darkness. She could see across fields to the tollway that trailed by in the distance. Electrical power cables ran between the transformers that lined the highway like giant soldiers standing at attention.

"I like the suburbs more than the city. I guess it's because I'm more familiar, and I feel safe near home or something. The city is kind of depressing to me," Sarah answered, and then wondered why she was even talking to Vi. She tried to stay removed, but she was actually beginning to enjoy the conversation. It felt like they were at a different level, standing here on the side of the road. They were just looking at the stars instead of showing off knowledge by naming constellations. No one was asking opinions for discussion's sake. The questions were true and asked in a need of guidance in the right course of action to take. Sarah wondered if it was time to see the rest of the world, the real world.

"Why is the city depressing to you?" Vi asked.

"I don't know. It's just all those people crammed together and trying to be unique around everyone else. It just feels..." Sarah trailed off. She was going to say 'fake', but tonight she felt perhaps it was her life on the wealthy North Shore that was fake.

"Is that what people want, to be unique? I thought everyone wanted to fit in." As she let out a cloud of smoke, Vi played at skeptical, but she was really just aiming at conversation. Sarah didn't answer the question. She could see Sean approaching, and it was time to put on heirs.

"Everyone does want to fit in, but they also want to be unique in the group that they fit in to." Sean pulled at his jeans jacket as if he was going to take it off. "Are you ladies cold?" he said to Sarah.

"I'm fine," Sarah said as her arms hugged her tiny frame.

"That's very gentlemanly of you, but I'm fine, too." Vi smiled, her leather jacket fairly warmer than Sean's anyway.

"I'm just trying to be polite. I think that you ladies slamming on me is going to teach me manners." Sean's shoulders lifted as he placed his hands in his pockets. He smacked his lips, wishing that he could steal a drink in the darkness, but he would settle for a cigarette. "Can I bum one, Vi?"

Vi pulled out the pack and the lighter and lit Sean's cigarette. "You smoke?"

"Usually only when I drink," Sean replied, wondering how long it would be before he could steal a sip.

"Oh," Vi responded. "You're one of those."

Sean squinted at Vi as he took a long drag. "Yeah, one of those. Now, what's all this talk about being unique?"

"Oh, nothing." Vi shrugged as she looked back up into the sky. "I was just saying to Sarah that I miss all the stars. You can't really enjoy a starry sky in the city."

"Really? What's the difference between being able to see ten stars or a hundred?" Sean looked at Sarah instead of up at the sky that he was currently insulting.

"There is a difference." Sarah paused, deciding whether she wanted to continue with the answer on the tip of her tongue. "The stars are unique to the people wishing on them."

Vi stopped and looked at Sarah with a smile and a nod. "That's poetic."

"It is?" Sarah asked. She smiled, pleased that she had reached a depth she hadn't thought was within her. "I guess it is. Thanks."

Hands in his pockets and holding the cigarette between his lips, Sean kicked at the loose stones in the road. He wanted a drink to fill his stomach and words to fill his ears. He needed distractions. "What does the 'Vi' stand for? Vicki? Victoria? Victrola?"

"Yes, Sean. I'm named after a record player." Vi's condescending tone shut the boy up, causing another round of unwelcome silence. "Are you guys almost done over there?"

"Yeah, hold your horses," William yelled back. He was holding the flashlight for Tom who was removing the lug nuts. The mysterious passenger seemed happy for the job at hand that took his thoughts away from the big picture.

"I'm getting a little cold," Sarah said, hugging her slight frame more tightly.

"In one more month, we'll really be freezing our asses off," Sean commented as his hands moved around in front of him. He wasn't smoking the cigarette as much as he was just holding it, watching the orange fire float around in the darkness like a lightning bug in July. He wasn't cold. The alcohol had installed its fake heat shield around him.

"Why is it that people only freeze their asses off? Or

laugh their asses off, for that matter?" Vi field stripped the cherry from her smoke between her thumb and index finger before throwing the butt into the weeds on the shoulder of the road.

"You make the weirdest observations," Sean commented as he attempted to distinguish his cigarette as Vi had. He managed to burn the side of his index finger before dropping the butt to the ground and stepping on it.

Vi looked over her shoulder and down at her behind. "Well, I haven't lost my ass in the last few cold winters." She looked over at Sarah who shifted her frame uncomfortably, conscious of the eyes upon her figure. "But it looks like Sarah did." Vi laughed. Sarah didn't. "I was just wondering who first said that." The three stood silent as two cars shot by, rushing air across their faces.

"What's that?" Sean asked as he pointed to a tower on a farm about a quarter mile back.

"It looks like one of those grain storage things," Vi answered.

"It looks like a water tower to me." Sarah and the other two studied the skyline, trying to make out the odd figure. It was a grain storage tower, but instead of being cylindrical, there was a shape on top. The orange ball with a smiling face was difficult to see even under the floodlights that lit it.

"It looks like a pumpkin, but it can't be." Sean stood on his tiptoes, squinting his eyes in disbelief.

"It's the Great Pumpkin, Charlie Brown!" Vi laughed at her joke, but no one else did. "Come on, everyone watched the Peanuts special when they were kids. Don't you remember Linus waiting up for the Great Pumpkin who never shows?"

"I remember, Vi!" William called. He and Tom were kneeling on the ground, replacing the lug nuts on the spare tire. "It is a pumpkin on a grain tower. I know, it looks weird, but it's actually pretty cool. These people have a huge pumpkin picking farm."

"What is it? A balloon?"

"No, it's actually part of the tower. It looks like that all year round."

"Cool," Vi agreed. "That's a great idea. Could you imagine living in a giant pumpkin's head?"

"I don't think that anyone lives up there," Sean laughed at Vi. "I think it's just a decoration."

"I know," Vi defended her point. "I was just saying it would be like living in a water tower." Sarah and Sean's foreheads crinkled in question, not knowing if they should take Vi seriously or if this was just one of those things she said to fill the space between actual conversation.

"What? Ever since I was a kid, I always thought that it would be cool to live in a water tower. There was this one small one that had rust on the outside, and I would see it on the way to the Axle Roller Rink. You know where it used to be over by the Harlem Irving Plaza? Anyway, it was the weirdest thing because there were houses all around the thing, and at the base there was a little chain link fenced around the lawn. I always imagined that the cars on the street belonged to the people who lived up in there."

Sean laughed so hard at Vi that it took him a full minute to catch his breath. "That's one whacked out mind you've got going there."

"What?" Vi waited for Sarah to stop staring before she continued in her defense. "I still think that it would be cool to live in a water tower someday. Especially in one of those giant oval fat ones they make these days. You could have an elevator up the shaft and lots of skylights, and maybe the floor could open up into a pool. Wouldn't that be cool?" Vi lost herself in her imagination as she described her dream house. "I think it would be cool."

Sean and Sarah tried to contain themselves, and Vi attempted to ignore their mocking laughter. "When are we leaving, William? I'm taking some abuse over here."

"In one minute," William yelled over the passing truck. We're finishing up now." He tightened the wheel locks as Tom placed the flat tire in the trunk. "What was that whole thing about 12:12?" Tom asked quietly as he took the lug wrench from William.

"Nothing." William stood and brushed the dirt from his slacks. "Okay, I'll tell you." William looked at the others to make sure they weren't listening, and Tom waited in his familiar silence. "Twelve is my lucky number. So I buy my tickets at 12:12, you know, for more good luck. I didn't mean to get angry about it, it's just that usually I get there with time to spare, and nothing has gone as planned tonight." William waited for Tom to erupt with statements of how ridiculous that was.

"You're superstitious, that's all." Tom shrugged, opened the back door, and slid to the center of the backseat in anticipation of sitting between Sean and Sarah.

"I am not superstitious. I just need all the luck that I can get." William waited for a car to pass before opening the driver's door. "Are you jokers coming?"

"Shotgun!" Sean yelled. As Sarah and Vi made their way

toward the car, Sean stole a slug of his vodka and replaced the flask before anyone else noticed it. He ran over to the Towncar. "Sorry ladies, I called shotgun."

Without argument, Vi climbed into the back seat with Sarah. Tom slid toward the driver's side, taking the seat behind William and leaving Vi in the middle. "William's superstitious?" Sarah asked as she closed the door.

"He is," Tom confirmed, a little nervous now that Vi was next to him. "He believes in lucky numbers."

"That's not superstitious," Vi defended William as he pulled the car into the right lane and proceeded northwest toward Phil's Breakfast and 7UP.

"Yeah," Sean agreed from the passenger seat. "Everyone has a lucky number. That's not paranoid. Superstitious is like walking under a ladder or breaking a mirror."

"Or black cats crossing your path," Sarah added.

"See?" Vi asked Tom as she looked to her left. His eyes were so green, and even in the dark, Vi could see them looking into her. Neither looked away, and Vi almost burst with excitement before remembering her music. It always brought her back. As appealing as Vi was finding Tom tonight, her music and her dream of Nashville would have to remain her only lover for now.

Tom smiled. "That is superstition. Are these numbers astrologically your lucky numbers, or do you pick them?"

"My lucky number is four," Vi defended. "And I chose it."

A wave of freedom mixed with actual happiness flowed across Tom's heart. "So it's not really lucky. You just like it." Tom was here, making his point to the others. He was speaking out loud, talking and responding. And he was sitting right next to Vi: not in the audience three tables back on the left, not on the bus ride home thinking of her, and not in his bed dreaming her face and her voice. He was sitting next to her, their hands practically touching. As he inhaled, the same magical air that she breathed out was reaching his lungs. It brought a confidence to Tom that he had never felt before. He could do anything.

"He makes a good point, Vi." William agreed with Tom, although he still believed that twelve was his lucky number. The argument did, however, make him feel better about missing his 12:12 A.M. deadline.

"Do you believe in all of that astrological crap?" Sean asked without turning around. "You probably call the psychic hotline once a day."

"What's wrong with psychics?" Sarah asked, nudging the back of Sean's seat.

"Did you ever notice that the word 'chics' is in the word 'psychics'? You women will believe anything."

"We would have to for a guy like you to ever get laid." Vi's comment stung at Sean, but he bit his tongue. Whether he liked it or not, these four people had become the rest of his Tuesday night, and he was trying to get along. He didn't want William to leave him on the side of the road, and he hoped he could convince them all to hit a bar after Phil's 7UP.

———

William drove on, believing that twelve really was his lucky number. He had picked it for his basketball jersey in sixth grade and had held on to it all these years. No psychic was going to pick luck for him. What did they really know, anyway? William's loopy sister, Jennifer, was into that voodoo stuff. She and her friends had sleepovers when they were younger, and they'd pull out the Ouija board and move the needle around, spelling things randomly. William knew that one of them had to be moving the piece, as he found it utterly impossible that a spirit would really want to make its grand reentrance to the world through a thirteen-year-old girl holding a séance in her pajamas. But on Jennifer and her friends went, answering their own questions, the same ones William sat alone and answered with his Magic 8 Ball.

When they were older, Jennifer took William to a palm reader. She had taken all of her siblings throughout the years. They drove together to a dreary part of the city and entered a dilapidated house that appeared as though it would crumble to the ground any minute. William had made a joke that the psychic knew nothing if her crystal ball hadn't at least told her to evict herself from this abode before she died in the falling rubble. But Jennifer, who was used to William's sarcasm, ignored him and pressed on into a dark living room that doubled as a lobby.

The incense choked him, and he had waited cynically, counting the mystic paraphernalia that littered the tables and the walls. After spending fifteen minutes with his sister, a middle-aged woman dressed in robes with a scarf wrapped over her head, 'the witch' William had named her in his thoughts, called to him. She brought him back into a small, dark room and told him to sit down and to clear his mind. There were cards and stones laid out on the table between them. William had looked around for her crystal ball, but found none.

After sitting in silence with her eyes shut, the witch lit some incense and decided on the bag of rocks. William waited as she emptied the bag and placed new stones in it. Then she handed it to William and asked him to roll the bag in his hands and to think of one question. He did this, trying to keep the topic in his mind about what he would have for lunch. But the silence took him in, and he wondered about his life and his death and the things in between.

The witch eventually took the bag from William and let the rocks tumble onto the table. William waited as she made her predictions, sometimes tilting her head and making indistinct noises with her throat. It was a strange feeling, not believing in what he was here for and also curious about what she had to say. People will gladly listen to anyone tell them about their lives just to hear someone else's version. A condensed story listing the highlights was always a better time without chronicling all the tedious tasks a human goes through each day. William was not a believer, but as he watched her stare at the stones, her cheeks wrinkling and then softening, he became interested.

In a room filled with William's hopelessness, the witch really had somehow dug into her magic rocks and brought an answer to his morbid thoughts. William was thinking about his father when he'd held the rocks, rolling the bag around on his fingers. At the time, the old man had been seeing a doctor about his relentless coughing, and although his parents had told no one, William knew that something was wrong. So his questions had been about his father's health, but the answer had not.

The witch, after minutes of staring at William, told him he was scared. This was something that few men will admit, and William sure as hell would not admit it to some middle-aged bat. So he sat and listened and tried not to hear what she had to say. The witch told William that he should learn to live with himself. She said that two plus one was three, and that he was the third. She said that someone was always the first to die, and someone had to be the last.

William, at thirty-seven now and single, found himself driving four strangers to his lucky spot and thinking about the witch. He was the third in a line of five children. His father had died after a brief battle with lung cancer, and his mother was holding on by the thread that her grandchildren had strengthened. It had been ten years since William had gone with his sister Jennifer to see the witch, and he was now thinking about the prophecy she had left him. He had learned to live with himself, and although he enjoyed being single, he thought that someday he might settle down.

He decided the witch had reinforced his lucky number twelve, one plus two made three, and he was the third child. It was the last part of her observation that bothered William. His father's death wasn't a question for long after he had met with her, but she had said that someone was always the first to die, and someone was always the last. He couldn't imagine life without his brother and three sisters, and yet one of them would have to be the first, and one would be around as all the others passed away until that one was alone. Only one could be the last. William didn't know if he would be the first to go, but he didn't want to be the last, the one left holding all the memories and no one to share them with.

"I saw a psychic once," William told no one in particular.

"You did!" Sean reacted loudly.

"My sister made me go. It was no big deal."

"I bet you're one of those people who reads their horoscope every day."

Sarah leaned forward. "And what's wrong with that?"

"It's not real. You're going to let some newspaper writer tell you how to act and what to feel all day?" Sean rolled up his window and the inside of the car was quiet aside from the argument beginning to boil on the passenger side of the car. "They're so obscure in those messages. 'Taurus: your day is a three. You should definitely go to work today, as it will help with your finances for the week. Romance is a bummer today because someone you love does something you don't like. If you don't have anyone to love right now, stay home and hide because anyone you meet will scowl at you.'"

"Come on, Sean. It's not that bad." Sarah defended her position, but her open smile made her less convincing.

"Do mine, Sean. I'm an Aries," Vi joined in.

"Aries," Sean thought for a second. "You will go to work and work hard, and some people will notice how hard you worked. Romance is a nine because when you step outside today, members of the opposite sex will fall from the sky into your lap. Wear an enormous hat and beware." Sean crossed his arms and smiled, pleased with his performance.

Vi laughed at the prophecy, wondering if Tom had perhaps fallen out of the sky. "What did your psychic tell you, William?"

"I don't remember. Not much, I guess. It was about ten years ago." William kept his eyes on the road as he shied away from the current topic.

"Santa's Village!" Vi yelled as she pointed to her left. "I

never knew where this place was. We used to come out here with my aunt every summer. It always seemed so far."

"Everything seems far when you're a child. Children live in dog years. Every year for adults is like seven for a kid." Sean looked at the park and remembered his own time spent on an indoor ice rink playing games in the children's ice hockey league. They had been ten years old but were tough, mean, little boys pushing and shoving and bleeding, their fathers cheering for them to push harder and to knock the other kids over.

Sarah couldn't see from her seat, so she leaned over, causing Vi to lean toward Tom. Vi caught her arm on the door and looked at Tom who stayed relaxed, looking right back into her eyes. They remained locked in time, their eyes less than a foot apart. Vi thought of his lips and then looked away for an instant, hoping her red cheeks remained invisible in the dark. She could feel her face burning in embarrassment and tried to push back on Sarah. Her glance strayed back to Tom. He was still watching.

Sarah had loosened up a little, and it felt good in a way. Among her family and those she called friends, life was always a show with a level of sharp competitiveness. But here she felt like one of the gang and understood what Randy might have been after in a place like Baker's Tap. These were the pieces of society she had seen having fun on television shows. They were nothing like the high society prisoners who Sarah had grown up around.

"I never went to Santa's Village when I was a kid. But my parents did let our chauffeur... I mean, they drove me fast through a really hilly area once." Sarah remained hunched over Vi until the park was out of sight.

"Was it fun?" Vi asked as she slowly pulled back from in front of Tom and straightened up in her middle seat.

"It was great." Sarah's laugh built from a chuckle and she went on for almost a minute before letting everyone else in on her joke. "I threw up on my mother. It was one of the best times of my life."

6

TRASH

William and Sean both stared out ahead and Sarah looked out the window to her right, but Tom's attention was on Vi. He had been looking directly at Vi since Sarah had pushed her into him. Vi turned to her left and let their eyes meet again. Most would have looked away when caught in the act, only to peer back when no one noticed. But Tom kept his gaze fixed on her, and Vi was the one to look away first.

Tom looked right into her, like he knew exactly who she was because she was part of him. He looked at her as a cat would, staring unabashedly, creating questions of discomfort in the object of interest. But Vi wasn't uncomfortable under his gaze.

Vi hadn't even talked to Tom until tonight, and it would have been wrong of her to think that he really knew any part of her, but he was opening her heart, and a sense that she had put away years ago resurfaced. The piece of herself that she rarely allowed was beckoning her, beating on its cage walls, and yearning to be set free.

Vi felt beautiful at that moment. She was sitting between two strangers, and her hair was still tousled although the windows were closed. The clothes she wore weren't the most feminine; nothing like the ensemble which, doubtless, must have taken Sarah an hour to put together. Vi liked to wear jeans and a simple blouse, her leather jacket bringing out the rebel in her. She never wore make-up, although they would make her someday when she hit the main stage. Vi was practical about her appearance, and she always felt like a hard shell holding a sensitive soul.

She knew who she was inside, but when it came to her looks, she just let them be. She was a tough girl, a brute, she thought, a protector. Not pretty like Sarah, surely not the small, petite, model type. She was a beast with a large frame, overweight but strong. She was smart, practical, and educated, but with fashion, she was at a loss. Picking out a wardrobe intimidated young women like Vi just as genuine conversation intimidated young women like Sarah. It hadn't occurred to Vi that she appeared different to the world than how she appeared in her mind. It hadn't occurred to her she might be beautiful. Distance from beauty was a matter of fact for Vi, and it surprised her when a man was attracted to her.

Vi could almost hear Tom whispering to her, leaning over into her ear and breathing: *You're beautiful.* She would believe it if Tom said it because he wasn't just looking at her body, he would be talking about all of her. Vi thought she could count the total number of words Tom had spoken since he had gotten in the car. But it wasn't about them getting acquainted. She was not naïve to their building chemistry and the fire that his stare was igniting. Tom had spoken to her, all those weeks of watching her play, all of those weeks of silence. His eyes expressed his need, although she could never see their color because the dim bar lighting had never done justice to the piercing glassy green of his soul. Vi glanced over at Tom who was still looking. She could swim inside his gaze, free and unguarded, allowing herself to be vulnerable in his presence.

Again the whisper, "You're beautiful." Vi looked at Tom in a question, her cheeks red, wondering if he had actually spoken aloud. She felt the gift of promise as a cool sensation rode up and down the back of her neck, leaving ripples of pleasure around her heart, a feeling amplified by the heat that unfolded her own longing. At this moment, in the wicked hours of the night, she rode along with a smile, knowing that Tom would see it, and hoping that he would know he was the one that put it there.

"Are there any more chips left back there?" Sean asked.

"I don't see any." Sarah smacked her tongue to the roof of her mouth and could still taste the Cool Ranch flavor. Tom and Vi scoured the backseat and the floor, but the bags were gone. "What happened to them?"

"I thought you guys were finished, so I threw them out." William said this flippantly, and he was obviously glad they were gone.

Sean looked at William for a long moment. "I can't believe you threw them out. I bought those, you know."

"They were practically empty." William shrugged off the complaint. "I'm sorry. I'll buy you another bag if it will make you happy."

"It will." Sean was angry, and no one else added to the conversation, as they didn't want to get into an argument with the temperamental Irish boy especially while he might still be drunk.

His last swig of vodka was wearing off, Sean knew, and he wanted another few sips to rid the lingering aftereffects that were chasing through his body, causing him to sober up. He had thought this would be a quick ride and maybe he'd get lucky with the beautiful Sarah. Then he'd go home, have a couple more brews, and crash for the night just in time to get up for work.

He wanted another drink. He needed it. Sean was twenty-four, out on his own, and he felt like a man. He liked to hit the bars and pick up women. He had no intention of keeping any of them. At least no longer than it took him to scramble his thoughts in their skin and relieve his tension in fewer strokes than at a good run on a golf course.

Sean had been truly and desperately in love before. She had been his best friend for years, and he let her go. He let her get married without a word of protest. Sean believed she would figure it out on her own. Hell, at the time Sean didn't know himself that he had these feelings. But he knew it three years ago, the day he left for the big city of Chicago. On that day, he couldn't say goodbye. He needed her. He wanted to call her every day, but he didn't want to get her in trouble with her nagging husband.

Sean had watched for a couple years in disgust as she stuck by her man's side through three other women. She had a possessive spouse who only turned his back long enough to step out on her. Sean dreamed she was now divorced and searching desperately for him. She had called him once when her husband was out of town, and they talked for two hours. It hurt to love someone who allowed herself to be trampled on when the promised land was waiting at the other end of the line. She called again later that week and laughed and then cried as her old drunken friend, Sean, confessed his deepest sin; to covet his neighbor's wife; to beg each day for one night of her adulterous affection. After years of keeping a secret that made him ashamed, bold, and cowardice in the same wish, Sean had never expected to hear her repeat his words. Yet she had spoken them aloud, after seven years of friendship. *I love you.*

Sean wanted just one beer. One would rid him of the sticky mouth that was developing around his tongue. It would take away the animosity that drove through him and the hurt he tried to hide from himself. The bottle befriended him where she had left off. It held his hand in the dark and told him she loved him, even though they were worlds apart. He knew deep inside that releasing the secret had killed what was left of their friendship. The alcohol painted pictures of a future that he had both given up on, yet was subconsciously waiting for.

Sean turned around and looked in the backseat, but the bags of chips were gone. He felt the metal flask under his jacket and knew that sneaking a drink here would be impossible. He shouldn't have called shotgun because at least in the backseat Sarah's legs offered a distraction, and now he'd just have to sit still until they got to Phil's.

"I can't believe that you threw out the Doritos."

"I said I was sorry." William rolled his eyes.

"That's okay." Sean sat still, looking at William. He hunted for a topic of conversation, anything but the silence would do. "Wait, it's not okay."

"What's the problem now?" Vi sat forward, ready to stop the argument that Sean had been working toward.

"I was just thinking…"

"That's a stretch." Vi laughed, interrupting Sean. She sat back in her seat, realizing that she would end up starting an argument faster than she could stop one. "Sorry, go on."

"I was just thinking that I hate the way we always tell someone 'that's okay' when they say they're sorry. People do some terrible stuff, and then they say 'sorry'. And that's supposed to undo it?"

"It was a bag of chips," William yelled. "I'll buy you another one!"

"No, I'm not talking about that." Sean sighed and unbuckled his seatbelt before turning around in his seat to face the back. William flinched, but Sean ignored him. "Why do we automatically say 'okay' even when we're really hurt?"

Sarah answered first. "Maybe it's because we're trained that way. Parents teach us that sort of thing. It's like 'please' and 'thank you'." Sarah knew her etiquette, if nothing else.

Tom sat still and formed his next remark. He was getting used to this talking, this opening up, this being social, something that he had banned himself from over the years. He cleared his throat to speak. "I think that it's more than our parents teaching us. I think we need to tell someone it's all right for ourselves. If we didn't say 'okay', then we'd just be carrying this anger around with us. We'd never let anything go." Tom knew about building up anger and not letting it go. It controlled a person. He also knew that some things were unforgivable, and a million 'okay's' wouldn't excuse them. The word 'sorry' could never make them better. Tom had learned this difference in the most terrible of lessons. *I beat you and your brother. I beat and raped your mother. I'm sorry.*

"It's maddening," Sean turned forward and buckled his seatbelt, glad for the diversion brought on by conversation. He dug in for more talk. "I still can't believe that you threw two plastic bags out on the side of the road. They call that littering."

"What do you care about the environment?" William shook his head at Sean's taunting him. "You live in a city where everyone litters. Besides, you don't live anywhere near here, so it's not like those bags will blow around your neighborhood."

"No, but there is such a thing as recycling." Sarah could have led this conversation. She had a unique appreciation for recycling. When she was in college, she had run the recycling program in her dorm the first year and in her sorority after that. It was an interest that had started early in life, before recycling was fashionable and picked up weekly next to the trash.

Sarah's mother had taken her to a garbage dump once to show her what the world's trash looked like, causing a young Sarah to come away with a sense of disgust for humanity and a larger appreciation for the earth. This would have been a good day's lesson if her mother had been trying to prove the positive effects of recycling and that nature should be revered and watched after. But the lesson that her mother was trying to teach that day was the importance of looking one's best. "When you let yourself go, this is how people see you," her mother had said over and over on their visit to the trash dump, their silver BMW shining amongst the filth. Sarah's stomach turned for the memory, and she knew that years of therapy would not undo her mother's influence on what she had become.

Sarah was beautiful and rich, and she was out in the world looking for a husband because that's what her mother had told her she should be doing. But she didn't think that she wanted a husband because that would eventually lead to having children, and Sarah was afraid that she would parent them as her mother had her. She knew that this was a possibility because she had heard her mother speak of her own mother with hatred in her words. Sarah listened to stories from her mother's childhood, which usually began, "You're lucky that you have it so easy, because when I was a child, my mother would make me…" Sarah didn't want that to be her in ten years, saying this same thing as her child looked up at her mother politely, inside feeling anger and hatred, hoping to wither away into nothing.

Sarah turned to Vi and then looked back out the window. She admired Vi, as hard as that was to admit. Earlier at Baker's Tap, Sarah had been insulting everything and everyone around her. She had really believed that they were all inferior. And now Sarah realized that years of her mother's coaching had made her exactly what she had vowed to hate. Sarah saw something ahead, something she'd have never recognized if Randy hadn't dumped her in the bar. It was change. It was the ability for her to take control of her life. It was a single chance on the only night she would be surrounded by people who expected nothing of her. These people she was with, they were real. They had lives and hearts and wishes of their own. They had personalities beyond money. Sarah saw Vi, pretty and uncluttered, venturing out into the world with only a dream. Where

Sarah felt like an object without spirit or substance, Vi had character. Sarah had grown up learning that you are who you know. You are who the world sees on the outside.

And the world saw a beauty in Sarah, with her slight frame, her tight legs and silky hair. She didn't feel that beautiful. It didn't fill her up and make her truly happy inside. The body that Sarah saw was hunched over a toilet bowl, destroying her stomach lining as she threw up what small amount of nourishment she had allowed herself. The woman she saw in the mirror padded her bras to give shape to the bony chest underneath her clothes. On and off over the years, she had lost hair and had suffered from skin discoloration. Still, she longed to be one of the magazine models that her mother constantly pointed out to her.

Sarah had been crying for help. She was in and out of hospitals that would pump her full of nutritional supplements and send the resident therapist to fix her mind. Sarah's mother was less concerned about her daughter's wellbeing than she was about what others would think, and Sarah's father showed little worry between board meetings. The nurses and doctors were the only ones who really seemed to care, sometimes even more than Sarah did. She would show progress but then relapse.

Sarah knew they expected her downstairs one day, in the morgue, her body frozen as cold as her heart was empty. This did not deter her battle to look pretty. She was never skinny enough, never small enough. Blonde hair, blue eyes, a soft demeanor. She had the perfect upbringing, always in training for her adulthood. The right clothes, the perfect taste and table manners. Yes, the world saw a beauty in Sarah.

Although she spent hours doing so, Sarah hated to look in the mirror. All she saw within herself was at the same time pathetic and horrific. She knew the words, her diagnosis. She could say them, she understood them. She was in a cycle of anorexia and bulimia. That was what they told her. They had tests and long explanations for the results, but they didn't understand what they were dealing with, not really. No treatment could fix her. Sarah could look in the mirror, she could see what was going on, and she had no intention of stopping. She could see her life and her destiny. She was alone, a little girl who had been on a suicide mission for ten years.

———

Tom pulled the switch on the door that made the window slide down. He let the glass move about six inches and then stopped it. October had been milder than usual. There was the rain and mist, and the frost had coated the grass a couple of mornings, but the temperature during the day had been reaching into the upper fifties, tricking everyone into believing that there was still a hint of summer in the air. Tom wished that Mother Nature would stop teasing him. He wanted winter, he was ready for the cold. This was the time of year when everyone in Chicago was sick because they didn't wear enough clothing. If it was sunny and fifty, people wore shorts with sweatshirts, a mixture of clothing that only made sense to Yankees. Tom never wore shorts; his bare legs would have blinded a baby if they weren't covered with fine black hair.

Tom put his elbow on the door and his hand on the top of

the window, the wind racing through his fingers. He remembered being a child and seeing his father drive this way with one hand on the wheel and the other in the window. Tom would roll his window down and try to put his arm up like this, but he was too small, and he would end up fighting the wind with his palm. His father would look over and laugh and one of the few tender smiles his old man had ever given would cross his lips. This was one of the few good memories that Tom had of his father. It was the one moment that Tom felt like a son, a child growing up like other children, his father coaching him and smiling; an affectionate moment. This, of course, was while Tom still thought the punishment he took, the abuse, was his fault. He'd spent most of those years trying to fix himself, trying to make his father love him, trying to create more tender moments of joy like when he would try to imitate his father by putting his hand up in the window. But there were no other memories like this one.

The vile memory built in his stomach and slowly made its way up toward Tom's heart as he took his arm off the door. The memory kept coming in with the wind, and Tom rolled the window up. He could see a distorted reflection of himself in the glass; his lips curled down in a frown, his eyes blank, showing no emotion. The way he presented himself to the world was how he learned to present himself to the drunken bastard. No happiness, no fire and hatred, just death.

As Tom stared, he noticed Vi looking into the same reflection, trying to see his face, leaving him wondering how she could have known that something was wrong. If she could read him so easily, she must have known that she held his heart. She must have felt it beating faster as the memories hung in the window, and she must have sensed that his soul was not at ease.

Tom drew a long breath, cursing himself for letting his father into the car with him. He tried to smile at Vi to show her that everything was okay. He should hide from her as he had from everything else, even life, for so long. Tom didn't want her to know his past, one filled with nightmares. But Vi was a songwriter. She looked into people and pulled melodies from their joys and pains. She could recognize the solitude of a tragic memory. Vi could read an expression as others did street signs. He knew he would tell her someday.

Vi tried to return Tom's smile, although her curled eyebrows told Tom that she could see him thinking and wondered what was wrong. He didn't want her worrying about his problems. He wanted to make her hopes and dreams come true, although Tom knew now that her dreams were the same as his, and they would grow their dreams together. Hand in hand meant something more equal than just pulling someone into his or her future. He continued to watch Vi watching him. She was studying his eyes, searching for her melody. Somehow, after four months of wanting, four months of silence, he finally had her attention.

7
ROBOTS

They watched Spring Hill Mall fall back on their right as William drove farther west. Route 72 merged in to a two-lane road, and the housing developments became fewer as they drove. The street was no longer lit, and William's four passengers sat in complete darkness on a road that they had never traveled down. They were all the way into Kane County. William enjoyed taking this drive every week. Sometimes, when the moon was full, he could see the countryside as if it were lit up around him in a bluish glow. Illinois was mostly flat. In some places, it appeared her Creator had taken a leveler to the earth, and one could see straight for miles. In other places, hills rolled over the land, and the trees were littered in clumps across the acres.

The night was clear and well lit by the moon. William kept the Towncar close to the speed limit so he wouldn't miss any of the turns. He knew this road by heart, but this night differed from any other because of those in the car with him. They took his mind off the road, and William studied his past and questioned his future.

Thirty-seven was a good age for a man. It was not too old to get married, and not too young for a confirmed bachelor. William hadn't gone through life searching for someone else to keep him entertained like his brother and sisters had. He still preferred to be alone. He answered to no one but himself. He wasn't afraid of marriage and liked the company of the women he had dated, but there was some reason he wasn't following the path of the many. William could imagine himself married, but he couldn't imagine himself with a wife. He knew the day would probably come, but he was holding out until the last second, the one in which a man decides that he needs to carry on his last name. It was the same finality that had sucked all of his friends into the world of permanent couple hood.

For the moment, he had the car he wanted, and a nice flat in Chicago with a killer entertainment center that his buddies drooled over. The spare room, the one that he would convert into a nursery after he was married, was William's pool hall. Sometimes William felt lonely, but he had developed rituals to keep his mind occupied. Like the lottery tickets. He had never bought one until his buddy Steve had coaxed him into it. Soon after, William had found Phil's Breakfast and 7UP and had made lottery tickets part of his weekly routine, so necessary that he actually felt bad if he missed a trip out to the diner. It had become a habit for William nearly a year earlier, and for a while he had been compulsive about it. Then, after a snowstorm in February forced William to stay home, the spell was broken. Sure, he still took the drive, and he had realized a while ago that he had become a little anxious about the timing of the purchase, but William didn't think of it as a real problem or addiction. He wasn't like one of those people that compulsively cleaned all the time or straightened the fringe on the edges of rugs. He just wanted what he wanted when he wanted it, that was all.

"Did you guys notice all those houses?" Sean commented.

"Single family homes, they're called," Vi added.

"They all look the same, and I don't know why they're called single family homes. In some countries, houses like that would hold one man, three wives, and eighteen kids."

William eyed Sean. "You want three wives?"

"No way!" Sean yelled. "Not at the same time, anyway. And I'm still working on the first one."

"You want eighteen kids?" Vi asked from the back.

"No." Sean moved to put his left foot up on the dashboard and then reconsidered, lest William flog him for passenger insubordination. "But I probably have that many out there, somewhere, lost in the world of one-night stands."

"How poetic." Vi's sarcasm was obvious, but Sean didn't respond.

Sarah became angry. She'd had a lot of one-nighters, more than she cared to admit, and they shamed her now longer than they had given her pleasure then. "I don't understand how guys can have one-night stands."

"Well, if we're having them, then you girls must be having them too." Sean smiled righteously.

"It's not the same," Sarah defended, unable to verbalize what she was feeling.

"Of course it is."

Vi came to Sarah's defense. "No, it's not. Women don't go to bed with someone thinking only of sex. Whether or not we want to admit it, we always think long term."

"I thought long term once," William smiled at Sean as he slammed his point home, "I signed a *two* year lease on an apartment." Sean laughed and even Tom snickered. Vi and Sarah scowled.

Vi dug in. "Listen, a man goes to bed with a woman, and, if he happens to even stay the whole night, he wakes up in the morning thinking, 'Thanks, baby. See ya'.'"

"So what?" Sean shrugged. "That's the nature of the one-night stand. Why bother getting all emotional about it?"

"Because, Sean, a woman sleeps with a man, and even if she does so knowing it might be a one-night stand to him, she still wakes up thinking, 'What are we doing today?' It's a curse, really. But we can't help it."

Sarah leaned forward and nodded in agreement. "We do that."

Sean ended the conversation with a huff. Knowing Vi was right, and remembering a few of the disappointed faces as he had walked out of their lives, he rethought whether he should continue to work on Sarah tonight. It was between her and a pint of vodka. He'd think about it.

––––––

Sarah opened her eyes, and it took her a second to get acclimated to her surroundings. She had closed them five minutes earlier to relax, to forget. She was tired and felt like rolling into bed, but she was countless miles from home with strangers, and matters in her life made no difference to her anyway. That was how she felt on most nights when she had a date. She sometimes ended up in a backseat flushed with darkness, and those times she usually wanted to be home, alone, falling into her dreams. She would stare at the ceiling before sleep and think of the life that she had really wanted to live. Sarah had a Mary Tyler Moore fantasy. She'd be out on her own in her perfect apartment, spending real time with her friends. She would have a job and her own income, and her mother would be a million miles away as her father had been for most of her life.

Sarah became a completely different person in these fantasies. She was still beautiful; she looked the same, maybe a little healthier, but her taste in clothes was a little smarter instead of the model-esque designs she currently wore. Her wardrobe was less cute and looked more businesslike. She was a woman about town, a self-assertive character. Sarah looked over to Vi who was propped up between her and Tom. Vi was less put together beauty-wise. She didn't wear make-up, and she didn't really seem to care about her hair very much. She didn't carry a purse nor have the same constant need for a mirror that most women did. Vi was just out there, in the world, not trying to pretend to be someone else. Vi wore jeans instead of slacks or a skirt, and her leather jacket fit her image perfectly, although Sarah could never wear that short biker's style, preferring a more elegant long, thin leather.

When Sarah dressed, she took her time and made a state-ment to the world. *I have money. I am put together. You can't touch me.* Inside, Sarah knew the message that she heard when she looked in the mirror was different. *I have money, and on the outside I look great, but I am as put together as a brand new puzzle in an unopened box. I am completely fake. Try to get to know me, go right ahead. If you find something, let me know. I have been searching for years.*

Randy had been looking, though. He had seen something. He had been willing to put up with Sarah's games, her whims and deceptions. He actually seemed to care about Sarah the person instead of Sarah the status. And although he had walked out on her tonight, Randy had begun a chain of belief within her, a pattern that grew stronger with each mile she was beyond her family and her home. Sarah looked objectively at the experience and at the people in the car with her. She allowed herself to let down a little more guard, to bring level her upturned nose. She thought that somehow the lesson was necessary, and it scared her a little.

Vi looked at Sarah whom had been staring at her for a few seconds. Then Vi smiled and looked forward, leaving Sarah to her observations. Sarah closed her eyes and tried to control her emotions. She wasn't clinically depressed, and she wasn't taking any pills for depression as her doctor had wished, but her mother was all too willing to get Sarah doped up on the same medication that she had used for equilibrium in her own unbearable life. But Sarah wanted the feelings; she wanted the tears and the lamentations. Sarah knew that if she let herself feel every second, she could make it out of her prison. Vi was proof of that to Sarah, proof that she could make it. Sarah's mother had kept her sheltered from other working class women. Men worked, and women spent the money or droned along and languished in their solitude. But Sarah's life could be different.

Sarah had been thinking about making a break for it, a run for her life. She had been contemplating her will to live for eight months, ever since she had refused the medication her therapist had offered, ever since she had decided that her parents would never really love her and that she'd have to love herself. It would be difficult, as her mother had kept Sarah penned in.

Sarah didn't think of killing herself, not once, although the anorexia and bulimia might have been a symptom of self-destruction. If it was a call for help, no one was answering. Sarah thought about waking up after death, getting on with her life after cutting all ties. No one back home worrying about her or hounding her, just visiting her stone and remembering her as she went on living her fantasy. There was one flaw that had stopped Sarah from planning anything too drastic: one thought that kept her on the breathing side of complete annihilation. Sarah knew that it was impossible to wake up dead.

"You know what this view reminds me of?" Sean asked from the passenger seat.

"No," William answered sarcastically, although it had been a rhetorical question.

"Well, I'll tell you. The way you see that farm passing by and trees and flat fields in the moonlight, but it's so gray that it's really hard to see. It reminds me of the Civil War." Sean sat pleased with his description. It lacked prose, but to a high school-educated boy, it was downright poetic.

"This reminds you of the Civil War?" Sarah asked as Vi leaned forward, interested in the topic.

Like most of the romantics she knew, Vi had always been

a history fiend. The way things were. Times you could study but never really know about, not having been there yourself. Trying to get to a place that no one could: the past.

"How do you get that impression from this landscape?" William asked. "Were you in the Civil War?"

Sean moaned, not prepared for the coming barrage of abuse. He was trying to be eloquent, and it had backfired. "It just does. The open field. And those guys in their trenches at night, digging in with their old weapons, sitting still in the moonlight. That must have been something."

William stopped the car at a flashing light. The sign read 'Big Timber Road', but there were no trees in sight, just corn-fields all around. "Sure," William said after a few moments of thought, "Yankees dug in up here in northern Illinois defending against no one because the Confederates never made it up this far. We already agreed that Americans don't know their history. This just proves it.".

"Hey, lay off. I was just making an observation. Haven't you ever imagined something or thought about anyone but yourself? It would be pretty scary to be in any war, don't you think?" Sean sat quiet and unappreciated.

William offered an apology, doubting he could really hurt Sean's feelings. The boy was truly a brute. "Pull over, please," Sean grabbed the doorknob and waited.

"He said he was sorry," Sarah added.

"I'm not mad." Sean swung around and smiled at Sarah. The countless number of drinks he had consumed in the last four hours pushed down on his bladder. "I've got to take a leak."

"We're almost there. Five minutes more, just hold it." William didn't want to waste anymore time messing around.

Sean shook his head in William's direction. "William, you either pull over and let me water some of this corn, or we'll be sponging the contents of my bladder from your soft leather seat here." William looked at Sean to gage how serious it was and then pulled over in resignation. He was already late, and no amount of complaining could change that.

"Thank you," Sean said as he darted from the Towncar, his zipper down before he reached the crop of corn. He took a step into the first row, hoping to steal a drink from his flask before returning to the car.

William, Vi, Sarah, and Tom sat silently waiting for Sean to return. Vi thought about Sean's reference to the Civil War. Although his context into history was inaccurate, his description of the men preparing to fight had stuck with her. The moon was bright, especially on this dark, country road. It bled a gray light onto the flat fields surrounding the Town-car. Vi imagined a fog rolling in. Not a thick, moist cloud, but the thin puffs caused by the burning powder fired from rifles and cannons. It was an eerie thought, and Vi imagined bodies of soldiers surrounding Sean who unassumingly stood in the dark and relieved himself. She shook the image out of her head as Sean returned to the car. William pulled back onto Route 72 west while Sean buckled up.

"Feeling better?"

"Yes. Thank you, William. You're the man."

"That I am." William concentrated on the road, a little happier that he had nearly reached his destination.

"Sean," Vi addressed him, her thoughts still trapped somewhere in the 1860s. "I think you made a good argument. The Civil War might not have been fought here on this land, but it was fought in America with American soldiers. I couldn't imagine what it could have been like to fight for your country, especially against your own countrymen." Vi lingered in a documentary that she had once seen.

"I was in the military," Tom offered. Vi responded first as her head snapped sideways to look at him. She was interested in this tidbit, and she waited along with the others for details. "I enlisted in the Navy when I was eighteen."

"Well, how was it?" Sean bellowed impatiently.

"It was okay." Tom looked at Vi who waited with the others for him to share more. "I worked on a carrier. I was a mechanic." Tom paused as if he couldn't remember the details of his enlistment.

"And how was that?" Sean asked, again too impatient to wait for the usually quiet man to collect his thoughts.

"It was hot," Tom responded, knowing that this would only goad Sean. The years rushed in, and Tom let the details out methodically. "I liked it. I was in for six years. I made some friends who I still talk to once in a while. It was nice to be part of something, part of a team. When you meet someone who was in the military, there's almost an immediate understanding with them, like you've seen the same things and have known the same life." Tom was slow and deliberate. He was lost in the past and the others tried to follow as far as they could, but it was impossible to truly know another person's history.

"I enjoyed being on a ship. Sometimes we'd stay out for a couple of months, cruising around from port to port. I got to see a lot of the world, and it is more beautiful than you can imagine. Every place is different from the last. Our country, the United States, it's young, you know. We've got two hundred years of history behind us. Japan has two thousand." Tom was smiling and then studying his thoughts, a stern look of concentration sweeping over him. "But now that I think of it, everything was almost the same. I mean, the people speak different languages and have different traditions, but they have the same expressions and a lot of the same mannerisms. We're all human, I guess. That's why you never feel completely out of sorts, why you're never too far from home even a few thousand miles away. Corporations like McDonald's, they're everywhere, and even though their menus differ a little, they still make you feel like you know exactly where you are. You can go into a completely different culture and still not feel lost. It's amazing."

Vi leaned in a little closer to Tom as though she would understand him better if there was less distance between them. "What made you decide to go into the Navy?"

Tom hesitated. His actual reasons were not suitable as conversation pieces. How could he tell these people that he had begged his mother to sign a release when he was seventeen, so that he could get away from his father? Tom wasn't staying at home. He had left a year earlier to live on the streets and in the shelters and anywhere he could rest his head. He could no longer take the abuse at home, and Tom knew he would kill his father if he saw him beat his mother once more. Tom sometimes wished that his brother had gone with him, gone away to another world. That's what the military brought to Tom. They didn't care where you were from at the start, on the first day of basic training. They broke you down to nothing and then built you up as a unit of soldiers, as part of something completely different.

What made him decide to go into the Navy? It seemed

the farthest away. Sure, the other branches of the service offered overseas tours, but in the Navy, on a ship, Tom was gone. He had tried to get a job on a submarine, the perfect place to hide, but it turned out that he had become a little claustrophobic, a result of the many nights spent hiding in cramped places as his father tore the house up in a rage.

Tom smiled, and the others waited patiently for him to turn the smile into a story, but he would keep these thoughts to himself. He was twenty-nine, and after six years tooling around the world, four years of college, and two years on his own, out in the 'real world', the only thing he still thought about was his brutal childhood, the one that had officially ended twelve years earlier when he raised his right hand and swore to defend the Constitution of the United States.

"I always liked boats," Tom answered as the smile slowly disappeared. He forgot what he had found so funny a minute earlier. "I was a crazy teenager, and I wanted to get away from my parents. What can I say?" His cheeks flushed and Tom looked down at his fingernails to hide.

"I hear that," Sean agreed.

"I'm still trying to get away from mine," Sarah added.

Sean laughed. "I don't think that the military is for you. Somehow, I just don't picture you scrubbing floors, shining boots, or firing bazookas. It would be like that movie 'Private Benjamin'." Sarah sneered at Sean, although she agreed she would be no good to Uncle Sam.

"You never know, Sean. I met some girls on tour who were doing okay for themselves." Sean didn't care, and Tom decided not to waste his energy on convincing him. He sat back and noticed Vi. She was still looking at him, staring directly into his face. She knew, he thought. She knew it all.

Vi didn't buy his cop-out answer as the others had. Maybe it was the smile that had tipped his hand. Tom didn't smile, ever. That was changing though, here, tonight.

"Was being in the military exciting?" William asked as he handled the Towncar through a few tight bends in the road where there was a baseball field and a radio tower on the right.

"I guess." It always amazed people at the lifestyle, but Tom didn't seem as thrilled with his enlistment as other civilians he knew had been. Over time, he realized that there were many who had wanted to join, but for reason after reason, they hadn't and he had, and that made him of interest to them. "We helped the Coast Guard out sometimes, you know, stopping other boats to check for drug smuggling and stuff. Then during Desert Shield, we parked in the Gulf doing all sorts of drills."

"You were in Desert Storm?" Sean asked incredulously.

"No, my enlistment came up during Desert Shield, and since there wasn't a shortage of engine mechanics and there wasn't a freeze on my job title, I got out and came back to the states."

"Why didn't you stay in? I mean, it was a war and all. Well, Desert Shield was a prelude to a war anyway," Sean prodded curiously.

"I guess I could have re-enlisted," Tom answered, as if it had never occurred to him before. "It wasn't for me, though. There are people who are suited for the military, and I'm just not one of them. Sometimes taking orders is a little hard. Sometimes you just want to do what you want to do, and the government has their own ideas about that. I did my time, got out, and went to school for free." Tom tripped through his sentences as he rambled on, surprised that he had so much to say on the topic.

"Did my time," William repeated. "It sounds like they sentenced you to serve time in prison."

Tom thought about the play on words. "It's not exactly like that, but sometimes it didn't seem all that far off. You're allowed to come and go as you please from a boat that they decide you'll live on doing a job that they decide you'll have. It's not prison, but it's a far cry from civilian life."

Tom remembered the day he PCS'd – Permanent Civilian Status. He was free, and it seemed awkward that he could go wherever he wanted for as long as he wanted, and no one cared if he got back in time or not. He had sat in his car outside the base for two hours the day that they took his I.D. and processed him out. Knowing that he could go anywhere was almost overwhelming after six years of being told where his days began and ended.

Tom decided to return to Chicago, and he drove the eighteen hours from Florida straight through. He had been back to his hometown only three times during his enlistment and had seen his mother and his brother, but avoided his father. He tried to pretend the old man didn't exist. And then, six years after he had gone, Tom returned to the hole that he had tried so hard to climb out of, tried so hard to run from. He stayed in a hotel two days before leaving again, this time for a degree, any degree, at any school in any town but his town.

"I think I would probably stay in and retire after twenty years," William commented.

"What is it you do for a living, William?" Sean kept the others talking to divert his mind from the commercial that ran over and over in his head: a large bottle of spirits poured slowly into a glass over rocks.

"I'm a bricklayer." William nodded to himself as he answered. "It's a difficult profession, hard on the body, but I enjoy it."

"Difficult?" Sean laughed and commented in his usual obnoxious, unfiltered ruse. "You mix the cement, plaster it on, and lay the brick on top. How hard can that be? It must be the monotony that makes it difficult."

"We build things." William defended the thing he did ten hours a day, five days a week. "Buildings are the structure of society. Think about where you work and live and everywhere you go. There's probably a little brick in every structure."

Sean threw his hands up in defeat, hoping William would return his attention to the dark, winding road.

"Who's going to put cities together? You? Please. You're what? Twenty-one?"

"Twenty-four."

"Sure, you have no idea what life is about yet. You don't know how many jobs there are out there. You don't realize what people will do for money. I'm not talking about prostitution or anything illegal either. I'm talking about the little Mexican cooks that work for nothing to put food on a restaurant table for your ungrateful ass. And what about garbage men?"

"Hey, when I was a kid, I wanted to be a garbage man."

"You'd be good at it. You talk a lot of trash." William stopped at a flashing light as he lectured Sean. "There are people out there doing everything from sewing buttons to fixing ships like Tom here did, so don't tell me that bricklaying isn't a noble profession. I've been doing it as long as I can remember, and my dad did it before me." William pulled the Towncar left onto Route 47 and into the gravel parking lot on the right. He stopped on the edge of the lot near a row of trees.

"I'm not saying that it's not an honorable profession. Hell, you got so charged up and defensive, I don't even know what I was saying." Sean sat still next to William, the three in the back seat silently waiting for round two. "You know," Sean continued, not knowing when to quit, "most jobs these days are being replaced with computers and robots. What are you going to do when they invent some big bricklaying robot that takes over for you, dissolves your union, and destroys your way of life?"

William stared at Sean for a minute before throwing the gearshift in park and turning off the engine. Vi, Sarah, and Tom held their breath in the back seat as he opened the driver's side door. It looked as though William would challenge Sean to a fight right here in the gravel lot out in the middle of nowhere. William slammed his door shut, but instead of calling Sean out, he walked toward a small rundown building that hovered in the middle of the lot behind two old gas pumps.

Sean opened his door and stuck his head out. "William, come on! I was joking. Although robots will change the world," he added under his breath. "Let's go, William!"

"I think you really pissed him off this time," Sarah said behind Sean.

"I was only speculating. That's happening these days, you know, computers are taking over the world."

"You just couldn't shut your mouth, Sean. Typical," Vi complained.

"Hey, you haven't known me long enough to use the word typical." Sean returned his attention to William who was almost to the door of the shack. "I'm sorry, William. Now let's go!"

William grasped the knob of an old scratched glass and steel framed door before turning back to the car. "We're not going anywhere, Sean. We're half an hour late, but we're here." With that, William entered the tiny store as Sean, Sarah, Vi, and Tom sat in the car, their jaws dropped in awe. This was Phil's Breakfast and 7UP.

8

NOWHERE

The five strangers had been travelling together for over two hours, and they had ended their journey at William's earthly version of heaven. Phil's Breakfast and 7UP was a tiny diner in rural Illinois, at the corners of Route 72 and Route 47. At the edge of the lot, closest to the intersection, an old fruit shack was left standing empty. The neon street lamps that glared from the intersection and beamed on the weather-beaten wooden structure lit it up. A sign advertising pumpkins for sale stood out by the street, and plastic streamers waved between the small edifice and its advertisement. Two semi trucks were parked in the back of the lot along the rows of trees that separated the diner from the adjacent farmland. The trees were half bare; the colors of the remaining leaves were inde-cipherable on this mild fall night. Almost naked, the branches moved slightly in the wind, scribbling black lines on the midnight blue backdrop behind.

To the left of where William had stopped the Towncar was an old picnic table. Hidden in the shadows behind the diner, it braved the elements along with a small junkyard of forgotten items. Two white propane tanks stood near the picnic table. Next to those were several old broken down heaps of rust looking as though they had stopped there so their owners could grab a bite to eat, only to be abandoned and left to rot. Used truck tires were discarded along the far side of Phil's, their insides filled with slippery, moldy grime. On the opposite side of Phil's near the street, a Chicago Tribune vending machine was lost next to an old ice machine, its paint peeled, the word 'Ice' in red almost gone. Next to the diner's front door, a billboard on wheels flashed an arrow accusingly through a payphone and into the building. The words underneath the arrow lit up, signifying sausage and eggs for $1.99, and a six-pack of 7UP for only $1.32.

Across the street from Phil's stood a brand new Garden Center that looked out of place on a corner surrounded by cornfields. It wasn't a typical flower shop. It was a warehouse for those farmers that ordered seed for their land in bulk quantities. The Garden Center inhaled the neon light and loomed at the small diner as if to say, "You were here first, and I'll be here last."

Vi was ready to jump out, but she waited in the car as Sarah and Tom had her pinned in the middle of the backseat. Sarah was looking around into the darkness, wondering how safe it could be, and she imagined a patch of fog rolling by the car. Several werewolf movies flickered through her head. Sarah had never been very superstitious, but ever since she was a child, her imagination had an affliction with the hairy beasts, the half man-half wolf. She gave no credit to vampires or ghosts, yet the possibility of werewolves seemed utterly real to her. Sarah shuddered, hoping that there was really nothing to fear.

The three watched Sean from the back seat as he strolled away from the familiarity of the car and headed toward the diner.

At first glance, the parking lot had seemed to be covered with gravel, but as Sean walked on it, he could tell that they had paved it at one time. The ever changing hot and cold of the northern United States left huge chunks of rubble to scatter back into gravel, the snow plows gouging huge potholes in the asphalt. His footsteps crunched on the rocks and were lost in the deafening noise of three passing Harley Davidson motorcycles, the rumbling of their exhaust rebounding after the bikes as they shot out from under the blinking light of the intersection.

Sean couldn't believe where he had ended up this Tuesday or how he had begun Wednesday, he thought. The world ended across the far street where midnight began, and he could see only blackness outside the bright lamps where the world fell into nowhere. Every few minutes a car would stop at the flashing red light and proceed on, this being Sean's only assurance that he was still in the real world, as if others verified his existence more than his own mind could.

Sean imagined a picture of the earth, her blue oceans converging around the red-brown bodies of the continents, white clouds swirling in her atmosphere. He zoomed in as he imagined a high powered telescope would, pictured himself walking across this ground toward Phil's diner, zoomed out in his consciousness, again back out into space. The earth was a vast world in his mind and yet he couldn't see past this place, this few acres that made up five people's final destination. "I'm on that," he thought aloud, picturing himself as a giant figure on a tiny planet. Then he saw himself moving among hundreds of other planets, now tiny cells in someone else's body, relativity changing on his mind's whim.

Sean caught himself contemplating his existence as he looked up at the night sky, his own mind staring back down from another world. He glanced back at the long blue car and noticed three figures still in the back seat, then turned his attention toward the diner, Phil's ludicrous Breakfast and 7UP, its large windows a contrast to its tiny size. His hunger began resurfacing, and Sean smacked his lips as he made his way to the door. Greasy eggs and sausage with a side of hashed browns were already on the tip of his tongue.

———————

Sarah, Vi, and Tom sat listening to crickets hum their anthem to the stars. Tom was still, willing Sarah to stay in the car, leaving Vi trapped in the middle at his side. On one hand, Tom hoped William would hurry and buy his tickets before Vi switched seats. On the other hand, he hoped that William would sit down and eat. Tom wanted this chance to get to know Vi, to make her notice him, to tell her who he was and who he could be for her. Vi had an idea about the world and who she should be in it. Tom's entire world was in this car.

"Do you think we should go inside?" Sarah asked. She had no desire to be in the filthy diner cramped close to the aroma of animals being fried up for animals.

"I was thinking of sitting over there at that picnic table and having a smoke," Vi pointed to the left. Sarah and Tom were quiet as they eyed the table. It was a harmless wooden rectangle, but placed in the darkness, it became an object of suspicion. Sarah opened her door, and the three stepped out into what had become a chilly October night, colder than it had been outside Baker's Tap, anyway. Vi slammed the door closed. Tom's door latch took as loudly, and the crickets answered with their silence.

"Do you mind if I sit with you?" Sarah asked Vi.

"Free country. Right Tom?" Tom nodded his reply at Vi as the two girls made their way over to the table. Tom stood by the car for another minute, like a child afraid to move away from the "glue" safety in a game of tag. He watched Vi expertly light her cigarette and prop herself on the tabletop, using the bench below as a footstool. Sarah milled around the table for a minute before seating herself on the bench. Tom reluctantly moved away from the safety of the car and made his way slowly across the lot into the diner to join Sean and William at the counter.

"I like Tom," Sarah admitted.

"You do?" Vi asked after a few seconds, her emotions remaining in check as she tried to seem uninterested in the conversation.

"He seems really nice. He came to my rescue back at Baker's Tap."

Vi pulled hard on the smoke before letting it out into the air. It seemed to disappear until it rose above the roof of the diner and into the light where it materialized again as if under the spell of a magician's wand. Sarah watched the tiny cloud dry up. "Don't you think that he's a nice guy?"

Vi flicked the ash from her cigarette before responding with another question. "Do you think that a nice guy wants to be a nice guy?"

"I'm just wondering what you think of him, Vi. I think he likes you." Sarah watched Vi turn her head into the darkness, her gaze lost across the field behind the Towncar.

"What makes you think he likes me? I thought that you just said that you liked him." Vi was hopeful but controlled her voice from sounding defensive. She found herself deeply attracted to the man who had confused her, the one she thought was a little weird, sitting in the bar staring at her, never approaching. Vi had her daydreams about the dark stranger, but never allowed her mind to go too far. She only anticipated the dreams she would make true, and those included only the ones she had lived in pursuit of since she was twelve. Yet Tom was a vision of mystery, and Vi was a being of curiosity. He'd held her interest since she had felt a pang of jealousy at him approaching Sarah's table in Baker's Tap.

Sarah watched Vi, two questions answered with questions. It was a ploy, really. Sarah was no psychiatrist, but she had been around enough of them over the years to understand certain anecdotes about characteristics that the doctors had shared with her. Sarah had played every game in the book, and she knew that answering a question with a question was a self defense mechanism, a smoke screen thrown in front of a cover-up. She could tell that Vi had built a shell around herself, a wall that few could get over.

Sarah was beginning to like Vi. She wished she had Vi's inner strength and poise, the beauty hidden beneath its hard, cynical, and sarcastic shell. Sarah wondered if she should, and then the gossip in her pursued. "I do like Tom, but not for me. He really opens up to you. I see how he looks at you. That boy's got it bad. I think that you guys would really look cute together." Sarah looked back into the diner. "Of course, I'm not that much of an authority these days on what men want and don't want."

Vi tossed the butt of her cigarette to her right, avoiding the propane tanks. "I don't think that he was responding to me. He's probably just shy, and he needed time to feel comfortable." Vi hoped that Sarah was right about Tom liking her, but she tried to hold her poker face. Never show your cards until everyone has bet. "What about you, Sarah? What about that guy I saw you with?"

"I can't believe you noticed that." Sarah shook her head and tried to laugh. "Weren't you supposed to be singing or something? I thought that you performers got all into your music."

"We do sometimes. But usually you're into the crowd when you have one." Vi watched Sarah until she was convinced that the rich girl would tell all.

"His name is Randy. I've been seeing him for a few months." Sarah stood up as though the added height would help her explain. "Yeah, well, I *was* seeing him. He got all freaked out though, like I was trying to control his whole life or something. What a joke that is."

"Why is that a joke?" Vi lit another stick.

"Because. I never called him. I never told him what to do. I just went out with him, you know? I tried to be interested in his interests. I tried to be a good girlfriend. Guess that wasn't good enough." Sarah was pacing now. "You know, all these men complain they can't get a woman to do what they want, and then when they get it, they're not happy either." She stopped pacing and sat on the bench next to Vi's feet, her back to the table. She looked over the parking lot.

"You make it sound like it's your fault."

"It must be. Here I am, single again. I'm an idiot."

"Be mad at this Randy guy. He's the one who left you at Baker's." Vi sounded righteous, a true women's libber. "What about Sarah? What are your interests?"

"My interests?" Sarah searched the rocks on the ground for answers, but there were none. She hadn't thought about what she wanted to do in a long time. It never got her farther than her mother's opinion, anyway. "I don't know. I like make-up and clothes. I'm interested in dating."

Vi shook her head furiously. "No, no, no. I mean your interests. Like, um, I don't know. Hobbies, sports, stuff like that."

Sarah had never discussed herself with her friends because they only talked about the men in their lives, where they'd been shopping, and the next big social.

Sarah thought hard. She wanted her answer to count. She wanted to learn how people talked, how they interacted beyond a fake smile and fabricated interest. "Randy liked rugby, and we went to a few matches. That was interesting."

Vi sighed. The problem with today's society of women sat next to her at this picnic table. "That was Randy's interest. I bet that you have always liked what your boyfriend has liked."

"I thought that's how it was for everyone. Like that's how it's supposed to be," Sarah answered without hesitation. She knew inside that there had to be something more. She hoped that there was lest she lived as a zombie until she gained enough courage to snuff her life out for good.

"Fifty percent of all marriages fail. That means that half of the people who jump in get divorced and are now littering the bars with long faces, wondering what went wrong." Vi hopped off the table and shoved her hands in her jeans pockets. "Women want families, so they have them, but we're too impatient these days. Everyone else is doing it, so we do. You really need to find *you* first. Figure out who *Sarah* is." Vi spun around, scattering her thoughts and reorganizing them. She liked to give ideas to others to help them try to experience different things. To take a chance is difficult, but to some, taking the chance itself is the reward no matter what the outcome. "You need to figure out what you like about you, and stop doing the things that you don't like. Even though you weren't calling Randy or nagging him, you were making yourself completely available to him. You occupied yourself with what he would want and what he likes."

"What's wrong with that? Aren't we supposed to be interested in who we date?"

"Yes, we are. But how can they be interested in us if we have no interest in ourselves and all we do is focus on them all the time? You're right, in a way. Love is about giving more than it is about receiving. If we really found ourselves to be so interesting that we were the best company we could find, then no one would leave their house." Vi swung her arms in front of her, imitating a mummy. "But people need variety or they get bored."

Sarah watched with a smile, trying to hide the tears that were beginning in her throat. This was it, the part that her mother had left out. Sarah knew how to make herself look pretty, and she knew how to make men feel good about themselves. Some felt great just having a beauty like Sarah on their arm; the prize. But Sarah didn't know how to feel good inside. She didn't know how to love herself beyond the mirror. She had learned guilt and hatred, and fear. No one had ever told her to be someone, only to be for someone.

A breeze swept across the parking lot, and her body was stiff. It was frail and aching, vacant of the proper nutrients, and worse, vacant of half her soul. She was alone, without a man to think of, no one to dream about marrying. She should have never begun this conversation with Vi. This strong-willed singer would tear Sarah apart, breaking her down like a fighter; one swing at a time, then a little dance around the ring, then another swing.

Sarah tried to look down on Vi, the lower class, but it didn't work. She had no conviction left anymore. She could make no distinctions. Her spite turned in on itself, and Sarah felt the years of emptiness coming to terms. The angst in her stomach that she had been trying to suppress manifested into tears that found her eyes and were born into the world, bringing with them a chance. Sarah put her hands over her face and whimpered softly, Vi's silence willing her on. There was so much she was crying for, but at that moment, Sarah had only one reason to let the tears go. She felt joy in acknowledging their existence on her cheek. For to have shed tears, she must have a soul beneath the gray pallor of her human form. She felt a whirlwind of grief, then anger, then more grief.

Vi had been there before, listening to the choked back sobs, not understanding what made others so comfortable around her. She knew she wasn't really doing anything for Sarah aside from talking and listening. The girl was making her own conclusions beyond what they said out loud, confronting to resolve her own issues on the inside. Sarah looked helpless, slumped on the bench, hiding her face. Her body looked as though it might snap in half at the will of the wind. Sarah shivered, probably from the tears, but Vi wasn't sure.

As pretty as Vi sometimes wished she was, the perfect beauty she and the rest saw in Sarah, the one accepted by the media and therefore the entire country, the image Vi herself would someday strive for, was three feet from her, breaking down, dying. Vi thought that she should sit on the bench and put her arm around the girl, or at least touch her lowered head. Some form of human contact to let Sarah know she was not alone. But Vi was not the personal contact type. She never had been with her family and wasn't now with this half stranger. It was hard to sit in the silence and watch though, so she removed her leather jacket and wrapped it gently over Sarah's shoulders.

"Anyway, I may not be the right person to discuss relationships with. I have been hooked on my ideas so long, I don't even remember my last kiss." The part about the kiss was a lie, but Vi didn't know what else to say. Sarah's crying didn't make Vi as uncomfortable as silence did. "It takes a long time to figure out what we want in life. You're a beautiful girl, and if you can stand up to Sean's bullying, then you can't be all that bad." Sarah was wiping her cheeks now. Vi couldn't believe that the make-up hadn't smeared. "If nothing else, you can always aspire to throw up on your mother again."

Sarah chuckled at this, her back rising in the same jolting motion as it had when she was crying, this time a guffaw leaving her lips. Right now, hunched over and crying in public, Sarah was completely beyond acceptable behavior by her mother's standards. On the grimy bench next to this disgusting diner, talking to such a common woman as Vi. But they laughed together, and Sarah made her way out of the rough waters and back toward shore, back to the parking lot at Phil's Breakfast and 7UP.

Sarah had never talked to anyone like this. She never felt comfortable enough, even with her friends. They were all proper friends, children of the iniquitous women that had influenced her mother over the years. But Vi was real. She was from a different part of town, but her songs were like therapy, her mere presence a shield to guard the weak. She knew how to fix things.

Sarah didn't want to be safe anymore. She wanted to get it out, to figure out where to go. She hoped Vi had the answer, and although she knew it didn't come down to one simple solution, she went on. "So I'm just supposed to find a hobby, and that will make me happy?" She brushed the remaining moisture from her cheeks. The dry air sucked the saltwater left in her pores and caused her skin to feel chapped.

"A hobby alone won't make you eternally happy, but it will keep you occupied until you're ready to get on to bigger things." Vi could see the light at the end of this dark tunnel as Sarah listened attentively. Vi thought about giving up pursuing the young lady's truth, but the feeling that she could look straight into someone always drew her back. Vi had spent hours at Union Station alone, watching the rest of Chicago go by. Those were the people in her songs. It was their stories that she was telling. She could have picked Sarah out of the crowd at the train station, thinking of where the beauty was going, wondering what kind of car she drove and what her boyfriend was like, but she had no frame of reference in her own friends, and surely would not have guessed the story that was unfolding in front of her.

Vi approached the edge of Sarah's nightmare and teetered. The girl could go home tonight and forget that anything different had happened. She could continue primping her shell in the mirror, or she could take a long look, underneath the make-up and expensive clothes, underneath the all-attentive demeanor of the perfect girlfriend, and make a change. Vi would have never picked Sarah as a friend, someone to talk to, but here she was, her confused face looking up in the dark for guidance. Vi couldn't choose the right direction, but she knew how to find the right buttons to push. She never walked away from an emotionally charged conversation unless it was about her. "First, you need some ice cream."

"Ice cream!" Sarah repeated. "I can't have ice cream."

Sarah paused, and Vi pursued. "Come on. You know the important role that ice cream plays in a single girl's life. It's a friend, a companion, something to drown sorrows in. You just get a carton and sit on the couch in front of the television with a spoon. Trust me on this one, I am a living disciple of the almighty god of ice cream. I've seen its healing powers."

Sarah's expression had started as a smile, but Vi slowly saw the frown returning. She knew the tears were not far behind the hint of fear that showed in Sarah's eyes. The beautiful, frail, insecure model folded back in on herself. Vi could guess what was coming. She had watched in the passenger mirror as Sarah had thrown the Dorito out the window. This child held so tightly to her image. The same feeling that Sarah got each time she had thought of food was what Vi experienced: excitement and shame swirling in her stomach. Only Vi would eat where Sarah wanted to throw up from pure disgust.

"I don't think I could eat ice cream." Sarah repeated, waiting for Vi to lead on, but Vi had discovered the power that silence brought to a conversation. Someone had taught her that if a person finished their thought and faced silence, they would continue on that same topic at first, but it always took a turn toward what they were really thinking. The longer Vi left them alone, the further they would go. She lit another cigarette and realized that she had been smoking more tonight than usual, but the cigarettes gave her something to turn her attention to, something to distract her as to squelch her own questions.

"I haven't had ice cream since..." Sarah brought the leather jacket in tighter. "I threw it up once. I ate it, and I threw it up." She expected to cry, but she didn't. Sarah had told no one that she had done that. Her parents knew, and the doctors knew, but they didn't count. She had never acknowledged it, and this was her saying it, telling the truth as she saw it. "I've done that a few times with food." The relief that came pushed the words out faster. "I'm okay, you know? But there were a couple times that I just couldn't stomach what I had eaten. I just didn't want it anymore."

Vi almost snapped her cigarette in half. She looked away from Sarah and saw the tires resting next to the restaurant: old; useless; crusty; garbage; rot. She couldn't understand what Sarah was telling her. She could hear the words, process the medical terminology, the diagnosis, but she couldn't fathom how someone formed a habit like that.

"It's stupid really, because I get hungry again and then I'm back at square one." Sarah chuckled a little. "I don't really know why I do this. I remember when I was fourteen and I wanted to be a cheerleader, and my mom said that there were a lot of other girls out there better than me, and that I needed to be the best. I just figured that she meant the best looking because she was beautiful and she was always telling me to look my best. It's not her fault; she doesn't throw up her food. Of course, she mostly drinks these days anyway."

Vi wasn't puffing on her cigarette, she was just holding on to it. How did people get so screwed up? How did they ever decide to pin their obsessions on such a stupid thing as being thin? It disturbed Vi because she had been fighting with these demons herself. She wanted to be a big star in Nashville, but what record exec would want to take the time to look through her rough exterior to the music inside when there were models out there who could sell sex to a deaf audience? That's where the world was, wrapped up in magazines.

So Vi hadn't gone, hadn't taken her chance. She would someday sing with the greats, write songs alongside them, but she wasn't ready to stick her neck out. She had heard that she was beautiful. She had even thought it herself a few times. Then she studied at the celebrities with their perfect hair and make-up, and she knew she wasn't ready. She realized she was hiding in Chicago until she woke up one day and was thin and beautiful. She had fallen into the same trap she swore would never get her. Beauty intimidated Vi, and she was wondering if it was worth striving for now that Sarah had shown her the ugly side.

Sarah stood and handed Vi the jacket. She was feeling good, warm, and free. She was sick and she knew it, but had never cared to do anything about it. Each time Sarah had stood up, her mother had reeled her in and re-initiated all of her fears, her insecurities. Now Sarah was standing next to a woman who was making her life happen on her own. There had to be a way in life for anyone who had the guts to try.

"I don't really do it much anymore." Sarah needed this lie for herself. She simply didn't purge her stomach as much because she didn't eat.

"Why would you?" Vi asked aloud.

"I don't know, Vi. I just feel like I have to. I can't explain it. It just makes sense to me."

Vi pulled her leather jacket on and replaced her pack of cigarettes in the pocket. This wasn't the time to worry about her own insecurities, not when she had seen the washed out face of affliction and humiliation.

Vi felt good about Sarah, and good about herself here. She wasn't worried about what this girl thought of her. She didn't have to use her dry wit to outsmart the stupid beauty. She could just stand, and not understand, and be happy about life.

Vi was a good listener because, although she would never understand stories like Sarah's, she could accept the words as fact. Even if they were half-truths, she didn't have to take away the pain as her own. Vi would listen to Sarah and try to impart some confidence in the girl, hoping Sarah would make it through and someday look back on this time as a lesson in life.

9
KISMET

Sean followed William's lead and ordered the two-egg breakfast special with sausage. He spun the salt and pepper shakers between his hands as he looked around the tiny diner. This was William's heaven on earth. Because of its desolate location, Sean could hardly believe that the place stayed open twenty-four hours. The interior looked as though it hadn't changed in thirty years.

They sat at the front of a three-sided counter that held five stools on each side. Two men sat on their left, and Sean thought they must belong to the semis parked outside. The linoleum covering on the bar shined in the bright lights, proving a rough contrast to the dull metal coolers that flanked each end of the bar's horseshoe shape. One was a Pepsi refrigerator with a nineteen inch color television propped on top, probably the newest thing in the place. The picture came in clear. A *Matlock* rerun was playing at one in the morning.

Oh, how insomniacs needed their sleep, Sean thought. On the opposite cooler was an "I Love America But Fear My

Government" bumper sticker. Both coolers kept the same coating of grease as a thin dull layer that had fallen over time onto the metal and would no longer wash off. Sean could imagine a cramped kitchen in back full of hicks and their rifles, waiting patiently for the next conspiracy to unfold. They would rush from Phil's with guns blazing. Sean chuckled to himself as a fork fell behind the bar with a bright metal clang. No one picked it up.

There was a baby chair in the corner, and Sean wondered who would want to bring their child into a shack like this for breakfast. It wasn't like there would be a Sunday morning rush of church goers mixed with the loud and mostly obnoxious Saturday night hangovers like the ones in the diner near Sean's apartment.

Opposite the kitchen wall were a variety of distractions. There was a cigarette machine flanked by a potato chip rack, and in the corner behind the door was a sunglasses rack. A condom machine next to the potato chips made Sean wonder if he was in the Twilight Zone. He held his laughter at the object. He wondered for an instant why it was out in the open instead of in the washroom. Then he remembered joking with one of his friends about the sanitary method of eating ribs with ten condoms rolled over his fingertips. The memory brought a smile, which distracted him from the feeling that only a tall beer could bring happiness.

As Sean contemplated a cigarette purchase, he thought that the room somehow resembled his mother's dining room. It was the cleanliness among the clutter; various objects taken hostage, mixed to form scenery like a prop shop on a movie lot. His mother had collected everything over the years, taking what she could get. They had struggled to keep their heads above the poverty line for most of Sean's childhood, and his mother had become somewhat of a pack rat. They always had two old vacuum cleaners, several lamps, rolls of various clothing materials, and other collectibles. These supplies were all for the proverbial rainy day whenever that turned out to be. As Sean and his siblings left home and his parents' savings account took shape, his mother was finally throwing items out, albeit slowly. The house looked less like a warehouse and more like a museum, unique items saved from destruction and left on display for those who dared walk the halls of mother Finnegan's three bedroom nick-nack palace.

Sean buzzed the cigarette machine and decided on the sunglasses rack instead. He tried on several pairs, modeling them in the windows that had turned into mirrors, the light from the diner reflecting on and masking the dark night. Sean swung around in different poses, mocking a model on a runway, showing off the shades and then his faded outfit. He put on a pair with red tinted lenses and eyed William and Tom who sat silently painted in pink at the counter. Tom looked back, slightly appeased at the jester in glasses. William ignored Sean, hoping that he, like a child without attention, would get bored and stop. The waitress returned from the back and placed two plates on the counter. Sean returned to his stool.

The waitress was Betty. She ran the diner that was owned by her cousin. Betty preferred the night shift as her husband worked days as a regional truck driver, returning home each evening after hauling packages every which way. Their schedules left little spare time for them, but they weren't on vacation. They were raising a family, and they saved money not having to pay for childcare. The highchair in the corner was hers for the times she had to come in with her kids, or when her husband had to drop them off when he had to work early. Betty was fit and lively compared to most other night waitresses that were pale and tired and generally lost. She ran the small shack with efficiency, and even though everything was old, it was clean.

Betty snapped orders at the chef just as she snapped replies to the customers. She didn't have time to breathe much less waste her words. She slowed herself down around William, though. "Anything else, honey?"

"I'm good, Betty."

"How about your friends?" Tom wanted nothing to eat as the chips he'd eaten in the car were still tiding him over. He sat behind a glass of orange juice, one he had ordered in haste. He would stare at it, stare a hole through the smashed pulp. Tom was fighting his way back into society right here at the breakfast counter. He looked at the juice but didn't take a drink. He looked over at Sean's plate of food, which looked exactly like William's, as this chef had prepared hundreds of Phil's breakfast specials. It looked like every other breakfast from every other greasy spoon in every other town after every other bar had closed.

Sean responded to Betty with his mouth full of his first bite. "I'll take some wheat toast."

"White toast, honey. You'll take some white toast." Betty leaned over the stainless steel counter dividing the dining area from the kitchen and barked the order at the cook.

The two truck drivers that had been staring at the tiny television moved their attention to Betty. She wore a white apron over a black polyester skirt, the thick support hose unable to hide her strongly defined calves. They ogled as she leaned forward, flexing the leg muscles. As she spun the coffee pot toward the men's cups, they returned their attention to the TV. The moment was orchestrated like a ballet: heads turning, eyes sweeping, no one the wiser for it. William didn't like the scruffy drivers looking at Betty like that, animals sizing up their prey, but he had no room to judge. He couldn't help himself either.

Betty delivered the toast to Sean with a small cart of jellies. He looked closely at Betty and realized that she was much younger than he had first thought. He had assumed that overnight diner waitress meant old and tired. She was probably close to William's age and Sean looked at the two and wondered if there was something between them.

"Pick your own flavor." She didn't really have a drawl, but her dialect wasn't choppy and exaggerated like it was in Chicago. She spoke a little slower than Sean was used to. Men who spoke that slowly sounded stupid to Sean, women were just more charming for it. The slower to say 'no', he guessed.

"You sure you want nothing to eat, honey?" Betty asked Tom who had barely touched his juice. He didn't reply, only shook his head. William and Tom watched as Sean smeared his toast with strawberry jelly and then slopped the yolks of his sunny-side-up eggs on top. When he bit into the toast, the thick yellow liquid poured into his mouth and some onto the plate. To Sean it was the only way, but it seemed a disgusting habit to William who liked his eggs scrambled.

The truckers paid Betty and left a tip for her on the bar before collecting themselves and heading out to the rigs that were parked out back near the tree line. One trucker stopped and eyed William. "Hey boy, you were late tonight. That has to be some sort of record." The driver's black beard covered a mocking smile as William kept his eyes on his food, his disregard bidding the truckers goodbye. "See you on Thursday, Betty," the larger of the two called.

"Okay, sweetie. Drive safe, now." When the loud engines growled to life out back, Betty cleaned the counter with one vigorous sweep of the dish rag, the dirty dishes left in a bucket behind the counter until there were enough to bother with the washing.

"What's with those two?" Sean asked between bites.

"I don't know." William tried to seem passive, but Betty knew the truth.

"They think that William here is a real card." She stopped her constant motion and set a cup of coffee for herself on the counter in front of Tom. She sipped it slowly, enjoying William's uneasiness. "They think that he's a little, uh, eccentric." Betty sucked down her coffee a third of the glass at a time, the thick steam leaving its residue on her cheeks. Anyone else would have had to wait another five minutes while the liquid cooled enough to be bearable.

"Why do they think that?" Sean was almost finished with his food, and he slowed his scarfing as he was more interested in Betty's story.

"Well, they've been coming around here twice a week for about six years now. This place is on their regular route, and they're always here late at night. They thought it was strange that a city boy like William would come all the way out here to eat, so I told them why he's really here."

"The lottery tickets?" Sean asked. He hadn't realized until

now that, among all the odds and ends, there wasn't a lottery machine in the place.

"Yeah," Betty smiled. "They thought I was joking for a long time, but William just kept coming back. They think he has a crush on me."

William's face was a darker shade of red when he looked at Betty. "You shouldn't tease like that, Betty. You're a married woman."

"Come on William, lighten up." Betty refilled her cup of coffee.

William didn't respond. He wiped his lips with his napkin, folded it, and placed it over the crumbs left on his plate. Betty took the plates from the counter and placed them in the bin. She dug into her apron for a few seconds before finding what she was searching for. "You almost forgot about these. Midnight came and went and you didn't show up, you didn't even call. That's not like you, William. I thought you were skipping out on us." Betty threw a small stack of lottery tickets on the counter in front of William who threw two fives into the pile.

"I didn't forget, Betty. I was just held up by these four nags." William shuffled through the ten lottery tickets as Betty pocketed the cash. Sean felt as though he was watching some sort of dope deal going down.

"Four?" Betty asked as she tallied up the food bill.

William looked around. He had forgotten Vi and Sarah hadn't come inside yet. It was a comical gesture as Phil's was too small to even lose your wallet in. "Sarah and Vi are outside."

"Sarah and Vi? Hmmm. Is one of those your girlfriend?" Betty razzed William.

"No, neither is my *girlfriend*."

"I don't know what you're waiting for, William." Betty leaned in toward Tom who was finally finishing his juice. "This man here could make some girl very happy. He's a gentleman, he's handsome, and he can have a conversation, which is more than I can say about most men."

As if on cue, a scruffy older man entered the tiny restaurant and stumbled around the counter to a stool on the far side. The four watched as he swayed a bit before planting his elbows on the counter. Betty let him get settled in before approaching with a cup of coffee.

"What do you say, Ray?"

"Hey, baby. You're a lifesaver." Ray slurred more than he spoke, which reinforced his drunken appearance. Betty placed a glass of water and a one page laminated menu on the counter.

"Take your time." She returned to Tom. "You see what I mean? You need to get out there and find yourself a girl, William. I wish you were around after my first husband. What a jerk he was." Betty meant no disrespect to her current husband, as he was the family man that she had been looking for the first time around.

"I enjoy being single, Betty. I don't have to worry about putting bread on the table for anyone but me. I can buy the things that I want, and I work a forty-hour week without having to pick up overtime to feed my family. I like it, and it's going to take someone special to get me out of this routine."

"You said it, man." Sean slapped William on the back in encouragement. Tom remained silent, thoughts of a future with Vi forming more clearly in his head.

"Do you agree with them, honey?" Betty asked Tom. He shook his head no.

"He never does," Sean added.

"Let me tell you boys something about marriage and family. It fills your whole heart, it give you a purpose." And then Betty was off, spewing about children and love and her husband, and everything joyous that made her world go around.

————

Sarah sat on the bench, Vi on the tabletop. After waiting in silence for the answers, Sarah decided that she, too, would sit on top of the table. It sounded so stupid to her, but Sarah wasn't sure if she'd ever done this in her life. It wasn't proper; it wasn't correct, but she pulled herself up on the table, taking a small but necessary step.

Sarah had connected to someone. She had connected to the improbable Vi. She had talked and listened and cried. And she decided she could never go back from here to the old Sarah, the insecure turtle hiding from the world. Sarah felt as if she had written her name on a block of wet cement next to Vi's. All she needed now was time for their symbols to dry, time for the changes to set in stone. Then they would be trapped in time, stealing a bit of history for themselves.

Sarah wanted to know something about Vi. She wanted to listen to the singer's stories and become part of her power. As Vi sucked on another cigarette, Sarah contemplated what she could say to draw the honesty from the cynicism. She wondered why Vi had been so adamant about not liking Tom. He was handsome, and Sarah could tell that he was smitten with Vi. Sarah looked at Vi draped in her leather jacket over her brown polyester-blend blouse, her black jeans not anything Sarah would choose to wear but fitting on Vi. She wondered about Vi, this woman who sang her songs and made snide comments to Sean and razzed William. And what about Sarah? What did Vi think of her? She had caught Vi looking at her in the past couple of hours. Had she been admiring or judging her?

"Do you have a boyfriend?"

Vi exhaled. "No."

"What about Tom?"

"What about Tom?" Vi repeated in a statement. She didn't have time to feel for this boy, but she knew that ultimately she didn't have time to ignore him either. She was nervous, and this was causing her to chain smoke. But she didn't care. No matter what she said now, Vi knew she was sitting outside with Sarah, waiting for Tom to come to her. She was planning in her mind what she hoped would happen and tried not to worry about the inevitable letdown. She had dreamt and dreamt, and most of the time she was hurt in the long run.

Vi knew that she was special because, unlike most of the population that threw excuses in the way, she would do in life what she put her mind to, and nothing less. But she had learned to tiptoe around her emotions because when she liked someone, she planned a future course, and when they let her down in the end, it was always her vanity that took the hit. Not pretty enough. Don't know how to dress. Too fat. Vi could see Sarah looking at her, trying to read her expression. Vi was frowning, and she tried to smile, which only made her lips quiver in indecision. She threw the unburned half of the cigarette away, not wanting the distraction anymore.

"Vi?" Sarah asked timidly. "Are you gay?"

Pushed by the wrinkles forming on her forehead, Vi's eyebrows pulled down over her eyes.

"It's okay if you are. I was just wondering." Vi sat still and heard Sarah out. "You don't seem to need anyone. I mean, you're so self-sufficient. And you have a style, it's kind of hard and tomboyish. And then there's Tom, who you're so adamantly against even considering." Vi was looking away from Sarah now. "I hope you're not mad at me for saying that. There's nothing wrong with it."

"I know there's nothing wrong with being gay, but I'm not." Vi answered sincerely.

"I'm sorry. I just thought that maybe..."

"It's okay, Sarah. You're not the first to think so. You know, I've stayed single for a long time because I want to be a singer. I've got to get my music out there, out into the world. It's what I've always wanted to do, and I don't want to give that up for anyone." Vi was more aware than anyone of how alone she was. She spent every minute with herself, sometimes content, sometimes longing, always focused on the future. Her family supported her dream, but her mother made it no secret that she wished Vi would at least need someone or want a companion.

Vi held to her convictions that a relationship would only cloud her judgment and steer her away from her goals. The truth was, she could picture herself as a wife and a mother with the church picnics and family vacations, the P.T.A. and days spent cooking and cleaning. She was a woman, and part of Vi longed for a brood of her own. But the piece of her who wanted that life wasn't big enough to win out. She had lost someone a few years before who had been looking for a family, someone she could have spent her life with, and it hurt her to the core when he walked away.

Vi wasn't writing off the possibility forever, but it just wasn't practical for her to pursue her music and date someone at the same time. Would a man want to move to Nashville so she could follow her dreams? Would a man want to stand on the sidelines as she worked the clubs?

Vi didn't want her visions of being a songwriter and recording artist to disappear. She didn't want to spend all her time longing for where she used to be, remembering the excitement and emotion, the anticipation and thrill. She didn't want to die wondering 'what if' and wishing that she had lived another life. This dream would never go away, and if she gave up singing to be anything else, she would live a lie. To Vi, there was no answer other than staying single until she was who she wanted to be.

She got lonely sometimes, out at a bar with friends, surveying the men, wondering who was who. And she felt stupid then, underdressed, not pretty enough. Then her defenses kicked in. The, *I am smart,* and *look at all I have done and will do's* running through her head like a picket line of chanters on guard. They would right the ship, make her okay with herself once more, comfortable in her own skin, confident until next time she took a hard look.

Vi wasn't bitter about Sarah's insinuation. She was amused. "What is it about independence that makes people think that you're gay? What do they think, that gay people don't need anyone?"

"Don't you need someone?" Sarah countered.

"No." Vi was undecided. "Yes."

"Which is it?"

"Yes, I guess. It's just that right now I am trying to get something going, and I don't need anyone slowing me down or trying to change my mind."

"How do you know that's what will happen?" Sarah had never looked at a relationship as Vi did, like it was a nuisance. It was always her goal to find a man, to live the life that she and most others were destined to live. Sarah was smart enough to know that one could not pin her hopes on the future, yet she was hopeful enough to do just that. She wondered if there could be a future without a man. "What makes you think you won't find someone who will be supportive?"

"That's just not how it works."

"Vi, you can't decide something like that right now. You don't know what's going to happen tomorrow or next week. You seem to have your whole life figured out, but the problem is, you can't sit here and know what your destiny is." Sarah looked up at Vi who was resisting the thought of a different outcome than the one she had dreamed up.

"Vi, you live your life through, and when you look back on it, you know you fulfilled your destiny." Sarah was a little overwhelmed with her speech. She was an educated girl with feelings, she just had never been given a chance to be intelligent about life. Not until now. She was giving advice to Vi, not really believing she could take it for herself. "The thing is, no matter what regrets we have, or what things we think we'd change, where we end up is our destiny. You don't get to do this all over."

"But why should I sacrifice my dreams?" Vi was reluctant

to understand. If she did, it would force her to face Tom and all the questions he brought with him. All the love that Vi had within her coupled itself with fear lest she let go of the ledge and take a chance on an undetermined path.

"You don't have to sacrifice your dreams. I don't think you're capable of that. You're self-programmed to do things your way." Sarah earned a hard look from Vi with that comment. "Just be open-minded. There's someone out there waiting to surprise you."

Vi thought this over, knowing that Sarah was right. Vi expected a lot of the future, and she tried to control every step of the way. She was always the one in control of the relationship, always the pursuer, secretly wanting to be the pursued. She could see now where she had sabotaged relationships, using her goal as the scapegoat. When she gave herself time to listen to her heart, Vi knew she was scared. She had spent so many years re-enforcing her walls, making sure that she remained grounded. For a hopeless romantic, she felt pretty pathetic.

"I guess I can try." Vi shrugged. "I'll consider the possibilities if you come inside with me and eat something." They both agreed, neither expecting that they were really telling the truth.

10
RESEARCH

Ray slumped over the counter, his head resting in his arms. The steam from his coffee seemed to rise from his hair, the gray strands thinning out at the top. He was wearing a long, black trench coat that looked as though he hadn't taken it off in ten years. He snored, the sound rattling its way around the cramped diner.

"You got anything else for me now, Betty?" the cook asked in broken Spanglish through his metal-framed window.

"No, I'll make a grilled cheese for myself a little later."

The cook disappeared.

"What's his story?" Sean asked.

"He goes to school up at Northern Illinois, in DeKalb. He's got some sort of scholarship," Betty explained to Tom, William, and Sean. "I've never met anyone who works harder than him. He's a good kid, late twenties. He came here about four years ago with his wife and daughter. He works here at night and goes to school in the morning. I think he works another job before he comes here, too."

"When does he sleep?" Sean was feeling tired, the effects of the food pulling his blood away from his brain to digest the grease.

"I let him sleep here. He does homework sometimes, and I help him with his papers. But usually he takes a little nap in back when there's nothing going on." Betty filled Ray's cup to the top before returning the pot to its machine to brew more coffee. As if on cue, Ray lifted his head, took a sip from the cup, put it down, and went back to sleep.

William shook his head. "And you wonder why I'm still single. That guy back there is running himself silly, and for what? His wife and daughter, and a life that he dreams of but will probably never achieve."

Betty stopped her fidgeting behind the counter and stepped square in front of William. Tom and Sean leaned back, waiting for the rage in her eyes to explode. William put his coffee cup down and expressed on his face that he knew he should be sorry for what he had just said, but he wasn't. William never was much of a dreamer beyond the typical wanting to grow old with enough money in the bank. He hated seeing others working like slaves, trying to keep their heads above water to support a family that would ignore each other in life and revere each other in death.

"You listen to me, William. That boy works harder than most Americans do. He loves his wife and daughter, and I'm sure that he feels he still doesn't do enough for them."

William sat back in his stool, taking Betty's venom like a pro. He had offended her sensibilities before, and he would do it again.

"He's tired, yes. But he's motivated like the wind and he's going to make it. If you're going to put him down like that,

I'd just assume that you didn't come around here anymore." At that, Betty walked back into the kitchen. They could see her through the counter window working in front of the grill, concentrating on her grilled cheese, determined not to look up at William.

"Man, William. And you guys think that I'm a jerk." Sean laughed as he sipped on his orange juice.

"I didn't mean anything by it, Betty. I'm sorry." William watched Betty through the window, waiting for her to look up and tell him that everything was okay. She added more butter to the hot grill, leaving burnt smoke to rush over her and out through the large overhead fan.

"I think that Betty's right," Tom added. William and Sean both looked at Tom who watched Ray sit up and drink down the rest of his coffee. William shook his head as Sean's belted a loud laugh. "Well, I do," Tom added with conviction.

"Tom, man. You kill me," Sean finally got out between laughs.

"No, but he should." William's mood took a downturn. He'd liked Betty since the day he'd met her, and he didn't like her mad at him.

William had been driving back from a college party late one night, falling asleep at the wheel. He stopped at Phil's Breakfast and 7UP for some coffee. Betty was there alone that night as their chef at the time was sick. She was standoffish at first, and when William had seen her looking through a stack of lottery tickets, he opened up the conversation.

He hadn't played the lottery much before, once or twice in college when one of his buddies would collect him on the way to the store and then insist that he play put some money into the pool. But that night alone with Betty in the diner, how she moved around doing things without even realizing that she was working. That was heaven for William. By the time the sun had come up, William had to leave so he could beat the traffic into the city. He could have left the diner for good, placing Betty on a list of other names that William may have remembered later, but probably not. But Betty's memory didn't let him go as other acquaintances had. She opened up a door. She told him that if he was passing by again next week to stop in and she would go in on some lottery tickets with him. So William promised to be there, and Betty promised to have the tickets, and it destined the two strangers to become friends.

The following weeks and months were a sort of flirting game between the two. They got to know each other, and William became familiar with some others who came to the diner regularly. He got along with a few, but usually the truckers gave him a hard time even though he could hold his own. William was a union bricklayer, and normally he didn't take any crap, but he was a child where Betty was concerned. A little pussycat caught in her spell; concentrating ridiculously hard, watching the ball of yarn, swatting at it, missing it again and again.

At first, William felt let down when Betty talked about her husband and her children. He had liked her, liked her for him, not some other man. But William held his feelings. He knew that if Betty was single, he probably would have never gone back, never chanced it. He tried not to date women he was too physically attracted to. It was a weird rule, but one that he followed. William knew that if he thought about it, he could probably pinpoint a reason that he did this. But he didn't care to probe, to feel too much. He cared to live, to get as far as he could without incident.

And here he was in the diner once more, angering Betty in front of two new strangers in his life. William didn't want Sean or Tom to be here in his place of peace. He wanted to be alone at the counter for Betty to talk to, her concentration on himself and not some kid who cooked in back and worked harder than the average American, harder than people like William. He didn't want Sean's probing questions and Tom's lingering silence.

––––––––

Vi had never known someone to be simultaneously lost and found, but she was lost in a maze of questions about her future relationships, and found in her music. She was good at taking action, and very decisive in the long run. She was a leader, but incapable of leading herself through the puzzle of choices. To go or stay, to love or not, to want or to ignore.

Vi stood outside of herself for a minute, watching. Strong. Able. Cute yet not beautiful. Her body was solid and fierce, a bit of a gut pressing forward against her jeans. Vi noticed this flaw most often in a world of hard bodies.

She studied her flaws, but she embraced her strengths. Vi was a spirit in the night fighting for what she wanted, strong willed in everything. She could play sports and fix a car and make others cry with her lyrics. She was diverse and loved and respected. There was no better way that she would want to have been born into this world. She couldn't imagine life as a girl like Sarah. Vi would have had little respect for herself, worrying about all things material and few things sentimental.

Vi could picture herself standing next to Sarah who sat on the picnic tabletop. The girl's face was made up perfectly, a beautiful specimen in flawless clothes. So she had problems, so she couldn't handle food. She had the look that appealed to most men. She had it easy in a vain world.

Vi lost her vision again. She was down on herself, then up, then down.

"I'd be a model if my mom would let me," Sarah said. "She doesn't think that women should work. She thinks everything is like it was back in the Ice Age with prominent society women and their parties."

Vi remained silent. The cruel smart ass inside her wanted to comment to Sarah that being anorexic qualified her to be a model. She didn't comment aloud, though. She didn't want to hurt Sarah, and she was glad that this wasn't one time where she couldn't help herself, couldn't stop her mouth from spewing what her brain allowed to pass as funny.

"It's not like I want to be a waitress or anything like that."

Vi held her tongue. Her first impression of Sarah was resurfacing, the spoiled north-sider who would marry rich and never work. The brat that used to scoff at Vi, the one who still was scoffing if she knew it or not.

Vi remembered her mother saying that everyone had his or her own story. She was ten and was crying because her parents couldn't afford to pay for basketball camp. It turned out that a family like Sarah's had donated money for those less fortunate, and Vi could go. So Vi was happy yet full of spite for the well to do. She didn't care if at one time, previous generations of the rich family had struggled for wealth or status.

"I don't know what I want to do anymore." Sarah continued, despite Vi ignoring her. "Should I keep dating? Should I go back to school? No, that won't do me any good, since all I did was party with my sorority sisters."

Vi restrained her judgement. She settled on a slight laugh and brought herself back from her inner eye, back to the parking lot. There was a tremendous difference between Vi and Sarah, but she could see that there were similarities: the self-confidence on the outside, lack thereof on the inside, and the need for something, anything, to happen. The longing for change and for success, and for more change. Yes, Vi's mother was right, everyone had his or her own story.

Sarah waited for Vi to return to the conversation, to donate her wisdom to those in need. Vi pondered the advice looming in front of her: the *wake up and smell the coffee* advice, the *get real* advice, the *you have everything, go with it* advice. But Vi knew that the best answer was an obscure one, an analogy perhaps, something to jump-start the one asking the question. As everyone had their own questions about life, they also had their own answers. No one wanted to trust himself though, so Vi figured she would just spark the fire. She set in, balancing her weight on both feet, digging into a bit of gravel with her heels. Her head dropped for a minute, and then she began in a soft voice.

"I used to walk real early in the morning. I'm talking 4:30 a.m. or so. The neighborhood was empty that early, and the others who were out, I would see every day. There was this one guy who would hang around the edge of a park in the neighborhood. There was a curvy pond in the park, a big nature space. This guy would dig through reeds and after a while, he would send a little net into the water. That's what he did every morning while the sun was coming up.

"I was always walking my dog, King. He was a big shepherd, a protector. Anyway, there were the joggers out, and King would always growl at their lycra tights when they ran by me in the street, just out of range of his leash." Vi smiled at this. She didn't much like the aerobic queens. At least she would never admit how much she wished she had looked like them.

"Anyway, there were a couple others walking their dogs, too. It was the same crowd every morning, about six or seven of us. The pond guy always said 'hi' no matter which side of the street I was on. Sometimes the others would make eye contact, but usually not. Most of them were just hoping that I could control King." Sarah smiled as Vi mimicked pulling back King's leash with her empty hands. "They all had their own things going on. Each of us returned to different houses and went to different jobs. We all had different families and different relationships."

Sarah gave a confused look. She was trying so hard to understand the answer that Vi must have been telling her, but she hadn't found it yet. Sarah thought that Vi was brilliant, and she must have been talking beyond Sarah's limit of understanding. Sarah thought she would hear the story out, say that she understood, and politely bow out of the conversation. But then she realized that's how her mother would have handled the situation, so Sarah stuck with it. Her forehead crinkled under a mask of concentration, and she tried to imagine each word that Vi was saying. Sarah could see the neighborhood, the park with the pond, the beautiful people floating by in their two hundred dollar Nike's.

"So these people," Sarah tried. "They were all out early in the morning. Do you think that would help me? To get up early and go walking or something?"

Vi looked at Sarah. The twenty-two-year-old sat upright on the table with a pleased expression, waiting as a dog would for a cookie after completing the correct trick. No, Vi did not think that taking a walk was the answer for this lost child. Sarah had been robbing her own body of proper nutrition for years and was probably too weak to make it very far anyway. Her almost nonexistent muscles in her frail and bony frame worked as hard as they could to keep her upright. Like a two-pack-a-day smoker running a marathon, the walking might kill her.

Except, Vi knew that taking a simple walk could become a spiritual event, clearing the mind and the soul. One was forced to think, to observe both surroundings and body performance. Perhaps Sarah would like the walks and that would help her decide to be healthier. Vi had seen a movie where the recovering bulimics performed some sort of physical fitness that allowed them to take charge of their appearance in a healthy manner instead of starving. She wondered if Sarah's mother would allow her to take walks. Perhaps if she was walking with a man, being courted in the proper manner of a lady. Vi tried not to laugh out loud.

"I don't know if that's what I'm trying to say. I guess if that's what you'd like to do, then you should do it. You need to think about if it's the best thing for you." Sarah didn't answer Vi. She was too used to others answering for her, telling her the best solution, and it would take her more than a few minutes to make up her own mind. It was difficult to decide if something was what she wanted or what she thought her parents would expect.

Vi continued. "There was an old man that I saw every morning on the way home from my walk. He was a good height for a man, and he carried a little weight in the front, but old men usually do. His posture was a little hunched over, only I don't know if that was how his back was shaped or if his cane was just too short for him." Vi questioned herself, remembering more vividly. She could feel the memory in her throat, her breaths coming quickly with slight pauses in between. It amazed her how well she remembered.

"He would walk up the block across the street from me, real slow and purposeful, as if he had been walking for miles through the desert and refused to give in to the heat." Vi could see his hat now, although sometimes he didn't wear it and his balding head would leave strands of gray flopping in the breeze. "Every morning he would get to the corner across the street from where I would turn to go home. He walked to the curb at the edge of the sidewalk, touched his foot to the curb, turned around and went back the same way. It was so unusual, you know? He didn't stop where the sidewalk turned onto the next street or even in a different place each day. He walked exactly to the curb and touched it." As her memory of the old man faded, Vi still wondered. It had been two years since she had walked to that corner, since she had moved away and had seen the old man in his morning practice. Yet she was sure that if she were to be at that corner in the morning, he would be there too, turning on the same spot.

She was good at making up stories for people. She was good at reading human behavior. But Vi had never figured this man out. She had thought once that his wife of fifty years had died and he was biding his time now. But then she thought that he'd had heart trouble and his doctor was making him walk to keep in shape, the best shape an eighty-year-old could be in. Once Vi imagined that in the old man's past, he had walked to that corner with someone who ended up getting hit by a car and had died because he wasn't watching like he should have been. And so, in Vi's mind, he made his way to the corner in the early morning when there were no cars and no one was watching, and he would turn around and head home with his memory, instead of letting them go out into the street to their death.

None of these explanations fit, though. The man walked to the same spot each morning, his frame bent over at the same angle, only his clothing changing from day to day, and that change was minimal for an aging gentleman who had acquired his favorite style and color over the years. Vi never could find the meaning in the old man's actions, and she didn't know why she was telling Sarah about him. Maybe she thought that Sarah's perspective on the story would help her decipher its significance. Maybe Vi was just looking for the most obscure story she could think of. And this was it, tucked away in the back of her memory, waiting to be solved, like a puzzle with pieces missing from the box after years of children's little hands losing them under couches and behind dressers. Waiting to be solved as Sarah was now.

And Sarah was nodding, smiling and ready to share her explanation. "There's something funny about a statue. Half of the time you don't even notice it's there, and when you take time to look at it, it's different each time you see it. Sometimes it makes you happy, sometimes it makes you sad. And sometimes you don't see it at all, you just wonder about the artist who made it, what they were like and what inspired them." Sarah took a long breath at the end of her account. She had been talking so fast that she hadn't even heard some points that she had just made. But something had struck a chord for her, and that was all Vi had wanted.

"I know what you're trying to say," Vi offered, and Sarah's eyes lit up.

Vi liked the statue analogy. She thought along these same lines a lot of the time. It was how she got into people's heads and wrote her songs. She couldn't help but wonder if Sarah even knew what she was talking about. Once Vi saw a little window on the top of a hospital, and while most people wouldn't have noticed it, Vi wondered about the janitor who cleaned the small room, the person who looked out the small round window on his own, maybe late at night, and worried about his daughter who was ill or his son who was causing trouble at school, or his wife who didn't want him working at night except they needed the money.

Vi thought again about the old man with the cane and wondered what he must have been thinking on all of those morning walks. She couldn't hear the answer, so she gave up once more and tried to concentrate on Sarah. The girl sat on the bench, holding her arms around herself for warmth. Sarah admitted to Vi that she had thrown up after eating, and this girl obviously had a problem with her appearance. Maybe it would be a bad idea for her to pursue modeling. Vi knew little about anorexia or bulimia, just what she had heard on talk shows, but she could tell that Sarah was too skinny, and in the same thought, wished that she had Sarah's body.

Vi often felt overweight, a product of the media age of skin-and-bones models, diet pills, and Jenny Craig. She thought once about purging her dinner so that she wouldn't gain any weight for it. The thought left at the same moment it entered, because Vi knew she had too much sense to hurt herself like that. She knew that *she* was the only way she was going to reach her goal. Vi had been on pills that stopped her hunger, a time in her life she spent running in circles because really they were uppers. She had tried a soup diet, and a carbohydrate diet, and a starvation diet. And here she was, overweight as determined by science and record companies. Still, Vi wouldn't trade her place with Sarah. All Vi had to do was get motivated. Sarah needed some therapy and a few years of self-exploration before she'd feel happy with herself.

Vi turned toward Phil's. She could see William and Sean talking, Tom watching as always, smiling a bit, his eyes shining in the fluorescence. *Where had this conversation started?* And then Vi remembered. It was Sarah prodding her about Tom. And Vi had dodged the questions pretty effectively, although she didn't think that she could much longer.

The moon lent its light to the shadowed side of the parking lot where the picnic table lived; the stars looking over the moon's shoulder like apprentices, learning the trade of lighting the sky. The five unlikely friends, the Towncar, lottery tickets, the conversation cascading among the silence. Yesterdays and destinies colliding. *What was it that Sarah had said? We don't choose our destinies. We look back on our choices and realize that what we got, and how we turned out, was our destiny.* That made Vi smile as she stepped toward the diner. She was here with these people on this Tuesday night, or perhaps it was Wednesday morning, and this would be part of the ride to her destiny. This would be a memory. It made little sense, but Vi had learned a long time ago that it didn't have to.

Sarah stayed seated on the bench and watched expectantly until she realized Vi was going into the diner. Sarah looked around, and although she was too old to be afraid of the dark, she knew that being afraid of the night was a completely acceptable practice. Her footsteps crunched across the parking lot after the singer who was almost inside.

11

BULLDOGS

William slumped his head as Betty approached the counter. She had made her point, had her time to stew, and now it was time to let him off the hook. She placed her grilled cheese in front of William and refilled her coffee. Two more truckers entered the diner and sat at Tom's left. Betty brought them both cups of coffee and their own freshly brewed pot, which she laid on a folded towel. They poured for themselves and were on their second cup each before Betty had menus in front of them.

"Hey, Ray!" one of them called. "Where'd you go tonight? Were you out at The Slingshot again?"

"I wasn't nowhere," Ray responded angrily. The truckers made no attempt to conceal their laughter, and Ray could only scowl back from the opposite side of the U-shaped counter.

Betty returned to her seat at the inside corner of the counter in front of William. She took a bite of the grilled cheese and William watched her chew in silence. She washed the bite down with her scalding black coffee and stared straight into William. "Are you through picking on those out there in the world with a dream?" Again, Betty crunched into the crispy bread and slowly pulled it away, allowing the melted cheese to break. William looked up.

"I'm sorry, Betty." William was sulking like a nine-year-old girl who would say anything to get her doll back from her angry parents. "I won't comment on anyone else's life again."

William waited for Betty to respond, and she took her time. "Yes, you will." She smiled and poured William a fresh coffee, who sipped the burning liquid lest he offend Betty again. And with one smile, he was off the hook. William sighed happily. He had his lottery tickets, his stomach was full, and he was feeling the effects of a long night. It was too late to get a good night's sleep ,and he would be dragging in the morning. He was the foreman at work though, so perhaps he wouldn't help the men on the job tomorrow. Maybe he would just show up and drink coffee and pray his over-tired self through the slow minutes of a workday.

"Betty?" Sean asked with a deceptive smile on his face. "You really like the cook, that's obvious. I'm just wondering what the two of you have going on back there." William leaned over and put his hand in front of Sean in an attempt to silence the boisterous and vulgar Irish-American. The two truckers next to Tom laughed, but one look from Betty shut them up. Sean continued, "You're so defensive, so touchy. To me, those are the emotions of a person hiding something." Sean smiled, and even Ray was waiting for Betty to leap across the bar and strangle the boy. But in the long run, Betty always allowed her razor sharp tongue to do the damage for her.

"You shouldn't insult my husband. He's all I need in this world. Besides, the only person hiding something in here is you." Sean looked questioningly as it was Betty's turn to smile. "You, hiding your head up your ass like that. It's a damn shame." Betty smiled into Sean who sat in disbelief. William, Ray, and the two truckers let their laughter ring through diner and even Tom snickered at Betty's comment. Betty took her grilled cheese off the bar and turned toward the truckers who high-fived her as she strutted by. She put her plate in the bin below the counter as the cook looked through the window, sleepy-eyed, wondering what had caused the customers to erupt. Betty dismissed him with the wave of her hand and he was gone again. She filled Ray's cup and gave him some milk as the others calmed down. She walked straight to Sean, reached over the counter, and grabbed his cheeks between her thumb and forefinger, squeezing tightly and causing Sean's face to pucker like a fish.

"William," she said, still gripping Sean's flesh, "don't bring your friend back here again. I don't like him." She released Sean's cheeks, pushing his head back a little. Sean put his hands up in front of his face and waved a white napkin in surrender. The others laughed again, the residual silliness exploding in overtired brain cells.

Both Betty and Sean were smiling. Despite her words, she did like Sean, and he knew it. Sean was a loudmouth and often disagreeable, but people liked to have him around. His comments made it into the world without a moment's apprehension. Without a filter, he had no conscience in offending another's ego. The laughter that his ignorance brought was more accredited to his value than his insulting remarks.

Sean decided to stop hiding and removed his flask from his inside pocket. He poured what was left of the clear liquid into his orange juice. He stirred the mixture with his finger before sipping. Ray watched, mesmerized, longing for his own drink. Tom watched Sean too, terrors beginning to run through his head, the anger and energy forming bile in the back of his throat. Over Sean's shoulder, Tom saw Sarah and Vi coming toward the door to the diner. He threw three dollars on the bar and jumped off his stool. Sarah and Vi entered the diner, Vi holding the steel framed glass door for Sarah, Tom managing to slip out between the two. He lingered in front of Vi for an instant, his image reflecting in her eyes before he disappeared into the same night from which she had materialized.

"Hey, William," Sean said not noticing the timeliness of Tom's exit. "Give me Tom's orange juice." William slid the tart liquid to Sean who added a bit more to his poison.

————

Vi was looking back, looking out the door at Tom. But when the door closed, he was gone, the interior lights of the diner reflecting off the windows and sheltering the glass room from the night. Vi wondered what Tom's eyes had said to her as he left. He seemed to be hiding, but his eyes were on fire. They were mixed with anger and the innocence of a child. Vi wanted to follow him out, but she stopped herself. Sarah was waiting at the door, and Vi wondered if the girl had noticed her lingering over Tom.

Sarah had her arms wrapped around her stomach, her attention intent on Vi. Sarah knew that the men's attention was on her, each man hoping that she would slide onto the stool next to him and make their world a prettier place.

Vi sighed and reeled herself back into the restaurant. She moved by Sean and William and sat on the stool where Tom had been. Sarah followed Vi, but instead of taking the stool between Vi and the burly, gawking men, she opted to stand at the corner of the bar between Vi and William.

"What have you two been doing?" Sean asked as he mimicked Groucho Marx, his eyebrows moving up and down. Vi and Sarah ignored his insinuations and turned toward William.

Vi smiled. "We have been discussing life, love, and the perils of being a woman in the nineties."

"Oh, gauwwd," Sean reeled disapprovingly. "I don't know if I can sit here and listen to this. Betty?" he asked. She was serving the truckers and checking on Ray who was content in his world between drunkenness and consciousness. "Do you have any aspirin back there?" Betty shook her head and left Sean to look around the diner at the kaleidoscope of objects for sale. "You have a condom machine in the dining area, you even have a sunglasses rack, but you don't have any aspirin? Come on, Betty. Help me out here."

William didn't like the rapport that Sean and Betty had going, this after less than an hour of acquaintance. But they kept it up despite the fact they had no idea William was jealous. He knew he shouldn't feel this way, but he did. *This must be what women do*, William thought. *They think you can read their minds, and they get upset when you don't.*

He held his breath as Betty produced a bottle of aspirin

from her purse and tossed it to Sean who caught it with one hand, removed two aspirin, and tossed it back. Phil's own circus act, Betty held her purse open in the air and let the bottle fall in before closing the zipper behind it. Sean placed the two tablets on the counter next to his drink.

"You're welcome," Betty said.

"Thank you, Betty," Sean sang like an elementary school student greeting his teacher in the morning.

"And who are these lovely girls?" Betty asked William.

"Betty, this is Sarah, and this is Vi." He introduced the two and hoped that Betty would behave.

"Are you two the reason that William was late getting here tonight?" Betty asked as she produced two menus.

"We're half the reason," Vi answered. "You already met the other half." Vi pointed at Sean and smiled. Sean bowed his head to the ladies and sipped his drink.

Vi liked Betty already. She was a working class woman who was in charge of her own world. She had a good sense of humor and the temper of a lion. Vi could tell that Betty was happy, but bet that she was never content, always finding new things to fill her time. And Vi saw the customers occupied Betty's time well enough when she was at work. The waitress moving back and forth in her cramped space behind the counter, giving everyone what they needed before they even knew they did. She refilled coffees, presented meals, poured waters, and collected tips. She was a one-woman machine. Vi felt as though she was reciting this woman's life off of an index card, but she knew people, and she liked what she saw here.

"It's good to get a couple more women in here at night. This place fills up with a lot of horny men when the bar closes, but that's about it." Betty continued her duties as she spoke. "You've been talking about men, have you? I love men with Australian accents. Men down under really get me going." Betty smiled like the devil, the double meaning of her statement lost only on Ray.

"How you doin' there, little lady?" one trucker asked in an attempt at the accent.

"I'm doing fine, but you should get your head checked."

The other trucker laughed at his friend, almost spitting his water over the counter at Ray. The old drunk squinted menacingly. No one was scared.

"I like their accents too," Sarah told Betty. Sarah didn't know what to think of the waitress. She didn't understand a world of long hours and hard work, the physical labor permanently hurting the back and the feet over time. Sarah wanted to fit in, to take the fact of work for granted, but she never would.

"I like their dimples and their charm." Vi hit the mark.

"They're nice to watch," Betty agreed. "They're beefcake." Then Betty whistled as a construction worker might. "Ooh, baby."

"You women are terrible," William interjected.

"Yeah," Sean agreed. "I feel so used and dirty."

"We're like objects to you." The truck drivers added to the air of men's liberation that rose up around the counter. "We're used up and thrown away."

Ray laughed at the burly truck drivers. "Yeah, you guys are really a couple of sex objects." The old man was rocking on his stool, holding his stomach, the laughter coming out in whips like a high-pitched whistle, his dilapidated organs wheezing for oxygen. His eyes teared up with laughter, and Betty tried to calm him with a tap on the sleeve.

The drivers were looming over the counter like two bull-dogs at the end of their rope where the old drunk was concerned. They were powerful men, beasts, and they were not used to being criticized.

"You shut him up, Betty," one of the drivers insisted.

"Oh come on. Calm down, you two. He's just an old man having a little fun. Eat your food." Reluctantly, at Betty's insistence, they returned to their heaping plates of hash brown, corned beef, three eggs, and four pieces of toast on the side for each.

"Calm down, Ray. I'm going to order you your breakfast now." The old man slowly regained his breath, his face red from laughing, his gaze on the drivers across the counter. His lips curled up in a half smile to goad them on, and he chuckled at the edge of being beaten to a pulp.

"I for one, am shocked that you women would treat us like this." William acted flabbergasted. "You complain all we care about is looks, and here you are drooling over men like they're pieces of meat."

"You can treat me like a piece of meat," Sean added, always ready for any encounter with a girl.

"We were talking about hot Australian men," Vi said.

"Yeah, you're just a bunch of pigs." It was Sarah and Vi who had the last laugh. Betty joined in for a moment, pausing only long enough to defend her husband.

"Don't egg them on, Sean. It's a double standard. If we were talking about how hot one of those 'Baywatch' chicks are, they'd be all over us screaming about how men treat women like dirt."

Sean spun a knife on the counter. "Lighten up, William. This must be what they talk about when they all travel to the bathroom together. Besides, they're inspiring me here."

———

William waited for the women to finish oozing over their favorite daytime stars. He turned on his stool and tried to make out Tom's figure through the window but couldn't see outside. He looked at his own reflection in the glass watching the strange people behind him. Ray swayed in his stool trying to be as human as possible, a task the old man had trouble with. The pungent drunk had come to Phil's almost every week that William was there. He would stumble in as William was getting ready to leave, and he would pass out at the counter where Betty would patiently wait for him to wake up.

Betty seemed to like the old man. Sometimes he would tell her about his night out at The Slingshot, a small hole in the wall where he could drink cheaply without being bothered. Most of Ray's words were incoherent, although he never broke into that drunken chatter of sad stories of life and times. He never whispered through tears a longing for an earlier time or another life. William wondered if Ray had a family or a job, or even a home. Ray was most likely one of Betty's hard luck cases, but William had never been interested long enough to care.

Sean was still sipping on his drink, slowly diluting the vodka more and more with Tom's unfinished orange juice. In the reflection, his long, straight strands of red hair bobbed over the bottom of his collar. William watched in the reflection as Sean looked around at the three women, his eyes lingering on Sarah. William remembered a time when the brain downstairs drove his life as Sean's did now. But that was years ago, and he'd never wish to go back. William didn't understand how Sean could be so forthright and overbearing, and he wondered how the boy ever got a woman. Of course, most of the women that Sean ended up with must have been drunk or out of their mind, or both, perhaps.

William was glad that Sarah had enough sense to say no to Sean. She was standing next to William. He could feel her shoulder touch his for an instant, their reflections in the window touching without feeling. Sarah was attractive to William. She was a knockout. She didn't smile too often. He had noticed that in the rearview mirror. Sarah was small too; she was thin, a twig. William wondered how many layers of clothing she had to wear in the winter to keep warm. Although, if she came from money as he thought she might, she probably spent little time out in the cold but going from the house to the warm car with a personal driver who would wait for her every command.

William thought about trying to talk to her, maybe trying to ask her out, but that would have to wait until Sean was out of the picture. He knew Sarah didn't like Sean, and he also knew that Sean didn't care.

Vi sat sideways at the corner of the counter trading opinions with Betty about some young stud. William liked Vi a lot. She was upbeat most of the time, and she was a sort of peacekeeper, although she never backed down from her side of an argument. William had talked to Vi at Baker's Tap a few times, and he enjoyed being around her. She reminded William of his younger sister, Christie. She was the one sibling who could keep the four others in line, always cracking a smile or a joke at just the right time, lightening up the mood before the third world war broke out among the five children and they were left screaming and pulling hair. William hoped Vi would accomplish everything she had set out to do, and he knew she would, with or without his confidence in her.

He watched her reflection, and her plainness seemed to create more color in the surrounding room. William knew Vi thought little about her looks; self-perception had been Tony's topic of discussion late one night at Baker's Tap. Tony said that Vi was what he called a little rough around the edges. It was no great explanation. Tony had said that about everything in the two years since he had sobered up. William thought little of it as he figured 'rough around the edges' was the way Tony had seen the world through eighty proof eyes.

William shrugged with the randomness of his thoughts. Vi might not have given much attention to her looks. They weren't a priority at any rate. But her beauty was all around her, and it had its own energy; the way she made those around her feel special, made them feel better than they really were.

The two truckers were hidden behind Vi's reflection. William didn't think they were Tuesday night regulars, although he was here later than usual tonight. Betty seemed to know them well enough. New customers were always greeted with a barrage of questions, but she served these drivers with a few short words.

The truckers peeked around Vi every few minutes to get a better look at Sarah, and their blatant drooling bothered William. But he had unconsciously been stealing his own glances at her reflection, and he hardly thought the drivers even recognized their own action. It was something men did, checking out a woman's figure. They looked women up and down. It was human nature when human was defined as civilized animals posing, guarding and surviving, the same as any animal in the wild.

"What'll you girls have to eat?" Betty asked as she turned back to the city crowd. Vi looked over the menu, Sarah still standing, trying not to notice the laminated plastic menu showing greasy meals on the bar in front of her.

"Nothing for me," Sarah said timidly. One look from Vi and she changed her mind. One look back at the menu, and she changed it back. "I'll start with a cup of coffee."

"Sure you don't want anything more, honey? You look like you could use some meat on your bones." Betty looked Sarah up and down, a different look than the men had been giving her. It was more of a knowing, conclusive stare, one that made the girl uncomfortable.

For a second, Sarah was angry at Vi for letting her secret out. Then she realized Vi hadn't said anything at all, and it was just her fear creeping up to the surface. The same fear that craved and then made her eat when she was alone, eat more than she ever would in front of another. The same fear that made her run the water in the bathroom sink to cover the sounds of her heaving. The fear that ruled her life and chanted a whisper in her sleep. *You are what you eat. You are what you eat.*

Sarah tried to smile at Betty, but at this minute, she hated the woman. When Sarah heard the expression 'you need some meat on your bones', she thought of pigs. It wasn't Betty's fault, really. It was Sarah's mother again:

prodding her as a teen, mimicking the sloppy sounds of pigs when Sarah asked for seconds, degrading the child in front of her father and the staff, making her afraid that she would grow up to be fat and useless, playing with the child's imagination until finally, Sarah was terrified to ask for food even if she was about to pass out from famine.

Sarah could see the child; see her sitting in silence and trying not to cry as her mother goaded her. The child was spiteful for a while, then quiet. She didn't want to lose her mother's love, needed forever to please. Then the child grew cold. She became defiant, a scared baby taking her first drink at age ten. She was lost after that, eating all she could one afternoon, trying to regain her spirit, trying to ingest what she was losing. Then she was sick. And she was sick. And she was alone. The child stopped eating, stopped fighting. She gave in to the battle, and the sound of running water became her friend as she purged her soul from her body day after day. She was shrinking. The child was trying to disappear.

Sarah cleared her throat to rid the image from her head. She was in Phil's diner, Phil's Breakfast and 7UP. She tried to breathe the worry from her face, calming herself one second at a time. The child receded, trying to be forgotten, trying once again to disappear. The child could not fight for herself, and she would not win this battle. She was ashamed for giving up but also ashamed for thinking that her way of life had been wrong. The child was weak, would never raise her fists or her voice. A new Sarah, this Sarah, would have to fight. She would have to be the one to stand up and take everything that was thrown at her. Sarah would have to accept change, change for the good, and change for the future. She wondered what this feeling was, perhaps hope, something she couldn't remember knowing.

Sarah leaned a little closer to Vi, feeling the strong-willed woman's words of encouragement swirl through her, thinking that her newfound self-determination must have been coming from Vi's store of energy. Sarah wasn't ready to do this alone, and she knew she didn't have to. The child would no longer go away, she would no longer allow Sarah to ignore her.

"I'm not too hungry yet," Vi said, her system still pumped with tar and nicotine. "Can I just have a Diet Coke and some bacon?"

"I think I need to get some Tums if I'm going to watch you eat that," Sean said as he picked up the aspirin. "That sounds like a pretty disgusting mix."

"No more disgusting than the way you ate your eggs," William commented. "Letting the yolk run all over your hands. Such manners." Betty rolled her eyes and retreated to the kitchen to throw Vi's bacon on the grill. The cook appeared in the window, but Betty shooed him off to go back to sleep.

Sean held his hands out to show that they were clean now, dropping one of the aspirin on the floor. He hopped off his stool to retrieve the white pill. "My hands are clean now, aren't they? It's not like I went and rubbed the yolk all over your precious car interior." Sean pick up the aspirin and popped the two small saucers in his mouth, ignoring the water that Betty had brought over. He washed the tablets down with the last of his drink.

"That's really gross," Sarah said, her face crumpling up in disgust.

"What?" William asked, thinking that Sarah was talking to him. He rubbed his face wildly with a napkin.

"Not you, him." Sarah pointed at Sean. "That aspirin was on the floor."

Sean had eaten worse from more peculiar places. "It's coated."

"Well, the coating touched the floor!"

"I meant my stomach." Sean laughed as he headed for the men's room.

12

THIEVES

Tom inhaled the fresh air, but all that his mind allowed him to smell was the hidden yet distinct odor of the vodka that trailed behind him. He walked around the back of the restaurant and into the trees, stopping only when he knew no one could see him. He grabbed his chest with his right hand, his left still tucked deep in his jeans pocket. He swore at the darkness and all of its nightmarish suggestions, and he cried.

Tom could taste the salt that seeped from the inside of his lips, leaving the bitter taste of crying in his mouth. He had forgotten about that taste, the pain and then the relief that it brought with it. Tom's hands were on his face now. He was down on the ground, down on his knees, letting the world slip down off of his shoulders and away.

He tried to release his demons, his memories, but the night was not ready to accept the responsibility, and it forced Tom to live through them once more. But this time, he resolved to let them go with the tears and allow him the relief he had earned through the years of his burden. Tom hadn't cried once since he was twelve years old. That was when he had learned anger. That was when he had learned to spite his father and steer clear of the world. That was when he had decided that he did not deserve to hurt.

Tom had thought of himself as a robot since then, mechanically driving through the motions of life, allowing people to come and go from his days without a second thought. The only time in these seventeen years that he had allowed himself to feel was when he saw a happy family at a restaurant or in the park. And he had allowed himself to feel something for Vi, although before tonight he had never intended to act on his feelings. Tom could hear sobbing, and he looked around for a moment for its source. Then he realized it was the animal deep inside his own body creating that noise, that pitiful weakness he couldn't stop if he tried. He turned back toward the diner to make sure that no one had followed him out. Then he let it go.

The first time that Tom had a drink, it was a screwdriver like the one that Sean had just made. Although Tom's wasn't made as civilly as Sean's had been. Tom's father had beaten his brother to the floor in the living room. He had poured orange juice over his brother's face, the pulp drying to the wood floor in a sticky crust. Tom's brother didn't cry, he never did. He lay on the floor against the wall and stared at their father; the spite beaming from his eyes like daggers. There were many times that Tom thought his brother would lash out, fly across the room in a fit of rage, and strangle the man. Tear his eyes from their sockets. But the boy never did, and now the grown man carried the family torch in his own home.

After their father had spilled out most of the orange juice, he filled the rest of the glass with vodka. This far into the bottle, there was never time to put ice in the drink, which would call for a trip as far as the kitchen. The devil knelt over Tom that night, the glass outstretched, Tom's arms pinned to the floor under daddy's knees, his head moving side to side, his neck not strong enough to push his weight back through the floor and away from this madness.

The drink came down on him, his father squeezing his cheeks, his jaw opening involuntarily. Tom fought his father. He fought the juice that ran into his mouth and down his cheeks. But in the end, Tom had to swallow the juice lest he choke on the same poison that had drowned his father for years.

And he did, the swallows of air coming in huge gulps of warm oranges burning down his esophagus, melting in his stomach. Tom would spit and choke, but his father would keep pouring the colorful rain onto his son, and his son would pray for the sting of lightning to end his nightmare. But this rain came with its own kind of storm and no promise of an end.

After the glass was empty, Tom lay inundated on the floor. His tears drifted into the puddle of juice on the floor. The lesson over for the night, his father backed off with a few parting words and settled into his recliner.

Tom didn't move. He didn't run. He let the tears run, and his father turned the television up and let it take him away from his evil deed. This happened several times during his childhood, but Tom remembered this one as the last time he had bothered to cry. It was after he pulled himself off the floor and wiped his eyes, while his head throbbed from the pressure of tears exploding out and his jaw being pushed in.

After being left on the battlefield alone, that's when Tom gave up his fight. He expected to hear his brother's screams, but instead he saw his brother sitting on the edge of the couch in front of the television. His eyes were open wide, yet the pupils showed no emotion. He was frozen, sitting there opposite his father, a glass of vodka in his hands. He was a statue when Tom first noticed him, and then he moved. Looking away, his brother voluntarily took a drink.

Tom ran from the house and down the alley. When he was out of breath, he stopped next to a garage, the darkness hiding his appearance. But the stench was there. Tom's hands stuck to his face and his clothes where the potion had dried in a sticky mess. He waited. He heard the leaves trickling along the pavement around him and nothing else. He found a yard with a hose and silently drenched himself until he felt like a prune. He left the water running and ran. He fell and cried again, covering his dry sobs in his wet sweatshirt.

Tom saw his brother over and over, saw him looking away, saw him taking a drink. Tom knew that was why his father hadn't come back at him with a second drink, hadn't wrestled Tom to the floor for more humiliation and abuse. His brother had caved in, had thrown himself in front of the train. He had given himself up in Tom's place. That was when Tom had stopped crying, stopped crying forever. That was when Tom had lost his soul. And here it was, in the leaves and the trees right where he had left it seventeen years earlier. It was out in the night, waiting out in the cold for Tom to take possession again.

He sat back on his feet, his knees dug into the soft ground from his unconscious swaying. He didn't know if he wanted to feel, if he wanted to be real yet. He didn't know if he could handle the responsibility of his memories or of his future. He was having a hard enough time in this moment to consider dealing with the rest of time that had delivered him here.

Shhhhh, the leaves said to him. *Shhhhh,* the tree branches whispered. Tom was silent. He was ready to listen. *Shhhhh.* He came pouring back into himself. Tom was finally home.

Tom leaned forward, his face an inch from the ground, his arms tucked across his chest. He hugged himself, felt his body working. He was no longer hiding. He was alive. Tom let go of his guilt. It was not his fault that he couldn't protect his mother. He was her child, and she could not protect him. It was not his fault that he couldn't take that drink for his brother, that he couldn't change the life that moment had created. It was no one's fault, no one but his father's. Tom didn't have to live in that shadow anymore if he didn't want to. He had to remember, and it would never go away, but what if Tom forgave it? What if he forgave himself for having to live this experience? What if he forgave himself for not being able to protect his mother and his brother? What if he allowed himself to go on?

Tom hated his father all these years, all of this time wasted running, trying to get away. All of these years of hating had allowed the old man in, had allowed the old man to make choices for him, and Tom had no more room for the hatred. It wasn't driving him to succeed; it was chewing at his insides and leaving him to rot. It was taking more out of him to hate than it would to love. No, Tom would never love his father, but he could choose to not hate him. He could choose to save his emotion for better things.

Tom sat up, his legs falling asleep underneath him. He moved to the side and allowed his legs to unfold. He was no longer curled up, no longer closed to the world. He breathed loudly, and he let himself and the night know that's what he intended to do from now on, to breathe. No more tiptoeing around what he wanted. No more fearing his intentions. The wind ran across Tom's neck and the black hair stuck out in a row of goose bumps.

Shhhhh, his mother said. *It's okay, baby. Go to sleep.* And Tom was free.

———

"Do you have any Kleenex?" Sarah asked Betty who was busy serving the other customers. Betty walked to the counter in front of William, tore a napkin from the metal dispenser, and placed it on the counter in front of Sarah.

"Nothing fancy in here, honey." Betty was off again to retrieve Vi's bacon. Sarah stared at the napkin before picking it up. She rubbed her fingers over the paper, feeling its rough surface, not wanting to put this sandpaper against her smooth skin as she was sure that it would undo her efforts of laboring in front of the mirror day in and year out.

"Here," Sean offered as he pulled a handkerchief from his pocket. It was soft cotton, the same type that a gentleman would carry. This surprised Sarah, and although she should squelch cordiality toward Sean, she decided that accepting the cloth would not count as accepting a pass. She hoped Sean would agree.

"Thank you, Sean. That's very nice of you."

"Well, I'm a nice guy."

Sarah patted her nose as Vi and William looked at Sean expectantly.

"What?" Sean asked in his defense. "Underneath this rough shell beats the heart of a true gentleman."

"So you admit that, in fact, you have a heart?" William beat Vi to the punch this time.

"Yes. Yes, I do. But alas, I carry it around in my handkerchief." Sean caught Sarah wiping her nose, and Sarah stopped with the new attention. She pulled the cloth away from her face.

"Not at all," Sean responded, his words and dialect mimicking that of an English gentleman. "Keep it."

Betty brought Vi's bacon out and refilled a world of coffee cups. "You really are a sweetheart, aren't you?" she asked Sean. She reached over the counter and patted him on the cheek, earning a spiteful look from William. "There aren't too many that carry those things around anymore. People these days are probably too scared that they'll catch a disease or something."

"Well, my mom and my aunts keep me pretty well stocked. They send me a lot of packages filled with the things they consider the staples in life." Sean finished his drink, holding the glass up in front of his face long enough for the last drop of liquid to make its way down through the ice.

"I love getting packages," Vi agreed as she chewed her bacon. "When I was in college, my sister used to send me boxes of food with popcorn, spaghetti, and cookies. It was cool, especially to a starving college kid. What else do they send you?" As Vi waited for the answer, from the corner of her eye, she noticed Sarah staring. The girl couldn't stomach the thought of the bacon, and yet she watched intently as if engulfed in the sight of a car wreck from which she couldn't look away.

"They send me whatever they think of. Sometimes my aunt sends me these hideous vases. She's into that whole clay pottery thing. I don't know where she thinks I put all the stuff she sends me. I could have filled a warehouse by now." Sean rattled the ice around in his glass. That was it, the end of his stash, the end of his liquor for the night. He had to do something. He needed to find a bar or a liquor store that would still be open, but he was doubtful. Sean imagined himself rummaging through the surrounding farmer's fields in the dark, and he wondered how long it would take to ferment corn.

"That's nice that they do that for you," Sarah said as she held the cloth out to Sean.

"Keep it, I was serious."

"Thanks." Sarah looked at the white material, turning it over in her hands. She noticed three embroidered letters. "What does S.C.F. stand for?"

Southern Comfort Fanatic, Sean thought to himself. "Those are my initials, Sean Finnegan." He hoped no one would ask.

"What's the 'C' for?" Betty followed.

"It's for posterity." Sean wasn't about to tell these people his middle name, and he also knew that they wouldn't let it drop. He wondered why there had to be middle names. He guessed it was in case someone didn't like their first name, like it was a second choice. Sean couldn't think of a single person he knew who advertised their middle name. He was convinced that the name was only there as a way for parents to torture their children from birth to death. Maybe the middle name was only for yelling, to gage how angry your parents were since the only time a child hears it is when he is in trouble. Sean thought Vi might know the history of middle names. She sang country music, and everyone in the south had at least two names.

"Come on, Sean. It couldn't be worse than any of the names we're about to make up." Vi finished her bacon and pushed the plate away.

"Oh yeah? What does 'Vi' stand for?" Vi stared a hole through his skull. "Violent."

William joined the prodding. "Tell us, Sean. An Irish Catholic boy like you. You've got to have a great middle name."

"I'll tell you my middle name after you bring me a drink."

"No way."

"Then forget about it."

Betty stood in front of Sean, but even her motherly stare could not make him tell. William patted Sean on the shoulder to prod the boy, but it was Vi's tactics that spilled the beans. Vi swung off her stool and made her way around Sarah and William before sauntering up to Sean. She approached from behind him, his eyes facing in at Betty, his concentration tight on not giving away his secret. Vi bumped Sean from behind, her right hand slapping him on the shoulder and encircling his chest, her left hand reaching down into his back pocket before she nonchalantly backed away.

"Tell us, Sean," Vi whined like a ten-year-old. "I'll be your best friend." Sean didn't respond.

"I'll leave you out here with no ride home," William added.

"Okay," Sean told William. "I'll live out here in Phil's Breakfast and 7UP like Ray here. Hey Ray!" The old man looked up from his plate in dismay as he did not know who in the diner would know his name, although everyone always did. "Ray, you got some hooch for me?"

Ray squinted and his face puckered. "I don't know what you're talking about." He returned to his breakfast, looking back at Sean a few times to let the boy know he was watching.

"Well, we'll have to work on that. What do you say, Betty? Can I move in here?" Sean smiled at Sarah and William.

"No. This is a restaurant, not your apartment. Now stop goofing around." Betty had cleaned the counter in front of the truckers and placed their bill between two full coffee cups.

"But your cook lives here." William hit Sean's arm to stop his loud mouth, but the damage was done. Betty lifted the tub of dirty dishes and disappeared in the back.

"That's enough, Sean Cassidy Finnegan," Vi spouted like a mother at the short end of a fuse. Sean's face turned red, and he slowly pushed his stool around to face Vi. William was already laughing. Sarah stepped over to Vi and took the leather wallet that contained Sean's driver's license and other personal items.

"What?" Sean asked as he frantically patted his pockets in search of his wallet, the one that Sarah now held. "How?" Sean reached for the wallet, but Sarah took a step back and gave a coy smile.

"That's it?" the truck drivers laughed. "Sean Cassidy is your name?" Betty was looking through the counter window, trying not to smile. "Do your parents *still* hate you?"

"My name is Sean Finnegan," Sean told the truck drivers with a scowl that said he was ready to fight over it.

"You leave that boy alone, Digger," Betty called. The truckers poured down their coffee, dropped cash on the counter, and left. They weren't small men, and they never backed down, but they liked Phil's in the middle of the night on their biweekly runs, and they weren't about to spoil things with Betty. They had seen her throw drivers and drunks out in a blink. For Betty, it was never about who was physically stronger. It was a battle of wills, and Betty would win as long as she was playing. After all, she was the one in control of what they were ingesting.

"Sorry, Sean," Vi said as she headed toward the restroom while she rubbed her fingertips across her thumbs.

"You picked my pocket!" Vi didn't turn around as she walked by Ray. He eyed her as he held his hands down over his own pockets in case the girl got frisky with him.

"She picked my pocket!" Sean turned to William in amazement. William was shaking his head. Sarah read the other stats off of Sean's license: red hair, blue eyes, five-feet, eleven-inches tall. He wanted his wallet back, but he didn't mind it in Sarah's hands. He wanted her to get to know him, to pry a bit into his life. That was what made a woman love a man: delving into his privacy, feeling as though she knew his the deep dark secret, the secret that all men hid. But the secret was that there was no secret. William smiled at Sean before turning his stool and his attention back to his coffee.

"What?" Sean asked in defense. "I didn't pick the name. They chose it for me." No one spoke, the silence only making the boy more defensive. "Come on. It was the seventies. Give me a break." Sarah's soft fingertips moved over the brown leather, and Sean wished for a second that he was his wallet.

———

Vi closed the bathroom door behind her. It was a larger room than she would have expected for such a small diner. The room was clean though, probably because Betty cleaned it herself or kept on some employee to keep it up. There was a colorful picture of a flowery field, a tampon machine, and a paper towel dispenser on the wall opposite the toilet. On top of the white porcelain bowl was an air freshener and an aerosol can of freshener. The sink and countertop crowded the door. There was a mirror above the sink, and Vi stared in it without seeing herself.

Vi lit a cigarette and leaned against the wall, each breath of smoke bringing in another old memory. She hadn't picked a pocket in years. It was a skill she had learned from a long-lost man in a long-lost story, and she rewrote every word as she tried to remember. Vi had dated him for three months after he had pursued her, picked her pockets, found out where she lived, and charmed her. He was a lot of fun. Her friends had agreed to that. The two would move personal belongings around a party, wallets and combs changing pockets until someone noticed they were missing something. And then it was time for everyone to spill their belongings and figure out whose was whose. Vi thought that it was funny the first few times they did this tag team party tricking. Her friends thought it was funny also, the first few times. But after a while it became that bad joke that circulated, and people laughed at something that had become irritating, laughing only because they had been raised to say nothing at all in the face of nothing nice. And then he was gone the way of her other boyfriends, the way of the wind.

Vi couldn't remember everyone she'd kissed in time, but she could remember the ones who had kissed her. They had pressed their lips to her heart, breathing their love in and out of her. They had left a print on her softest spot, the one with the heaviest shielding and the most guards. She lived on these memories when she worried she would never find love again. Vi knew how to love. She had done it before. She could picture the object of her affection and her happiness, but like an accident victim who had lost the use of her legs, she could not take the steps needed. Her drive to be someone in the world crippled her love life.

Vi wasn't sure how to be in a long-lasting relationship without being married and then divorced time and time again, like every other celebrity. It didn't matter that she had not achieved public recognition yet, she was sure that she would. Vi didn't know how to pursue the woman she wanted to be and to let someone in at the same time.

She laughed as she threw her cigarette butt in the toilet. Was this her concern? To live beyond the confines of this moment? To worry about being in love in the future? To juggle her heart between her music and her lover? It was ridiculous, but she couldn't help letting the wonder creep into worry. Here it was again, the funny from the serious, the laughter from nothing nice to say. Vi forgot how she had come to be in this john dwelling over history and her future. Then she remembered what had brought it all back. Somehow, Vi's memories must have gotten into Sean's back pocket, and she had lifted them out when she lifted his wallet.

She wondered where Tom had gone and why. He would return for a ride home, if for no other reason. Vi wished she could pick Tom's pockets, to pick his brain. She knew him already. She wondered if he knew what it felt like to be in love with someone, if he knew what it felt like to be loved. It was such a unique feeling, an undefinable glow protecting hearts from true reality. When begun, it was pure, and when over, it was a lie, a mirage, gone.

Love was more wholesome to Vi than a newborn. For even a child that is a day comes with expectations upon its shoulders. It has to live out seconds and hours and years, triumphs and beginnings and endings. Vi left her expectations in the past where love had begun and ended for her. Either she or her partner would inevitably change, or the unavoidable questions about the future caused rifts. The details varied, but the honest, deep glow of love never changed. It burned on.

Vi thought about how naïve it was and how grown up and beautiful it could be. The only time love had really been pure to her was when it wasn't preceded by questions and doubt. When it was a baby. When the concerns were who loved who more and not about where they would live, or who would make a bigger income, or if they would want children. When it was not about the future but about that very moment, the eyes and the touch and the heartbeat, the breathing and the knowing and the peace. Love that good had come into view and hidden time and again. Vi could see it coming now, approaching her as a question. She shrugged love off and, in the same thought, wondered again where Tom was, and if she could take his heart as easily as she had taken Sean's wallet.

13
REIN

Sarah shivered. She sat on Vi's stool, drinking her ice water. William had been prodding Sean about his name for five minutes. It was funny at first, but the redheaded fireball was getting worked up.

"Okay, I've never heard *that* joke before." Sean stewed. He would have pummeled anyone else who shined on and on about his name, but he didn't want to get into it. William was the driver, Sean's ticket home, and the only one who could get Sean to a liquor store so that he could continue the party.

"Sorry, Sean. It's just that your parents made it too easy." William chuckled and turned his attention to Sarah. "You look cold, Sarah. Are you okay?" William was prepared to pull his sweater off and give it to Sarah, because that's what a gentleman did. So his sisters said.

Sarah smiled. "I'm fine, William."

"You've been shivering for ten minutes," Betty said. She placed a cup of hot water in front of Sarah and removed a tea bag from its paper wrapper. "I know that you don't want anything hot to eat, but you drink this and warm up a bit. It's got no calories and it will pep you up." It was no accident that Betty had mentioned there were no calories in the tea. She saw Sarah, feeble, tiny, and wanting. She knew the girl, the young lady of the late nineties, trying to be the goddess for every man that would look in her direction. And they would look, only not in this light where the yellow florescence turned Sarah pale white, her skin pulled so tightly to her cheekbones that the base and the blush could not cover the sharp shadows cut into her face. This girl didn't look like much of a knockout to Betty, not at two in the morning in Phil's. No one could though.

Sarah wasn't sure if she would drink the tea even if it was calorie free. It was something other than air and water, something more substantial served in a standard white restaurant style cup, a cup heavier and more suspicious than the flowery porcelain that Sarah was used to. "Thank you, ma'am."

"Nonsense," Betty said, placing a spoon in front of Sarah. "You call me Betty. Come on, drink up now." Betty stopped in front of Sarah as though she was going to watch until the girl drank the whole cup down. Sarah pictured a cartoon witch fattening Bugs Bunny for her stew. Betty's stare only lingered for a few seconds before she moved back to the kitchen.

She couldn't know, Sarah thought. *She couldn't because there's really nothing to know.*

Sarah gently withdrew the tea bag from the water and let it rest on the spoon. She wrapped the string around the spoon and then the bag, allowing the last bit of water to fall back into the cup. She meticulously placed the spoon and the tea bag on a napkin. Sarah wouldn't have minded some of the tea, but she decided it was too hot to drink and just cupped her hands around the hot mug. The warmth raised the hairs on her body, and Sarah knew she must have been shivering.

She didn't know why she hadn't brought a coat with her tonight. It wasn't cold when Randy had picked her up on this beautiful October night with all of Chicago enjoying what would be the last Indian summer of the year. Sarah thought that the only time she might be cool was between the car and the restaurant or the bar. Randy would surely have valet parked anywhere they might have gone. Sarah did not know they would end up in a diminutive bar on a crowded street. There were so many other places to go in the big city, yet Randy had chosen Baker's Tap.

She saw herself in the window's reflection, a humble figure in a tight miniskirt underneath a baggy blouse. The skirt made her look hot, her tiny legs and miniature calves accentuated by her two-inch heels. Her cream-colored blouse covered her lanky torso and the ribs that poked out at the skin. Her collarbone jutted out from her tiny neck, and her skeletal elbows joined her arms together in four slender sticks.

Sarah could still taste the cool ranch flavoring from the Dorito, and the thought of the chip almost made her stomach convulse. The tea appealed to her now. She pulled the cup to her face and pretended to drink. Betty stopped coaching Ray long enough to look at Sarah, her eyes telling the girl to drink. Sarah did. Although it was a warm sensation, soothing, Sarah pictured the bit of tea in her stomach mixing with the chip. She waited, imagining her body slowly puffing up, but nothing happened. Sarah felt foolish. She took another sip of tea and calmed down. She was coming alive again. Sarah wanted cake and ice cream and chicken and green beans. She wanted hordes of cookies and bologna. She wanted to be sneaking into her kitchen and gorging, standing at the refrigerator, tasting everything from which she had been fasting. She didn't want to think about the twenty minutes she would spend in her bathroom on the floor, on her knees, the faucet behind her keeping her company, soothing the jolts her stomach caused, keeping track of her penance.

Sarah knew this could be a defining moment. She smiled and pretended to pay attention to Sean and William who were sharing a joke. She tried to pay attention, but she didn't want to leave her thoughts, not yet. This was it. This was the moment of change that Vi had been talking about at the picnic table. She had asked who *Sarah* was, what *her* interests were. Sarah saw only herself now, in front of the refrigerator, in front of the toilet. This is who she was. She was a masquerade of events: never eating in front of a man, wanting to stay thin and beautiful, her mirror image hiding the disgust she felt for herself. Then later, without reason, pulling the food in for comfort, pushing it into her mouth, her throat still sore from the last time she had let it out.

Sarah could see her past clearly. Her only interests had been her mother's: to find a man and to be pretty. No wonder her father had no interest in her. Sarah was a shell. She was worried that there wasn't a soul inside. She had tried to change. The doctors had helped her try to understand, but Sarah had misunderstood. She had made her boyfriends her only concern, and she had convinced herself that they were only engrossed in her looks, and that was as far as she had let them get. *Look at me. Put me on your arm and show me off. Forget about me.*

Sarah thought she understood why Randy had left her, why he felt crowded and trapped, bored by the lack of feeling, by the lack of verbal intercourse. Was it too late to change? Sarah didn't know if she could stop herself.

The tea was cooling, and Sarah could feel the shivers returning. She needed to ask for something, but she couldn't for the lack of knowing what it was she wanted. Perhaps a ride home, a ride back into oblivion. Sarah didn't know, and Betty brought it anyway, warming the cup of tea with fresh water and placing a plate with freshly sliced banana and a fork in front of the girl.

Sarah looked up at Betty, the same ten-year-old girl who had been at the garbage dump with her mother, the twelve-year-old girl who had tried to escape in vodka for a while, the fifteen-year-old girl they had hospitalized for malnutrition, the twenty-four-year-old girl who was lost for years. Sarah couldn't look at Betty, but she couldn't look away. She needed the waitress' strength, her silent encouragement. She needed to decide now. *Who is Sarah?* Then Sarah surprised herself by picking up the fork and eating a slice of banana.

————

Vi smiled in the mirror, her head tilted down, her eyebrows cutting into her brown eyes. She left the tiny room after her second cigarette and returned to the counter. She saw Sarah eating the banana and looked away not wanting to watch the girl, not wanting to make her feel self-conscious. Vi sat on the stool next to Sean and patted him on the back. "I apologize, Sean. I just couldn't help myself."

"That's okay," Sean responded. "Next time I'll just make up a different name and that'll be the end of discussion. What's Tom up to?"

Vi blushed defensively and asked Betty for a hot chocolate. "How should I know? I was in the washroom."

"I thought he might be back there."

"He went outside." Everyone seemed to glance out the window, but no one could see through the reflection.

Betty placed Vi's hot chocolate in front of her, the whipped cream towering over the side of the glass. "Are you cold too?" Betty asked Vi who shook her head. Betty continued, "You dress sensibly. No one dresses warm enough anymore. That's why everyone gets sick these days." Betty was obviously referring to the clothing Sarah wore, but it wasn't a putdown. Betty was everyone's mother, and her opinion had to be accepted because she spoke with some authority on all matters. "I wonder when the term overdressed changed from elegance to quantity of clothing. Women run around practically naked these days. I don't like it one bit."

"I do," Sean said with the look of a vulture. William didn't comment either way, but his expression showed that he obviously sided with Sean on this topic.

"You're a couple of dogs." Betty shook her head. "You're the problem."

"What?" Sean asked innocently. "I don't dress anyone but myself."

Betty shook her head at Sean, but it was Vi who fielded a response. "But you buy into it. Men gawk, and it affects us. If

I were standing in a bar next to Sarah, you all would gawk at her. She's very pretty."

"I think that you're pretty, Vi," Sarah said a little self-conscious, still tasting the banana.

"Thank you, Sarah. But you see, men would look for you. You're like a picture. The television and magazines, they print these ads that make us feel inadequate, as if women weren't competitive enough already. It affects us all."

"You got that right," Betty added as she checked on Ray, asleep on his stool again, his head resting on the counter. "Clothing used to mean something. Now the dresses come as low to our cleavage as possible, and we spend the entire night tugging down on our skirt and up on our tops. It's insane."

Sean foolishly commented on a discussion where the women outnumbered the men. "Well, if you don't like it, then don't wear it. You can't bitch at us for your clothing choices."

William jumped in with both feet. "And if you're trying to look so nice for men by dressing a certain way, why are you complaining that we actually notice you? We didn't get rid of those giant prairie dresses women used to wear, and in some countries, women have to be almost completely covered to go outside. I know a girl that was sent over to Baghdad during the Gulf War, and she said that they wanted her to be in her full uniform all the time because Americans didn't want to offend the locals. You could live a life like that. One hundred degrees and clothed from head to toe." Sean agreed with William as he drained the empty glass once more into his mouth and was left to suck on an ice cube.

"Now you're being ridiculous." Vi shook her head as she

spooned the whipped cream from the hot chocolate. "Look at the difference in clothing in just the last one hundred years. The media has a huge effect on how we choose to look. It's all about sex. You guys ogle until you're ready to settle down. Then and only then are you willing to look around at the real world of single women available to date you."

Sarah knew no one had meant to offend her sensibilities. She was what men were looking for, and the moment Vi had said it, Sarah had given up on changing. She didn't need these strangers confusing her. "How much do I owe you?" Sarah interrupted, fumbling in her purse.

"I've got it," William told Betty who added the total to William's check.

"Thank you, William, and thank you Betty for the tea and the banana." Sarah had eaten four of the slivers of banana, and while that wouldn't have been enough for anyone else, it was enough for Sarah. It could have been a good start, but now she knew it was a mistake. Sarah stepped off her stool and turned to William. "I'm kind of tired. Do you think that we'll be much longer?"

"No, I don't think so. You look exhausted. Do you want to go lay down in the car?" Sarah shook her head and smiled at William who lingered for a moment, liking the attention of a beauty on him.

"I couldn't go to sleep in the car, William, but thank you." Sarah didn't think it would be proper to sleep in a car. She wished she could, though. As inappropriate as her parents might have thought it was, she could think of worse things she had done in the back seat.

"Go on, Sarah, get some rest. We'll be leaving soon anyway," William reassured. "There's a blanket in the trunk.

You can open it through the button in the glove compartment."

"Thank you." Sarah left the diner, her eyes on the ground. She was physically tired, but mostly it was mental exhaustion. She hadn't thought about herself as much in the last five years as she had tonight, and she was only more confused about her progress.

Her doctors would be proud of her. Her therapist would tell her that this was the one small step she needed, the turning point. Sarah hoped this was just that, even as she felt herself letting it go. She had made progress before, tried to fix herself, but now it represented more. It was change. It was becoming who she wanted. She could see another Sarah in her mind, a Sarah that these strangers had helped her find, a Sarah that they let her be. They had no expectations of her. They didn't imagine who she should be. They just left her alone, and they talked, and they listened. And somehow, Sarah realized, they cared.

————

"Good job, Sean," William said as soon as the door closed behind Sarah.

"What? What did I do? She said she was tired. You were the one spouting off about women's looks and their clothing choices. I just agreed."

"You started it."

"You boys sound like my eight-year-old." Betty cleared the tea cup and browning banana.

"I think Sarah was just tired. It's been a long night for all of us." Vi didn't think that she understood everything Sarah was going through. She never had an eating disorder herself, but she'd made changes in her life that had taken a lot out of her, and she knew the stress it could cause. Sarah eating something was good, a sign of willingness, but Vi hoped Sarah wasn't going outside to flush what she had just eaten. Tom was outside, and maybe he could be the company that Sarah needed.

"Besides, you guys proved my point for me. Sure, we decide what to wear all by ourselves, but we're influenced by what goes on around us. And if the guys we like are drooling over beautiful women, then that's what we want to be like. Everyone needs attention." Vi ended in conviction, and William and Sean paused to regroup.

"Times are changing! You've got that right!" Ray yelled from his stool, his head springing from the counter, his eyes landing on the surprised faces of the city crowd.

"Keep it down, Ray. I thought you were sleeping." Betty brought Ray another cup of coffee.

"Can't an old man participate here, or is this just a conversation for youngins?" Ray swayed a bit on his stool. He intended to have his say no matter what, and he didn't wait for anyone to answer. "I was born in 1936. I'm sixty-two years-old, and that's the only credentials I need to comment on any topic of discussion."

"How about menstrual cycles?" Sean asked. Ray ignored the boy's remark.

"It's going to be a whole new millennium soon. Your kids are going to look back someday with surprise that you were alive in the 1900s. Can any of you appreciate that?" Betty and Vi nodded slowly. William and Sean waited for the old coot to finish his speech. Then he would surely pass out on the counter and they'd be on their way.

"I remember going to the movies when I was a kid, and there were respectable people then, respectable people with their clothes on. There wasn't any of this swearing or sex on the screen. That's your problem right there. You're all in so much of a god-damned hurry to please other people, to get everyone's attention, that you forget about what's really important." Ray paused, and everyone waited for him to tell them his version of what was important. He sipped his coffee, concentrating on his hands that shook the cup when he set it back on the counter.

"Well?" Betty asked Ray when it was apparent that he had stepped off his soapbox. Ray had forgotten that he had started, and he looked back at William, Sean, and Vi, who stared at the old man in disbelief. He had a point in there somewhere. They were each sure of it.

"Pay no attention," Betty told them under her breath. "He can rant and rave about sex and the media as much as he wants, but he's a fraud. I caught him back in the bathroom once with a Playboy magazine." The four cringed at the thought as Ray prepared for another nap, his gray whiskers hiding a majority of his wrinkles. They would have each guessed Ray's age was closer to eighty. His lifestyle must have accounted for his time in dog years.

Ray had made his point about being alive in the 1900s. Sean used to wonder about history and how long men had been on the planet. It was one hundred thousand years, that was the current accepted scientific count. One hundred thousand years, and that was only for Homosapien, the walking and talking form of humanity. Sean was a speck, a meager life in the billions that had passed before him. A meager life in the billions that would come after, that was if his generation didn't contaminate the planet and make it unlivable. And he was supposed to be excited about the year 2000? The only significant time that Sean could recall was the time he had spent with her. Now it was the time that he spent thinking of her. And whether it was the 1990s or the 20 nothings, Sean would still sit alone wondering where she was, waiting for her to call out of the blue, hoping that she was happy, and praying that she was miserable without him.

Sean felt his flask inside his jacket. He could use a drink. No, that wasn't it. He wanted a drink. He didn't need a drink. That would make him closer to alcoholism than he cared to be. Sean looked back at Ray and wondered what the old man really knew, or anyone else for that matter. They were on the planet with millions of others in a life that would pass slowly and quickly and end up as a spot on some timeline printed by his great, great, great, great grandchild.

It amused Sean that everyone found such importance in themselves. He knew that he affected others' lives somehow; started a chain reaction by his movements. Hell, he had gotten into William's Towncar with intentions of shagging Sarah, and here he was instead, at a counter in a diner in Somewhere, Illinois, feeling miserable about his life, trying to keep his chin up until his next drink. Sean didn't need a drink, but he had left his apartment hours earlier with intentions of having one with him until he fell asleep. And he was still awake; he was sure of that.

———

Tom heard his name being called. He thought it was his mother's voice calling him, trying to wake him up. *Shhhh.* It was the trees soothing him awake. Tom heard his name again among the rustling leaves. He sat up, lost for a moment, then found in the single row of forestry along the diner's parking lot. It was Sarah calling out for him. Tom brushed the leaves from his cheek. He wondered how long he had been out. He felt as though he had been asleep for years; the gravity pulling him down into the soft ground, his frame leaving an impression among the dead colors.

"Tom, are you out here?" Sarah was holding her arms, trying to stop from shivering. The temperature might have been in the sixties, but not even in the summer could the moon warm the dark side of the planet.

Tom stood up and brushed his fingers through his hair and down his clothing. He stepped out of the darkness. "I'm here!" he called. Sarah turned toward the voice as Tom walked into the lit parking lot. He didn't explain what he had been doing, and Sarah didn't ask. "Is everything okay?" Tom walked by the picnic table and looked into the diner. He could see Vi, William, and Sean still seated at the counter. Sarah used Sean's handkerchief to brush her running nose.

"You look tired." Tom removed his flannel shirt and Sarah let him place it over her shoulders. It hung like a drape from her body, the large flannel becoming a blanket to Sarah's petite frame. She wrapped the flannel around her arms and noticed the way Tom's t-shirt hugged his wiry muscles.

"I was going to sit in William's car and maybe nap. I think we're going to leave soon."

Tom tried to keep his attention on Sarah, but he couldn't

help glancing into the diner at Vi. He didn't want to leave yet. He had been asleep in a dream, but he was fully present now. Not in his childhood home, not under his father's angry fist, not in a bath of liquor, not running away. He was here, somewhere in America with Vi, and he wanted more time with her. Tom was free now, free to choose, free to be chosen, and he needed time to let her know before his opportunity slipped away.

He could wait. He could hope that she'd come over to his table after playing one Tuesday night, but Tom didn't want to wait, he couldn't. He didn't have the patience anymore to sit back in the darkness and hide. He would not covet from afar the life that he wanted, afraid that he would hurt or ruin someone with his baggage. And there she was, sitting at the counter in Phil's Breakfast and 7UP. She had to be waiting for him, waiting for his love and his assurances and his protection. In Tom's mind, there was no better explanation for this night.

Tom returned his attention to Sarah who had been watching him watch Vi. Sarah smiled knowingly. "Go talk to her." Tom looked back into the diner at Vi. "Go talk to her, Tom. I know that she's interested in you." Tom squinted at Sarah, an expression she confused as doubt for a moment before she realized it was the hurt, pain, joy, and love that came together with the fear of realizing a dream. It was his heart that Sarah was seeing on his face.

She hadn't seen Tom react to anything this way. In the couple of hours she had known him, he had intervened between her and Sean, and she was grateful. But even then, even when Tom was spelling things out in an authoritative voice, he wasn't emotional. He was strict; he was decisive, but he was separate from it all, aloof, as though nothing really affected him. Tom had been a robot, going through time without committing to emotion because he was either too afraid of it, he had forgotten it, or he had never known it at all.

"I don't think that Vi really wants anyone to get in her way right now. She has a lot going on." Tom was thinking, and more exceptionally, he was trying to feel. The things he had wanted in life but had repressed came back to him. All those afternoons sitting on a park bench watching the normal families, the parents coaxing their children, the children's laughter spreading joy all around. All the stories that his buddies had told him in the Navy about their families, and the care packages that they received and shared. All the people back home worrying about their children in harm's way but no contact with his own family. All of this stored sentiment he had ignored came pouring over him. He wanted to tell Vi, to show her. She had brought him this far, her words and her eyes, her energy and her being. He had stared for weeks and she had let him. Tom, the only way he knew to be, alone at his table with her words. She had come back to Baker's Tap for him, Tom was sure of it. Sometimes she looked into his eyes. She watched him as he watched her sing *his* heart out to the bar. She discovered him before he had even discovered himself.

Tom's face twisted up in indecision. Sarah was still smiling at him, like a teacher to a confused child on the verge of discovery. She handed him back his flannel shirt and made her way toward the blue Towncar. "You'll never know if you don't try." It was a simple sentence for Sarah to give away. It was much easier to say those seven words to Tom whether she believed in them herself. Sarah opened the passenger door and unlocked the trunk as soon as she found the button that William had told her about. She walked to the back of the car where Tom was standing silently, his face relaxed and peaceful, and Sarah knew she had helped him. He lifted the trunk and removed the maroon and white wool blanket.

"Are you going to be okay in here?" Tom asked. Sarah nodded as she sat in the back seat and unfolded the blanket over her legs, while Tom pulled the blanket to her chin. She looked into his eyes, which seemed to flash and pierce the light. Although he was seven years older than her, Tom seemed younger to Sarah now than he had when he first sat at her table in the bar. He was relaxed, unguarded, and more handsome as he wasn't trying to blend into the woodwork.

Sarah closed her eyes and tried to picture herself with someone like Tom. A strong man, one with values. A gentle-man, one with the key to her being, one who could accept her as she was in her own eyes and not as her mother expected her to be.

Tom locked the doors and shut Sarah safely into the car. He waited a few seconds to make sure that she would be all right by herself, and then he made his way back toward the picnic table. He should go inside and see Vi. He should ask her something, anything. He'd had his one-nighters; a girl in every port, but Tom hadn't been out on a proper date in his twenty-nine years. It would seem unfathomable to some, but he'd had his reasons. And now he was beating his fears or rather overcoming them.

Tom had thought he was a man when he first left home. Later, he thought the Navy had made him one, then college. But there had been something missing all those years, something personal. He hadn't been a man. He had been a coward, running and exhausted. Running.

He thought he had escaped his father's memory by going away, by not choosing the same path, the one that his brother had gone down, by not feeling anything. No pain, no love, no hatred. Tom needed to be human. He needed to live. And not for the sake of breathing, as so many did. Not hating the world, or living because he feared death. He had finally accepted his childhood, beyond the parking lot, beyond the light and in the darkness of the trees. He had allowed himself to put the past away.

Tom could see Sean placing money on the counter in front of him, and he worried that he was out of time. He stayed on the picnic table, though. He sat and anticipated Vi, her smile, her eyes, her curly brown hair. He wanted to go inside and tell her and make her understand, but he needed the dream for a little while longer. He needed the hope and mystery to keep him company for a few more minutes just in case she didn't understand, just in case this was the last night that he would know her.

————

Sean put some cash on the counter for Betty and moved to the cigarette machine. He looked at the ten symbols, changing his mind several times whether he wanted to smoke, and changing his mind about which brand he would if he did. He didn't need to smoke. He didn't like to feel his lungs pounding out the breaths of air the next day on the job, and he didn't like the headache he would get from the combination of smoking and drinking. But he wanted something now, something to lift him up, the chemically induced buzz that would take his mind off of himself. Sean decided he had to talk William into driving to a bar or a liquor store. This would be a delicate operation, as he was sure that William's partying days were over and probably his understanding of them as well.

"Is indecision ruling the day?" Vi had been standing behind Sean, waiting for him to make a selection.

"What?" Sean asked as Vi inserted her money into the cigarette machine.

"I asked if indecision was ruling the day?" Vi withdrew her fresh pack from the machine and removed the cellophane wrapper.

"What is that, Shakespeare? 'Thou art thee'," Sean mocked.

Vi wondered how to ask Sean in his terms. She had never really concentrated on her word choice before. "Can't decide, huh?" she asked stupidly, flashing a mocking look. Sean retaliated by reaching over and stealing a cigarette from her new pack.

"You're not smoking that in here," Betty warned from the kitchen window.

"No problem." Sean conceded, his arms up in the air, the cigarette protruding through his right fingers. "William and I were just about to leave anywho." William looked at Sean, his eyebrow leaning up toward his hairline. "That's right, my boy. You are going to escort me to the nearest bar or liquor store." Sean gave William a pat on the back and smiled.

"I am not."

"Well, I can't very well walk there. How's about giving me your keys?"

"No way."

Sean stalled for a minute. "Betty, I need to ask you something." Betty returned from the back and approached Sean who was standing next to William, his hand resting on William's shoulder. "Betty? Can you tell me the nearest place to quench my thirst? I'd like to have a drink, a nightcap if you will."

Betty thought in all directions around the diner before answering. "The closest package store would be off of Route 20, over in Pingree Grove."

"Is that far?"

"No, about five, ten minutes. William knows where it is."

"Oh, he does, does he?"

"No." William tried to turn from Sean, but the boy was adamant. "Why don't you check old Ray over there to see if he has any? Whatever he's been drinking seems to work as a good nightcap."

"He doesn't," Betty interjected. "He knows that I'd kick him out if he did. By the time he gets here, he's had enough already."

"There's no way that they're open," William argued. "It's after two o'clock."

"They're open all night. It's a kind of liquor store and convenience store in one." Betty smiled at William before returning to the kitchen.

"You're not helping me here, Betty."

"I know that, honey." Betty waved over her shoulder as if to tell William to give up the fight. William shook his head at Sean who was staring objectively.

"Come on, William. We go, we're back in twenty minutes, then we leave and head back to Chi-town. Piece of cake. I just want to have a little fun, man. You know what I'm talking about."

And William did know. That's why he didn't want to take Sean for more alcohol. But it wasn't like the boy could cause too much trouble between the five of them. William decided he could take Sean in a hurry, and then they could head back to Baker's Tap. It would be closed by the time they got back, the city would be as quiet as it ever got at 4:00 A.M., and William would have to bring Tony his share of tickets a day late. The Italian bartender would understand. It was his fault that William had gotten mixed up with these people in the first place.

"You know that I'm going to complain until you take me." Sean buttoned his jacket, ready to leave.

"Go smoke your cigarette," William told Sean who placed the stick in his mouth and borrowed Vi's lighter to light it.

Betty was nowhere to be seen, but her voice yelled a warning from the back of the store. The eyes in the back of her head must have been as strong as his mother's when he and his siblings were out terrorizing the neighborhood.

"I'm going!" Sean yelled back as he headed toward the door, a cloud of smoke parting in front of him. Sean winked at Vi as he opened the door. "I'll finish this and then we'll go, William."

14
ADVOCATES

William expelled the air from his lungs through his lips, creating a pattering noise in the air. Vi was trying not to laugh. If she had been William, she also would have wanted to strangle Sean. But she wasn't, and she didn't. Vi had no intention of going on a liquor run this late on a Tuesday night. She'd just as soon hang out in the diner to keep Betty company.

"Don't look at me like that," Vi said to William who was trying to lay the blame for his next escapade on her shoulders. "It's not my fault. I'm not the one who let that guy in the car."

William's head dropped in defeat, resting on his arms that were folded on the edge of the counter. He moaned before looking up. "Come on, Vi. I don't want to leave Sean out there for too long with Sarah asleep in the car."

"Tom's outside," Vi said quickly, catching herself. "William. Couldn't you go to the store with Sean and then come back for me?"

"Sure. Everything okay?"

"Yeah, no problem. I just thought that I'd maybe eat something more substantial than bacon. I wouldn't mind keeping Betty company, either." Vi didn't want to be in the car yet. She didn't want to go back to Chicago and back to her life, back to the menial job and the menial paycheck, back to wishing for the next Tuesday night. Something was happening around her and within her, something in this ridiculous diner, or maybe in its beaten up lot. There was a song there, Vi was sure of that. She couldn't hear it yet. She didn't know what it was about, but she wanted more time to find it, more time to search herself for its melody and its story.

"I guess we'll be back in about half an hour. You sure you're okay?"

Vi nodded as William stood and retrieved his key ring from his front pocket. He pulled down his knit sweater that had bunched up over his pants. "William?" Vi asked before he turned to the door. "Can I ask you something?"

"Sure, Vi. What is it?" William waited for Vi to form her question. She looked uncomfortable, as if she might squirm right off her stool. Vi didn't ask for advice, she didn't ask for anything. Yet here she was, trying to ask without seeming weak. "You can ask me anything you want, Vi."

"Well, I was just wondering, in the car when we left Baker's, you said something to Sean about me." Vi hesitated.

"I didn't mean to offend you." William was on the defensive, although he couldn't remember what remark had put him there.

"No, you didn't say anything derogatory." Vi laughed, her nervousness trying to escape. "It's just that you said I don't date men. You said that I'm not the type to waste my time. I was just wondering what you meant by that."

William squinted, the corners of his eyes crinkling into the crow's feet that had developed after thirty-seven years of laughing. "I just meant... I just meant that you have a lot of goals, a lot of dreams, and you pursue your goals instead of wasting your time on men. You won't allow yourself to be tied down." But Vi was tied down to her goals, tied down to her dreams, tied down to her songs, and tied down to the notion that she couldn't and wouldn't be tied down.

"You're really put together, Vi. Look at you. You know who you are and where you want to go. That's great, that's what counts. People like Sean, they're just going to run around the world until they can't run anymore, and then they're going to shift gears and try something else. They're never going to accomplish anything. But you, you've got direction. You don't need anyone. You're going to make it." William was stern in his conviction. He had seen Vi playing in the bar, and they had talked with Tony about who she was going to be, and he believed she would do it. He thought he could encourage her, that this was what she needed now.

"You see girls like Sarah? I think that she's beautiful and all, and I know little about her aside from her name, but I saw what went on at the bar tonight. I know girls like her who spend their whole lives trying to look pretty, trying to please a man or find someone just so they will have someone to take care of them. I think that's ridiculous."

"Is that why you're still single?" Vi asked quickly. It's not what she wanted to say, but to fire back with a question, to make the other person think about what they were all about.

It distracted them from her. And although it was a valid question, she wanted to take it back.

"Maybe," William answered ambiguously.

"I'm sorry. That's not what I intended to say." Vi looked at the counter for the answer, but it wasn't there. She looked to the window, her reflection staring back. She saw William facing the kitchen, waiting for Betty and her inevitable input. Vi thought that perhaps the answer would spell itself out on the glass. She saw her figure, her muscular, square build, her wild, uncontrollable hair, her pale face sticking out over her dark leather jacket. She was beautiful. Staring, looking, watching her life go by.

Vi couldn't remember where the knowledge of what she wanted out of life had begun. It was different now though, different than a week ago or a day ago, different from five hours earlier when she sang her first song of the night. She was thinking of Tom. She was thinking of a relationship with Tom.

Usually, when Vi noticed someone who piqued her interest, she would have taken a second look and then she would have put it out of her mind. But she was reacting differently to Tom. He didn't make her worry about her future. The thought of being with him didn't make Vi worry about eventually saying goodbye to him. Maybe it was the way he came to watch her while saying nothing to anyone. He never turned away. He never missed a word. And soon, all Vi could concentrate on was the moment, this thing that was happening, this feeling.

Vi tried to convince herself. "Look at Betty. She's happily married. Her focus is on her family. There are millions of people out there looking for love like that. Don't you think that there's more to relationships than just work?" Vi knew that there was more. It was called love. It was something she had given and received in the past, and she wanted it at this moment in her life. She wanted it forever. She wondered if she could follow someone else, dream his dreams, but it had always been impossible for her. Vi could only be one person, and if she gave herself up to anyone else, it would be a mistake.

So Vi had asked William a question that she knew the answer to. She was alone. She was motivated to pursue her goals, but William had been wrong about one thing. She wasn't smarter than Sarah or all of the other women out there in the world dying for love and affection. Vi was just more afraid of it. She was scared to let herself go, to take any chance that she couldn't control.

Some would look at her dreams and say she was crazy for aiming so high. Her family and her friends and those who had heard her perform encouraged her. They really thought that she could make this happen. And Vi knew that chasing these dreams, making them into realities, that was the simple part. It depended on *her* to make it happen. She had to persevere, and it would all come true because Vi was unstoppable, relentless. To say that it was easy to achieve success in the music industry was an overstatement, but it was the straightforward route for Vi. Success in love took two people, and in that case, Vi would have to depend on someone else. She would have to allow them into the place she kept this courage and ability to fight, to give them half of her breath and all of her soul, to count on someone other than herself to believe in her. Trust was not her strong suit. Neither was vulnerability.

So the thing that William had praised her for, her ability to follow her dreams, it was not the hardest thing in the world. It was all she knew how to do. It was normal in society for the woman to wait for the man, to follow him in pursuit of his goals, to support him. But for a man to stand behind a woman, to step out of her way and to carry her, that was a rare mix. Perhaps William was right about Vi, and perhaps he was wrong, but Vi didn't have to decide this moment. She could go home. She could wonder about Tom until he was gone. She could let this one go by as she had the others.

————

Sean had been talking at Tom for over ten minutes straight. He was wired, anxious, and impatient. He had told Tom that they were going on a liquor run, there was a store about ten minutes away. Tom didn't disagree, but he knew that there was no way he would go to a liquor store. He could be around alcohol, hang around in bars like Baker's Tap, go to parties. But he couldn't handle driving around with someone drinking. The way it stunk the car up, the way the air seemed to close in, thick and moist, poisonous. He would become claustrophobic, angry. And then he would have to get out. He would have to get away from the stench of the memories that clogged the air.

Tom had felt something when he awoke from his nap. He was relieved, cured. It was his acceptance of his childhood, his acceptance of his father and who the old man was, but not an acceptance of what the bastard had done to him. It was a realization of times that he had lived through. He hadn't been physically abused in years, but the mental anguish that he tried to hide from the world had stayed with him. He felt as though it was time to move on.

Tom would never become his brother, he had never conceded to his father's will. He had chosen the beatings. He had chosen the abuse and humiliation. Now his brother lived with the anger and the hatred, but the line of tainted blood was not in Tom, and he knew it. This night had given him that relief. These strangers had made him realize himself. But as much as Tom would not hide anymore, he didn't think that he was ready to get in the car with Sean. He didn't even know why he was here, listening to the Irish pest rattle on about nothing in a bottle. "I think that I'll stay here. Maybe I'll get something to eat." Tom was speaking quietly and in control.

"Oh, come on," Sean whined. "You could have eaten before. Come on, man. Wouldn't you rather go get a beer?" Sean smiled and hit Tom in the shoulder, his manly salute of camaraderie. If he was fishing for a partner in crime, Tom was not biting. Sean pointed at William who was at the door of the diner. "Look, William's leaving and he has the keys. Let's go."

Tom waited. He would walk back, take a cab, any other way home. He would not spend his night in a liquor store.

———

William was ready to leave. A banging on the diner window startled the two. It was Sean. He pressed his face up to the window and yelled at William through the thick pane of glass. "Okay!" William yelled back. "I'll be right there!" He looked at Vi. "I'm sorry if I didn't help you at all."

"You helped, William. I was just wondering how you knew." Vi returned her attention to her empty hot chocolate.

"I knew because Tony and I discussed you one night."

"You what?" Vi stared at William, embarrassment showing through surprise.

"Sure. We all talked about how a lot of guys come through Baker's and comment on how pretty you are or what a great person you are, and you'll have nothing to do with anyone. Tony says it's because you're in the midst of being a professional and you don't have time." William pushed open the door.

"Where are you going? You can't just tell me that and leave." Vi was blushing visibly. Curiosity swirled in her reluctance to study her looks, and William's comment brought forward the inkling that she might be pretty. She had always thought that her sister was beautiful, and she was finally noting the times when people would comment on how similar they looked.

But to have them talking about her, Tony and William and whoever he had meant by 'we all', that could stop her indecision. It was ironic that she was trying to break into an industry that profited on appearances, and she had never really thought that she was pretty. She still couldn't believe that someone had noticed her.

"Are you coming?" William held the door open for Vi. "Because if you want to continue this conversation, it will have to be on the road."

"No," Vi answered, still in the revelation's wake. "I think I'll stay and eat something. See you in about half an hour?"

"Sure," William said. "You know Vi, you're always so unshakable. I can't believe that I actually caught you off guard. This is great." He chuckled in Vi's direction before calling out his goodbye to Betty. William stepped into the parking lot and allowed his eyes to adjust from the bright neon to the pale orange glow of the dim lights.

"Tell him we're going, William," Sean said before the door to the diner was closed. William approached Sean and Tom, the loose gravel trickling around his feet.

"I'm not going," Tom told William.

"Okay." William walked toward the Towncar. At first he couldn't see Sarah in the back, but as he approached, he saw her lump under the blanket in the back seat.

"What do you mean, okay?" Sean asked as he walked around the car.

"He doesn't have to go if he doesn't want to. I have to come back to pick Vi up anyway. We'll be back in about thirty minutes, Tom." William opened the driver's door. "What's the problem, Sean?"

"Nothing," Sean answered, his hand on the passenger door handle. "I just thought that this would be a fun thing for us guys to do."

"Riding around the middle of nowhere looking for a liquor store. Sounds too good to miss, really." William's sarcasm was apparent, but Sean didn't comment, not wanting to jinx the fact that he had actually talked William into taking him somewhere.

"What about Sarah?" Tom asked. William shrugged as Sean smiled and moved to the rear passenger door.

"I'll keep her company," Sean volunteered, a hunter

setting up for the kill. William could see Tom's shoulders rise, and he knew he needed to diffuse the situation.

"You!" William pointed at Sean, the devil's grin still on the boy's face. "You'll ride in front and forget that Sarah's in the car, or we all go straight back to the city right now. Do not pass a liquor store, do not collect two hundred dollars." Sean slumped his shoulders and dropped his head to the ground in disappointment as he moved toward the front. "She'll be okay, Tom. It looks like she's asleep. She'll probably never even know that we went somewhere," William reassured. "Sean won't get near her."

Tom relaxed as William pulled away. "Last chance, Tom," Sean yelled out the window. "It's between us and the Twilight Zone." The color of the car blended with the darkness as William pulled away, the car disappearing under the train viaduct on Route 47. Five more seconds into the night and they were gone, the roar of the well-kept engine rising and falling as the RPMs fought with the transmission for control.

Tom relaxed in the chilly breeze as the moisture in the air began to fall and collect on the objects below. He wondered about Sarah but knew that William could handle Sean. The question that lingered was whether William would if the situation arose. Tom had seen some of the despicable things that even soft mannered men were capable of, and he took no one's intentions for granted.

Shhhh, the trees told him again. He sighed and took his sights off the road. Tom's attention was needed here, with him. His wishes were being heard. His past and future were colliding on this spot. Like some sort of miracle, Vi was still here with him, stranded on this island.

Vi's eyes fixed on the muddy brown chocolate in the bottom of her mug, but her mind looked elsewhere, trying to see into her future, trying to understand what William had said. Trying to separate what she expected from what everyone else expected of her. She looked back into the window of the diner, the interior light reflecting off the glass, the large pane still acting as a giant mirror. Others had noticed her, men had wanted to date her. Vi wondered which ones had said something to Tony or William. She wondered if her ears had been ringing when they did.

Her reflection was the same as before, but now Vi was sitting up a little straighter. She was smiling to herself, yet her forehead was curled up in a question. She was confused. She had always thought of herself as a brute, a personality. She had looked out onto a world of beautiful people and never counted herself among them. It had never really hurt her. Vi didn't have time for people who couldn't have an intelligent discussion, and most of those people, she thought, were the pretty faces.

But others were talking about her to each other, when there were so many other topics to be had, so many other women to discuss. Remarkably, the world saw Vi completely different than the way she saw herself in it. She had always thought that the world would never really know her. It had not occurred to Vi that she would never really know herself, not through the world's eyes.

Vi could see Betty approaching behind her, and she turned back to the counter and put the mug down.

"They left you stranded, huh?" Betty asked as she refilled the empty glass racks.

"No," Vi replied. "They're coming back. I just thought that I'd stick around and maybe grab some breakfast." Vi had forgotten that Ray was still in the diner. She could see his disheveled gray hair sticking up over his coat sleeves, his head still down on the counter. She wondered what had become of Ray. How had he ended up at Phil's Breakfast and 7UP over and over? When had he decided that drinking was the way to live life? She wondered if Sean would end up the same way.

"Well, we have your basic breakfast stuff, so let me know what you decide on." Betty slid the laminate menu across the counter and went in back to retrieve a stack of saucers. Vi sat quietly on her stool and listened to the refrigerator's hum. That and Ray's snoring prevented total silence in the tiny diner.

"William was wrong, you know," Betty stated as she continued her restocking efforts. "Not about you being pretty and a topic of conversation, but about you and love." Betty paused for a moment as she refilled the sugar holders. "See, no one's really too smart for love. Some people know when they need to stay single, like after a long relationship. Other people rush in and out not really knowing what it is they want. That's most people for a long time, I think." Betty smiled at Vi as she finished her work. "But some people, some people are just too scared. They're afraid to give up anything that they think they want. They're too scared to risk it."

Betty wasn't one to mince words, and she wasn't one to be wrong either. Vi was listening. "I was like that." Betty nodded at Vi's disbelief. "I was racing around in a circle, and it took me a long time to realize how tangled up I was. So I stepped back, and when I met my husband, that was it for me. Something was different about him. I knew that as long as I was with him, I would be okay. And that's when I stopped worrying about myself or worrying about what I was going to give up if I gave in to him."

Ray lifted his head from the counter to interject. "You know what I think?" he asked.

"Go back to sleep, Ray," Betty told him loudly.

Ray griped with a look, but instead of putting in his two cents, he opted for the bathroom.

"What do you know anyway?" he grumbled to no one.

Betty walked around the counter and sat on the stool next to Vi. She flexed her ankles and rubbed her right calf as she spoke. "For some people, Vi, it will never happen. They will pass up their chances, and the person they end with will burden them, and the only reason they'll stick with that person is because they'll be too scared to be alone. But if you're lucky, and if you're patient, you won't have to give up one inch of who you are or who you want to be because the man you find will make you twice the person you are today." Betty patted Vi on the arm and returned to her restocking work behind the bar. Vi sat still, trying to digest the wisdom of someone older and wiser.

"How will I know Betty? How do I find someone that won't drag me down?" This was the question everyone wanted the answer to, but no one could provide.

"Well, it's a feeling more than a conscious decision. Have patience and be choosy. There's no genuine answer. But there is one secret, one thing that will help." Betty hesitated, leaning in to Vi. "Make sure that you have your eyes open. When you spend all of your time looking ahead, you miss the things around you. With your eyes open you'll have a better chance of spotting him, whoever he may be. There's nothing to worry about then because, with your eyes open, you'll know what's right and what's wrong." Betty took one last tub of dishes back to the kitchen and left Vi swimming in her advice.

Vi wondered how Betty could have known the exact right answer. How could she have seen that this was the advice, the reassurance that Vi was looking for? Vi knew that people talked all the time. They asked for advice; they offered advice, and they wasted their words and the air around them because more often than not, no one was paying attention. But Vi, here and on this night, had been listening. She wanted someone to tell her to follow her heart, and Vi knew that if she was smart, she would go with her instinct.

Tom watched Vi through the window of Phil's. She had looked straight at him for a few minutes before Betty had returned to the counter. She had looked right into him without even knowing he was there.

15
TRUTH

William turned left onto Route 20, his high beam headlights on, the road clearly visible in the bright moonlight. He watched the reflectors on the road fly by. Sean had the radio on a rock station, and he was slapping his thighs to the beat. By some miracle, Sarah was still asleep, and William hoped they would get back to the diner before she even knew they had departed.

"I love this song!" Sean exclaimed between verses, words that he sang with passion if not tone. "Come on, William," he coaxed, his beating hands reaching out to the dashboard. William looked over dryly before turning down the radio.

"I don't want to wake Sarah up." William nodded to the back seat. Sean turned around and looked at Sarah. She was lying down under the blanket with her back facing forward.

"Sarah," Sean sang in a playful voice. "Sarah."

"Sit down and shut up or we're going back to Phil's right now." William clicked the radio off, and Sean looked at William and judged that he was not playing around. Sean rolled his eyes as he sat forward in the seat, looking at the reflectors pass by in the night.

William wasn't angry with Sean. He remembered what it was like to be twenty-four, young and playful, every move inconsequential to the last. William was glad that he had made it through those days, with all the running around and the gags that weren't really funny. At the time, it seemed that was just how he should act. He was young and wild and free of burdens or remorse. It was liquor runs and all-night parties. It was the slamming beers and passing out for three hours before bouncing right back the next day at work. It was the swearing off of alcohol mid-sickness and then picking it up again by the weekend. William never wanted to return to that time in his life. Those were the days that had shaped him into the man he was. They had made him strong and decisive, and they had kept him single. William liked to be single, although he didn't like his reasons.

Sean didn't understand, but he would someday. He'd look back on something he had done, the thing that not even the alcohol could make him forget, the thing that straightened him out once and for all. The twenties were tough. You were reborn to the world out on your own, feeling free, feeling like an adult yet still a child, easily persuaded to do things that would have been unacceptable three drinks earlier. William was glad that he would never have to go back to those days, the days when he was out there trying to prove himself to the world, trying to prove himself to himself.

"How far is this place?" Sean asked, the silence beating at his ears.

"It's a couple miles up." William turned back to see if Sarah was awake, but the blanket hadn't moved.

"Are you okay, William? If I'd have known that this would piss you off, I wouldn't have pushed you into going." Sean was lying, of course, but he could see concern on William's face, and that brought back the nice Irish boy his mother had raised.

"Yeah, I'm fine. Just leave Sarah alone." William didn't know how a quiet guy like Tom could step into a situation and keep the peace as he had between Sean and Sarah. He wondered if Tom had been through what he had. He wondered if Tom harbored some guilt. William knew he wasn't angry with Sean. He was angry with himself for a choice he had made fifteen years earlier. He didn't want Sean to make the same mistakes.

"William, I'm not going to do anything with Sarah. I'm just joking around."

And that's where it starts, William thought.

"Besides, I know that you and Tom would kick my ass if I started anything." Sean laughed to himself.

"It's not funny, Sean. It's not a joke." William's face set a hard mask, his jaw circling as he let his subconscious grind his teeth away. "I used to mess around when I was your age. I used to go out with my buddies to the bars, and we would drink and drink and then hook up with some girls."

"All right!" Sean chimed in excitedly, still not understanding William's intention.

"Yeah, all right!" William mocked Sean. "But when is it time to call it quits? When is it time to stop?" William subconsciously followed the curves in the road, but he wasn't in the car, he wasn't driving. He was a young man in college again. He was a drunken frat boy among all the even more drunken sorority girls. He was primed and ready like all the other over-sexed college kids, and there she was, waiting for him. There she was in his buddy's bedroom, naked, lying in wait. There she was for him as she had been for his frat brother less than ten minutes earlier.

"You're not really making too much sense to me, William." Sean watched the expression on William's face turn inside out like a child's. The new input caused surprise and fear to melt into one.

"She was beautiful. I mean, she was always the center of attention. I would see her walking on campus or on the Greek Row bus after class. Her hair, it glowed all the time. It was so blonde. It was that white blonde, you know. It glowed during the day and at night, and indoors. In the darkness too."

William smiled and exhaled quickly through his nose, a gesture that could have been mistaken as a laugh, but Sean recognized it as the disgust William was feeling. Sean didn't want to listen. He didn't want to know what he had already guessed William was going to tell him, but he couldn't speak. William was already halfway through a time that he would never forget, a memory that he could never suppress. Sean had to listen. He needed to listen.

"You can't continue to treat women as objects, Sean. They have feelings. They're not just here for you. They have lives of their own." William was stalling. He didn't want to say it, never wanted to hear it out loud. He was a victim of the silence he had sworn with his fraternity brothers. But Sean needed to hear it, and William needed to say it. "I was just upstairs on the third floor having a beer, using the bathroom. I was kind of resting up before I went back to the party, you know?" His grin came and went with the memories. "This guy, Brett, he came out of the bedroom and closed the door. He was beaming. You know that smile, that stupid 'I am the man' grin? He sat down next to me for a minute, wanted to tell me, to let me know whether or not I cared. He wanted to share the wealth.

"After he went back down to the party, I sat in front of the T.V. for a few minutes, but I couldn't stop thinking, couldn't stop wondering..." William's forehead crinkled as his mind's eye made his way back to the bedroom. "I knew it was her the second that I pushed the door open. I saw her hair swirled in the sheets, draping the pillows. It was kind of glowing under this red lava lamp. It was kind of moving around with the wax. I stared at her for a long time. I wanted to wrap her up because one of her legs was pulled wide to the right and nothing was covering it." William's hand pulled the sheet over the dashboard before returning to the wheel.

"So what did you do?" Sean was anxious for the details.

"I went into the bathroom again. You know how beer flows right through you, and I had to go again. I stayed in there for a while thinking of what to do. Brett had told me to go in there with her. He told me she wanted more, that she wanted me. And I believed him until I saw her lying there, out cold. But I couldn't just leave the room. I couldn't just go back downstairs to the party." The words were speaking themselves now as William sat back and listened with Sean.

"I wish I had stayed in that bathroom all night, but I couldn't. I went out and looked at her again. I was still drinking, swallowing the beer in gulps. It was so easy to believe that she was there waiting for me. I mean, she was beautiful. And the few times that I had talked to her, I really thought that she might actually like me. She seemed interested. The alcohol made her seem interested in everybody, I guess." William pulled the Towncar into a small strip of parking lot along Route 20. Dimly lit from the inside, it was difficult to tell whether the store was really open. The car kept running in park, William wanting to finish his confession before they got out.

"I wanted to cover her up, then I wanted to leave, but then I decided I would just wake her up and ask her. What's the harm in that? So, I sat on the bed and finished my beer, and then I pulled the sheet over her leg and looked at her hair and her face and her shoulders. I must have been sitting there for a while before she opened her eyes. She looked right at me and smiled, Sean. She smiled!"

Sean nodded, knowing the smile William spoke of, the smile that could lure a man to his death.

"I thought since she smiled, she must have wanted me there, so I started kissing her, feeling her warmth and her soft skin everywhere. I really wanted to be with her. Her eyes were closed again, and I just kept going, kept kissing and rubbing and undressing and pumping. Her hair smelled sweet and strands of it were sticking to my arm." William pulled the key toward him and the humming of the engine was gone. "She opened her eyes and looked at me again. She didn't smile, she didn't cry. But she looked at me with a question on her face, like she didn't know who I was or what I was doing. And it didn't really matter because I was done, and I was off of her." William was relieved as the film in his mind ended. "She fell asleep again, passed out. And then I was gone."

"Man, that sounds like a close encounter of the first kind!" Sean was revved up. He wasn't sure that he had understood William, but he was certain that he didn't want to. He left the Towncar for the tiny building that ran along the road, a small paved lot with no designated parking spaces. William sat in the driver's seat, addressing the fifteen years of guilt that reigned over him. Sean had listened, but he clearly didn't care.

William knew the booze had played a part in his own boldness that night. He was also certain that it had ruled the three others who had raped the same girl. She had smiled at him and said yes with her embrace. He didn't hold her down. She had never uttered the word 'no'. He didn't hit her or unwillingly detain her, and the others hadn't either, not as far as William knew. And the girl said nothing after that night. She never pointed a finger or scowled at him. She didn't seem to change at all. She might not have even known then, might not have even remembered. But William knew, and he remembered. And it had changed his life.

"Where are we?" Sarah startled William from the back seat as she sat up and pulled the blanket off.

"We're at a liquor store. Go back to sleep. We'll be back at Phil's in no time." Sarah watched William's face in the rearview mirror. He was pale, unnerved.

"I think I'll check it out." As Sarah moved the blanket onto the seat, William watched her blonde hair in the mirror. It wasn't bright. It didn't shine in the light like the platinum hair in his memory. He watched Sarah step out of the car, the way her shoulders automatically hunched in reaction to the chilly night air, the way she pulled her arms across her tiny midsection, trying to keep her head up but lowering it against the cool breeze instead. She pulled the heavy door open and stepped into the convenience mart, her hair blowing back and then loosely following her inside.

———

Vi wasn't hungry. Her mind was busy with the seeds of thought planted by William and Betty. She stepped out of the diner for a cigarette, the cherry lit before the door was closed behind her. It was cold, and Vi zipped her jacket up and took a drag before she noticed Tom who was sitting alone at the picnic table. She was surprised that he was still there, left behind. She almost forgot to exhale and coughed out the smoke as Tom smiled uncharacteristically. Her feet stopped in the same spot where Sarah had told her that Tom liked her and that she should go for it. With that thought, Vi immediately gained the defensive, but something Betty had said pulled the shield away again.

Vi knew she should keep her eyes open. She should try to trust someone, try to trust herself. And in Tom she saw safety. This man hardly said a word, but he had been talking to Vi for weeks with his undivided attention. Opposites. She sang, he listened. He gazed, and she inhaled his regard. Now she would expose her jugular to the jaws of chance. But in Tom's presence, Vi didn't feel exposed, didn't feel like she needed to be armed and ready for battle. It scared her, preparing to make a leap at Tom's request, ready to ignore caution so as to not talk herself out of him. *Why not take a chance?* Vi asked herself. *There is no one here to observe failure but for two hearts and the night.*

"Hey," Tom said.

"Hey," Vi answered, her iris' opening up to let in the light. She noticed Tom's shoulders were settled, and he looked relaxed. Although Tom was always quiet, Vi had noticed that he always seemed tense and ready to spring. But now he sat leisurely at the picnic table, his legs outstretched, his back against the table's edge, his elbows behind him on the table-top. She felt her eyes observing his lean frame and moved her gaze to stare at the two large propane tanks. They were white at first glance, but upon studying them, Vi noticed the metal and rust under the chipped paint on the bottom. It was like so many things, beautiful to the virgin eye but decrepit and unkempt upon further study. Like some people she had spent time with, nothing was perfect, Vi knew, and the least of all herself. Vi wanted to run back into the diner, into the light.

"You'll never lose your creativity," Tom said. His voice startled Vi who stood frozen, trying to ignore the pull she felt toward him but unable to stop it.

Tom was surprised at the chance he was now taking, yet he was unwilling to turn back, no longer willing to let the past control his future. He would jump and hope Vi would catch him by jumping as well. "You said earlier in the car you were afraid that if you moved, you might lose your creativity, but you won't because it's inside you. It's part of what makes you so beautiful."

Tom was smiling outwardly, and Vi took ten seconds before she looked at him, her cigarette dropping to the ground, her ears wanting desperately to believe his words.

"And you are beautiful, Vi. The way you smile at everyone and laugh at things no one else sees, and the way your hair gets in your eyes and you don't even notice because you are too busy thinking or feeling."

Vi looked back at the propane tanks, back at the diner, caution and anticipation both swirling through her body. She wanted to pinch herself, to wake up. No man had ever told her how he felt, not like this. Instead, they walked away, and when they didn't, she did. Tom's honesty, and this wanting to have her for himself wasn't part of her plan, but it was happening, and she couldn't stop it if she tried. Vi chose silence in her confusion. She had wondered if he would ask her on a date, and there they were, five feet apart yet intertwined in intimacy. Vi took Tom's confession and wanted to offer herself as his penance.

Tom stood, letting his words crash into her. He had tapped a part of himself that had been dead for years and was presently overflowing. Tom was never taught moderation. He either took things as they were or he ran. Here with Vi, he poured out of himself what he wanted her to hear, unafraid of the outcome. "I have been watching you for two months. I have been listening to you sing, and your songs are so wonderful. I don't know if anyone understands you the way I do. I would love to be around you when you are writing, the way your soul must drip all over the page."

Vi remained still as Tom moved in closer. The earth became a gray mist as her tears blocked her view from everything but the moment. He was under her skin. He was tearing down the walls she had spent years building, the walls she had been peaking over for the last two hours.

"You have helped me, Vi. You have helped me discover

the person I thought was dead, and I love you." Tom waited for a reply, a sign. He stepped within inches of her and stopped. He wanted to reach out, to hold her, but he couldn't bear to hurt her, to do something she didn't want. So he waited.

Overwhelmed, Vi cried, and then surprised by her tears, she cried more. This was not her style, to be weak and assailable in front of anyone, to show the outside world the person she knew. That she could be this way with Tom was the one thing that had stopped her from turning and running. He was making her twice the person by allowing her to trust this chance.

Vi could hardly believe what he was telling her. She never imagined that she would be loved. She could hardly remember hearing the words before, saying it time and again within her own walls, but never feeling it as she did at this moment. Vi didn't know what to do, but Tom offered the ease of her not having to choose her next move. Vi didn't have to think about the future. She simply had to give in, to let go. She tipped her head forward and rested it on Tom's chest, allowing her tears their course down her face and onto the ground.

They christened Tom in the freedom of his truth, in the wind and the stars and the moon, and in the faith of a woman whose heart was now his. He raised Vi's face and dove into her eyes. He pulled her in and kissed her, the warmth of their lips opening communication into each other's soul. Tom's arms wrapped around Vi, and he held her together as she fell apart in the night.

————

Sarah entered the combined convenience and liquor store. She could see Sean near the large cooler of twenty different brands of beer, each tasting a little more unusual than the previous, some slower, some faster, each causing the same effect. A clerk sat perched on a stool enshrined in a cave of cigarettes. The little man opened his eyes as Sarah entered. He surveyed Sean, then Sarah's figure, then decided there was nothing of interest in the vicinity. He crossed his arms and rested them on his belly, trying not to fall back into his nap.

Sarah crossed the store quickly. She wanted a washroom, and she wanted to find it before Sean noticed her. He seemed content to open cooler doors and then close them when his eye would catch a better choice. He was like a child in a toy store, his parents telling him to pick out one toy and one toy only. Sarah spotted a faded paper sign above a door that signified the restroom. She reached for the knob as Sean caught her reflection in the glass doors of the large refrigerator. He spun around to look at her, but before he could get one word out, she was gone.

Sarah locked the thin, brown door behind her and stood completely still in the darkness. For a moment she thought that there was someone in the tiny room with her, a steady breathing entering her ears. It was her, panting from the stress of the walking, tired even after her nap. She flicked the light on and waited for her eyes to adjust to the oppressing fluorescents. The small room was clean with nice flowered wallpaper, bright tile floors, and shiny porcelain sink and toilet. The closet sparkled with care and scrubbing. Sarah was relieved until she caught a glance of herself in the mirror. Her dirty blonde hair frizzed out toward the walls, her skin was pale, and her eyes were half open, little bags pulling at the bottom, the lids fighting against the brightness. She couldn't believe that a complete stranger had seen her looking so scruffy. She hoped that neither William nor Sean had noticed, even after the story she had just overheard William share.

She had been hiding under the blanket from Sean's advances when William had started his story. She listened above the noise of the car, careful not to move or make a sound. Sarah couldn't blame William for something he had done to someone else at another time in another life. He had learned from his mistake and had to live with his remorse. But she could blame Sean. He had heard the same story and hadn't listened to a word of it.

Sarah returned her attention to her reflection on the wall. It was more than her hair or her face that bothered her. Sarah was fat. She had eaten some banana and drank some tea, a false need for food brought on by a Dorito. It was in her right now. It was pushing her hips out and rounding her stomach. All of this was Betty's fault. It was Vi's fault. It was her own fault in the end. Was it four or five pieces of banana that she had eaten? Sarah had broken the first law, the rule. She had to know how much she ate to know when it was time to stop, time to give her stomach and her throat a rest, time to clean up and stand up and go back out into the world refreshed and beautiful.

Sarah started the faucet, careful to avoid the mirror that stared back from above the sink. The sound of the faucet and the water spilling into the sink and running down the drain, it soothed Sarah. It kept her company. It almost made her excited to be alone in her sanctuary.

Sarah crouched in front of the glassy white toilet bowl, glad that this washroom was clean and kept up, still not wanting to kneel on the floor. The seat clinked as she let it rest against the plumbing. She could hear the sink making its noise, covering her own motions, deceiving anyone who might be eavesdropping. Sarah pulled her hair back and stuck her other hand into her mouth. Her index finger did as it was told, however reluctant it might have been. Her mouth watered and her stomach jolted. She didn't make a sound, only expelled air in her uncomfortable motions. She was a pro, trained and seasoned through practice. Sarah knew that the running faucet was a useless precaution. She hadn't needed the cover for several years. She was in control of her stomach and her gasps, in control of her purging.

Sarah felt the heat that came with the sweat, perspiring each time a little less. She could not blame her body for this reaction. She knew exactly what she was doing. Sarah poked again at the back of her throat, this time holding her finger there for several seconds, the nail rubbing roughly on the moist skin, the muscles contracting back and then forward into the finger again. Sarah pulled her hand from her mouth when she could feel her esophagus cooperating. A clear yellow mush dropped into the toilet bowl followed by some of the tea. Sarah was patient as she waited for the rest to leave her system. Then, wiping her mouth, she stood up. She didn't feel sick or that she might need some help. She didn't feel pathetic. Sarah felt good. She felt right.

The toilet flushed out her worries, and Sarah could once again look at herself. She was disappointed that she had let two women that knew nothing of her persuade her to eat. She was weak and a little angry. They had no right to know what was best for her. They had less right than her mother had. It must have been the combination of Randy leaving her, and Tom protecting her around Sean's ogling, and William's gentlemanly manner amongst his own nightmares that had made Sarah so vulnerable. They had tricked her into changing what should have been left alone. They had been tricking her the whole night, offering her drinks and potato chips, and spending all that time in a diner eating food, and offering her food, and offering to pay for it, wanting to make her feel like part of the group, tricking her into thinking that she wanted to be one of them. Sarah came from a whole different world. She had money; she had status, and she had better things to do with her Tuesday nights than feel wrong about her life.

Sarah saw herself in the mirror as she turned the water off. She was pretty once again, her frame returned to its natural thin shape. Sarah didn't notice her pale grey skin, her brittle blonde strands of hair hiding her stunted neck, her puny extruding bones, nor her dying body beneath baggy clothes.

16

RELIEF

The sound of the crickets fought with the wind as it blew southeast through the trees. One car went by, and another rig followed it east toward Chicago. The red light on the corner continued to flash, whether a car waited or not. *Stop*, it screamed. *Stop*. The dim glow spread across the pavement and reached toward the diner, but Phil's interior lights flushed it out before it could get inside.

The field of corn across the street pulsated in the breeze. It was ready to be harvested. It had been for weeks. The stalks were drying, turning yellow brown and shrinking. The fertile smell of dirt drifted through the air and around the propane tanks.

Vi was holding Tom, her arms stretched around his flannel shirt at the waist. Tom kept her head in his hands, his fingers disappearing in and out of her curly mass of brown hair. Vi was through crying. For a moment, she had let go and forgot where she was, who she was. But it was all returning now. Vi was pushing out the need for a companion and was back to accepting the wanting. There was no hope in the having. She didn't believe anyone could keep up with her chosen lifestyle.

It had never entered her mind that it wasn't a matter of someone keeping up with her, it was a matter of being there for the entire ride. And Tom was there, holding her, keeping Vi from the edge. And he would be, he could be. Vi had consumed his days and nights from the moment he had seen her through the window of the bus. He knew her from the first song he heard her sing, and there was not one thing that would stop him from having her. There was no place too far, no task too large, no emotion too strong. He knew that there was no love so great as this, and there was no one who would keep him from it, not even Vi herself.

"I'm all right," Vi said, muffled in Tom's chest. She wiped her face and pulled back, and Tom held on tighter for a moment before releasing her.

"I meant it, Vi. I love you." His eyes were hopeful as he let her go.

"I know you did." She looked up into Tom's smile and played with the moment, imagining that he might have been telling her the truth. She wasn't able to play the game in her mind that would distance her from him, because she knew he was sincere. His piercing eyes were so full of green honesty.

Vi wondered about this man who had watched her all of this time, never speaking to her until this evening and then telling her exactly what was on his mind. He saw them as a couple. He saw a future. She didn't know what changes this night had made, but she knew he was different now. He was older and wiser and outside his shell. He hadn't been this way at Baker's Tap. He wasn't like this in the car. Sarah had sensed something as Vi herself had, only Vi had thought it, Sarah had said it out loud.

"You can't imagine how you make me feel," Tom told Vi who had turned from him to face the line of trees to her left, the trees where Tom had been recreated. "I have been coming to see you play, and I always wanted to talk to you, but I never knew how to. You were looking at me once. At first I thought you were just looking around in the crowd, but you were looking at *me*. I could tell." Tom was excited, his voice rising, a beacon in the quiet twilight.

"I noticed you, Tom. You're right. I saw you watching." Vi was deliberately trying to distance Tom by placing herself back on the stage, back at home in the light, Tom stuck three tables back on the left, never telling, only watching. She stood still in the parking lot listening to nature keep itself company and tried to bring herself to reality. "I just don't think that love is the right word for this infatuation." She was purposefully degrading Tom's confession.

Vi had stepped up to the line and stepped back again, closing the door. She was afraid of what her heart might be capable of. This was no time to test her will, to change her motivation. She needed no more baggage, didn't want a different dream. But now Tom was part of the dream she had been changing and reforming since she'd gotten into William's car. Tom would be there whether or not she wanted him to be. Vi looked back, half expecting him to be gone, but he was behind her, smiling right into her, ignoring her words, not hearing Vi pushing him away.

Vi shook her head, shook away her need. Tom could either become the one she held or the one she longed to hold. It was her choice. His stare pulled goose bumps to the surface of her pale flesh. She tried to give in to the moment, tried to make herself return to his arms, to settle this forever. She could go it alone, climb, scratch, force herself along to the top, alone yet no longer wanting to be. She turned to Tom who waited as he always did, waited for her to notice him watching her.

Tom no longer smiled, but his serene face gazed upon her, enclosing her in its protection. He loved her. He had said it out loud and would again if that alone would convince her. But it wouldn't, and Tom knew he would have to wait for Vi to accept his fate. She needed to come to terms and acknowledge her beauty, her power of presence, and her need for love. Nothing could accomplish this but time. Vi stepped away and walked across the empty lot. Without a word, she returned to the sanctuary she had found inside Phil's Breakfast and 7UP.

———

Sean stole a glance at the clock behind the counter. It read 2:10 A.M., a far cry from an early night in front of the television and then to bed, a far cry from Chicago. He was done looking over all the brands of beer; the thing that dreams were made of for a twenty-four-year-old man out on his own. He moved away from the coolers and back toward the eighty proof, back to the vodka and the gentle burning and blurry relief. He had to wake up the old clerk to purchase the pint of cheap liquor and a large fountain lemonade. The man kept his eyes open long enough to close the register before returning to his coma. Sean shook his head. He could have helped himself to anything in the store without a care, anything but Sarah. She was still in the bathroom, although the toilet had finished its gurgling five minutes earlier.

Sarah was just what the doctor ordered, small, thin, dressed just so, her skirt almost short enough to be indiscreet, her lipstick thick enough to leave hundreds of small advertisements of affection all over his body. She had money and attitude, and she had time on her hands, time that Sean would like to have helped her spend. But he decided against pursuing her any longer, knowing that after William and Tom had their way, he would surely need a doctor. And deciding against pursuing her even after William had told his story, whatever it had meant. Sean was sure that he hadn't understood it well enough to draw a conclusion. Any girl sprawled naked in front of him was deserving of his medicine, deserving of the same prescription William had administered in his own pleasure.

Sean removed the lid from the pint of vodka and inhaled a gulp. The clear liquid burned all the way to his stomach where it formed a pool of forgetfulness that would soon disperse throughout his body. He removed his flask from the inside of his jean jacket and filled it to its complete capacity, a trickle escaping from the top as he screwed the lid back in place. Sean wiped the flask on his pants just inside of his right knee and returned the shiny metal to its hiding place. He chased the shot with some lemonade, making room in the forty-four ounce container for a mixer. There was a little left in the bottle, enough for Sean to raise it in a toast. He gestured in the air in front of the sleeping clerk. "Cheers," and then it, too, was gone. Sean leaned over the counter in search of a garbage can where he dropped the empty vodka bottle. The clank startled the old man who opened his eyes in the face of the smiling Irish boy. The clerk squinted at Sean who almost laughed out loud as Sarah finally emerged from the bathroom.

"I was beginning to worry that you had drowned," Sean said as Sarah looked around at the product displays for a distraction.

"Why would you say that?" She didn't think that she had been gone too long, but Sean lived within his own idea of time and space. He couldn't have known what she had been doing in the small room. She had always deceived the nurses paid to watch her, to make sure she kept her food, and there was no way this bag of drunken hormones could have caught a professional.

"I need to use the john, too. I heard the water running a long time," Sean answered. "It made me want to pee." He smiled at Sarah's disgust.

She had a mouth on her when she wanted to, but she was hardly used to overt vulgarities. Her family's status protected her from that displeasure. Sean left his vodka-lemonade on the counter and walked by Sarah for the bathroom. She leaned over and sniffed at his drink, hardly needing to bend too close to the potent mixture in order to decipher its contents. Her eyes almost teared up as her stomach protested. Sarah stepped back and exhaled as if she had just smelled a skunk, trying to hold her breath for a few seconds afterward. She eyed the sleeping clerk, his white hair pushed out in all directions, his double chin supporting his face over his chest. What a life this must be for him, being paid minimum wage to sleep in a store each night.

Sean was back before Sarah's mind could paint too horrid a picture. "That was fast. Did you even wash your hands?"

Sean walked toward Sarah, his hands up in a cupped shape, moving closer to her chest with each step.

"I washed them. Do you have anything I could dry them on?" Sarah turned on her heels and practically ran from the store.

Sean hummed the old country tune that played from a small portable radio behind the clerk. As he shuffled by the counter impersonating a dancer, he leaned over and palmed two boxes of Marlboro Lights from the upper racks of cigarettes. He looked at the clerk who took no notice outside of his dreamland. "Yeah, Sean *Cassidy* Finnegan. What about it?" One box of cigarettes fell into Sean's open sleeve, the other he pushed into his pocket. Vi wasn't the only one with hidden talents.

———

William was leaning against the Towncar when Sarah emerged from the convenience mart. She almost stumbled off the step as she looked back into the store, loathing in her expression. William opened the passenger door, Sarah taking her turn in the front seat. "He's disgusting, William. Can't you teach him some manners?" Sarah didn't expect an answer as the door trapped her words in the car. William waited outside for Sean.

The boy needed to learn some manners, this was certain. He had one of those maddening personalities, constantly saying exactly what he thought, usually with breath strong enough to intoxicate the person next to him, getting away with all of his whims because he had an edge of charm that disarmed. He was comical. He would strike out, be offensive, piss you off, and then he'd smile, and that would have to make it okay because you didn't want to fight him either. Sean wasn't big, but one could see by his forward stance combined with his forceful personality, he was scrappy.

William wondered what it was in Sean that he recognized so well. The boy was trying to be a man, his age and independence only the first signs of growing up. He wasn't smart enough to realize that he was unhappy, struggling to be his own person and fit in at the same time. And it would be a long time before Sean recognized his discontent. He would probably go on for years, searching out a drink and a better conversation, convincing those around him that he was satisfied. There was only one way for Sean to recognize his unhappiness, and that was to live through his limbo, to get to the next stage of life when he didn't need a bottle as company, when he felt that he alone was good enough. Only then could he look back and recognize the impatience and foolish pride. The unrest was necessary though as one could never be truly happy without the sadness. One could not recognize the peace without the war, the value of life without the death, each needing the other to gain its true meaning.

William had found his peace about a decade earlier, and he was now content to work and to be his own man. For a long time, he hadn't thought about the incident in college that had kept him single. It must have been tonight and the crazy ride with these random passengers that had him thinking about the past and the present. He saw a bit of his past in Sean, the way the boy wanted Sarah, how life was a party. William had reached himself, a place for which Sean was still searching.

The boy was wasting his days, but he knew no better. It was the only way he knew to live, to get to the future when he would grow up and take stock of his life. Maybe then Sean would care to understand what William had been sharing with him in the car. But William knew he had told the story for himself, told it to get it out, off his chest. It amazed him how many times one could relive a memory, how long a mistake could haunt him. He hoped he could teach Sean his error lest the boy live through the horror himself. He hoped he could make his point before a man's cravings ruined one more girl.

"Let's go!" William yelled to Sean who was standing in front of the store sucking on his drink. Sean was looking back into the store trying to decide whether it was time to leave this place, wondering if he had enough party in him to last the entire ride home. The food was soaking up the alcohol now, and he could feel the sand in his eyes.

"Isn't there a pumpkin patch out here somewhere?" Sean asked as he took his place in the car behind Sarah.

"Somewhere." William was no longer in the mood to play along. He had come this far free of incident. He had four strangers and his lottery tickets. It was time to go home.

"Let's get some pumpkins for Halloween." Sean's drink slowly disappeared between sentences. "Look, it's the Great Pumpkin, Charlie Brown!" Sean waved his hands in the air as William drove out of the quaint, barely populated town of Pingree Grove and headed back to Phil's.

"Some other time, Sean. I think we should just pick up Vi and Tom and get back to the city."

Sean sat back and watched the rows of corn slip past the car. His head was spinning, the vodka regaining control of his body. He was happy, warm, and mellow. His medium length red hair fell onto his face, but he didn't move it away. Instead, he lifted the straw through the straight strands and sucked out his juice. He wanted to get out of the car to cause some trouble. He wanted to break into a farmhouse or sneak into a barn. Sean wanted nothing specific, just the rush, just the story he could tell the next day at work. He gave up though, gave in to William. Sean didn't tell himself that he had no choice. He knew he could do anything he wanted, and he chose to ride along.

"Vi and Tom are alone at Phil's?" Sarah had the sing-song tone of a matchmaker.

"Yeah. Sparky here," William pointed to Sean, "wanted to go pick up a beverage, and they didn't want to come with."

"Sparky?" Sean complained from the back seat. "Sounds like the name of a dog." He protested and they ignored. No one cared but Sparky.

"They didn't, did they?" Sarah was asking the questions as answers. She had put the couple together in her mind and had tried to convince Vi that there was something there, and now they were alone at the diner. It was weird to think that there were other lives going on at this moment, that there were other ways to live the same seconds. Sarah hadn't thought about her parents or friends carrying on in their days without her, but they must have. They changed over the years and became different people with time. They must have had their own problems and trials and romances. Perhaps they felt the same way Sarah did. Perhaps she was just a recreation of what they had already lived through. This must be what they meant by someone hearing a tree falling in the forest.

Sarah was not the philosopher type, and the speculation became less interesting to her when she stopped to analyze the consequences. She wanted to get back to Phil's in a hurry. She didn't want to go inside, to go near that disgusting greasy smell or Betty who would undoubtedly force-feed her again. Sarah simply wanted to look through the glass and see inside a fairy tale, to see for herself what love was like up close.

Sarah had seen security, she had seen what society expected, and the fake smiles created by the fear of what others would think, but she had never seen genuine affection. And here it was, playing out at Phil's. It was Vi's fairy tale, one that Sarah wanted a part in.

"Where are we, William?"

"We're just about five minutes southeast of the diner."

Not knowing where the diner was in the first place, Sarah was still lost.

A right turn and they were back on Route 47. Just under the bridge was the diner, and an hour after that was Chicago. In the light that guarded the four-way stop, William noticed a scar that ran across the back of his callused hand. It had been there since the day a piece of shattered porcelain shredded him like a steak knife through warm butter. Blood had streamed from the wound before William had even felt the cut. And here was this scar, his scar. It was a trait, something left of a memory that only he had.

He had made an honest living for seventeen years, and there were scars all over William's hands. Some stayed with him for a few years and faded, like he needed to remember them for a while, like he needed that moment with him as a lesson and once learned it was to be left in the past. Other scars like this one across the back of his hand had faded but not gone, giving unintended texture to his dark peach flesh. William was fond of these scars, the physically noticeable ones. They reminded him he had made use of his time, that he had contributed. But it was the mental scars, the uninvited memories; those were the ones William needed to let go.

———

Tom had followed Vi into Phil's. He was unaffected by her attempt to shut him out, to leave him in her wake as she moved on, because she wasn't moving on. She couldn't without him. And that's why she had walked away. She had no cards to outplay him with. Tom was affected by holding her in his arms, quelling her tears with his heat, soaking up her confusion with his strength. He had seen her cry. He had been both the cause and the effect of her relief and her confusion. Vi had shown Tom vulnerability, something that she hadn't even done for her parents. Her passivity when she had walked deliberately by him and into the diner was the lie, it was her cover up, and Tom knew it.

Sitting at the counter next to her, Tom couldn't control his urge to smile. He had left his lifelong cage and was born again into Vi's life. As a child would follow its mother, and as its mother could never completely turn her back, Tom and Vi were attached. He had pulled his stool close to hers, their arms and legs pressing together in the close space. She didn't look at Tom, but she hadn't pulled away this time either.

Betty returned from the kitchen at the same time another flannel clad trucker entered the diner. He was dressed neatly in new jeans and a royal blue flannel with a leather vest. He reminded Vi of Harley owners that costumed themselves in new leather to fit in with the rest of the bikers. Vi liked the idea of driving all over for a living, always going, seeing everything and being on the road. She wouldn't want to drive the same route in a city every day. She would want to be out on the open roads, seeing sunrises and sunsets, seeing stars and places she would never live. She would be a bird, moving, changing, returning to her habitat long enough to leave again. This was part of her dream, to be on a bus on the road, to keep her life in motion, to outrun it all.

This new trucker ignored the eleven other free seats and perched himself on the stool next to Ray. He stared down at the back of the old man's head and waited for him to notice. When the old man didn't wake up, the driver flicked through the ruffled, grey mane at the drunk's ears.

"Leave Ray alone now," Betty chided.

Ray peeled his eyes open, intending to dispel his wrath upon the unwelcome intruder. Instead, he smiled and greeted his friend as Betty produced a round of fresh coffee. She smiled at Tom who gleamed back.

Vi looked at Betty and then at Ray, avoiding Tom's engulfing eyes at all costs. He was winning, and Vi knew it. He didn't have to say anything, didn't have to convince her. She enjoyed holding on to him in the darkness. She liked that they had made their first contact when she was her most defenseless because that was when she was unhindered by her drive and it left her heart wide open.

He said that he loved her, and she believed it. Vi had known for weeks that there was a connection between her soul and Tom's. She ignored it, as she ignored most men beyond a dance or a kiss. But he didn't go away, and he didn't appear he ever would. Vi pushed her left thigh into Tom's, causing him to lean back into her. She didn't want to look at him. She wanted instead to sit next to him, to feel his presence on her skin, to feel his spirit within her. Vi didn't know what would happen when William returned with the others. She didn't know how quickly she would pull away from Tom, how hard she would try to escape. But she knew it was an impossibility now, here, with only his eyes to look into and his voice to hear.

"I'd like two eggs, scrambled, and some toast, please." Betty wrote her order on a ticket with Tom's, his breakfast twice as large. Betty winked at Tom who smiled wider. She had winked at Vi too, the girl trying to ignore the direct innuendo. Vi stopped pressing on Tom's leg. The words she had tried to leave in the parking lot made their way into her.

I love you, he had told her.

Years had gone by, a lifetime full of hopes crashing into that moment like a tidal wave, travelling, building, waiting for its shoreline. Vi was that shore, a rock, a cliff, receptive to the blow, pieces of her wall crushed and left to tumble along within the bubbling fury.

"You kids still here?" Ray hollered five seats away. "They've been in here talking politics all night. Think they own the place or something." The driver laughed out loud, his baritone bellowing its approval of the sarcasm in the statement. "Something funny?" Ray shouted to the large man on his left.

"Every time I come in here, Ray, you're here. Do you think that you own the place?"

"Aagh!" Ray bit back like an elderly man at the bottom of a flight of stairs.

Vi smiled at Ray. Tom smiled at Vi. He reached up and placed his palm on the back of her neck, causing shivers on her spine. His touch was cool at first, but warmed quickly with her heat. Tom stroked her milky skin a few times, leaving his hand on the side of her neck, the part reserved for the tender softness of a newborn's head. Vi didn't move away. She was excited and her heart should have been racing. It should have been in her throat, but it beat just the same. His touch comforted her, relaxed her senses.

Vi felt safe. She had always worried that love was one dream and her career another. Men came into her life and ultimately felt neglected when Vi turned down dates to work on her music. Her boyfriends would eventually leave, but that wouldn't happen with Tom. Vi could picture him sitting still for days at a time while she worked, waiting in the corner for her affections, wanting her more with each word of each song, yet having the patience to wait for his prize. She could see herself exhausted, finding fresh energy for him, and forming from that a new poem. Vi had never heard the music clearer than she did now. She had never felt such a sweet melody as the one her heart was giving her at that moment.

17
SLEEP

"I bet you never expected a night like this," Sarah told William as he pulled under a bridge and out the other side. They were back at Phil's, one step closer to ground zero.

"I've never had anyone along with me for the ride, and to tell you the truth, I don't know if I will again." Sarah smiled at William as he parked the car, this time stopping right next to the diner.

"We're not that bad."

"Not all of you are," William replied to Sarah as he pulled himself out of the car and closed the door on Sean, a caged animal.

William could see Vi and Tom through the window. They were eating breakfast, their stools pushed close together, their legs and shoulders touching. If Phil's had booths, Vi and Tom would have been a couple, sitting on the same side, the other side free for their feet or for the emptiness. But there were no tables here, no booths to cozy up in. So they sat, perched together at the counter for all others to speculate on, keeping the secret they wore plainly on their faces with each glance.

William could see why Vi had been so concerned with everyone's impression of her and her personal life. He also knew why Tom had elected to stay back at the diner, even when William could tell that Tom wanted to go on the liquor run in order to protect Sarah from Sean. But Sarah was no longer the focus of Tom's night, no longer the object of Tom's attention.

Sarah left the car, wanting to talk more to William. She had heard what kind of man he was on the way to the convenience store. Although, forcefully or not, what he had done to that girl was wrong. But he felt regret, and he was no longer the college aged boy that Sean was.

William wasn't the young men Sarah dated either, the polite fast boys with their cars and money, the ones who sucked up to her parents and then used her up in the dark. Randy hadn't been like that. He actually had honorable intentions, but he too had his own agenda, and Sarah didn't seem to fit into it.

"Hey! You just decide to walk away, to leave me out here alone?" Sean yelled after them as they entered the diner. "Who am I? The cop who gets to tag along just to tape around the dead body?" Sean was talking to himself, making a spectacle in front of the large glass, a one-way mirror that no one inside could see through. His hands flailed about when he wasn't drinking his lemonade, and he paced back and forth.

"What kind of job is that, anyway? To go to a crime scene and tape around a body? That's probably where all of our tax dollars go. But someone's got to do it. Right? I mean, there's someone for every job out there. Like there is garbage collecting and waitressing and office jobs. And there's brick-laying like you, William." Sean stopped pacing long enough to realize that he was drunk again. He was losing his spark, tiring himself out, and he didn't care that he was alone ranting to himself. He sucked on his drink until all that was left was ice, and then he threw the plastic coated cardboard as far as he could across the lot. The cup landed short of the trees, the lid popping off, the ice scattering across the concrete, imitating Sean's brain cells that were bouncing around in his head.

He looked back into the diner, saw Vi and Tom eating, saw William talking to Betty and Sarah hanging on behind the rest. Sean wondered where his place was among the others. He wandered into this thought, the one he usually drank to avoid, but in this case drank to find. He wondered where he belonged, the question every twenty-four-year-old had, the one that every thirty-year-old had fought through. Sean would have felt better if someone was around to tell him he was supposed to feel confused at this age, but no one was, and no one did.

Sean watched the others in the diner like a puzzle fitting simply together, each piece dissolving into its surroundings as if life was great and this minute mattered the most. He watched Tom who was quiet, even annoyingly so, but Sean liked him because he could hold his own. And here he was, making his moves on Vi right under everyone's noses. Vi was a bitch, a know-it-all. She could have a conversation, unlike most of the girls Sean liked to hang with. *Shut up and look pretty. Shut up and open your mouth.* Vi could open her mouth all right, and all of her words bit down hard on Sean's ego.

She was too intellectual for Sean's tastes. Tom was in for a ride.

William was cool. Sean thought that if he was thirty-seven and had some cash, he would go out and get a different chic every night. He would live it up. *Lay chics all night, lay bricks all day.* Sean laughed out loud at that. What was it William was saying in the car on the way to the liquor store? Don't get caught, that must have been it. It was that girl's fault for being drunk, for being naked in bed and smiling, and it was William's problem for feeling guilty about it. Sean had spent some tall stacks of cash in the past trying to get drunk girls into his bed, and he would continue to do just that for as long as there were bars and beer.

At that, Sean noticed Sarah again. Her image spun around in his drunken head until he closed his eyes tight and reopened them. Through the window and in the overhead neon light, Sean took a good look. Her skirt was short enough to arouse, yet long enough while she was standing to remain respectable. She had little chicken legs, and tiny, tight calve muscles pronounced because of her heels. Sean wondered if there was enough muscle on her to hold her body up. He hadn't noticed before how tiny her frame was. Sean worshiped what society told him to, and that included the little boy frame of a bony model, the nothingness about her flat stomach and butt, the unreal fullness of the silicone that hung from her chest. Sean couldn't see Sarah's chest. Her blouse was all baggy and wrinkled after her sleeping in the car. Still she looked sexy, put together well enough for Sean to take apart.

He leaned toward the window and pressed his face onto it, licking the glass. Betty saw him and threw a wet towel over the others at his face. She yelled something, Sean laughing and licking a little more before moving away and stumbling around the Towncar into the shadows. He didn't know why he was here with these others, out here at Phil's ridiculous Breakfast and 7UP. Maybe he just needed his time spent for him. It was better out anywhere with anyone, away from his apartment and his life, away from Baker's Tap and another one night stand.

Sean could taste the vodka in his mouth, the ever-present medicine. He thanked God for it, for the way it made him social enough to forget how helpless he felt, how alone he was, and how accepted he longed to be. The vodka jiggled his thoughts and he dragged his feet along the ground, skating around on the gravel.

"He's crazy," Vi commented as she returned her attention to her breakfast plate.

"He's lost," Sarah added.

"He's drunk," Betty accused as she stared into William. Sean had stumbled away from the window and back out into the night where he was again invisible from inside the diner.

"What?" William exclaimed. Betty seemed to loom over the counter at William, scolding him as a mother does her child. "It's my fault that he's drunk? He's been drunk since he got into my car at Baker's Tap!" William's shoulders pulled back and his hands folded up to prove his innocence. It couldn't have been his fault that Sean was out of control. The boy had followed Sarah into the car, and he wasn't William's responsibility.

"You didn't have to take him to a liquor store."

"You told him where it was!" William shouted defensively.

"Well, I didn't think you'd actually drive him there. The food was working it out of his system. I don't mind his company when he's not out of control." Betty poured coffees again. She seemed to do this without even realizing the effort, over and over, night after night, and customer after customer.

William added a packet and a half of sugar to his cup and avoided Betty's stare. He liked her looks; he liked her company, and he went there Tuesday after Tuesday, collecting his lottery tickets and wishing that she wasn't happily married so he could have his chance. But it was moments like this that she would haunt his conscience, and William knew it would never work, and they were better off as acquaintances, as friends. She could control his emotion. She had the power to make him feel like a man and then a minute later like he was three years old.

"William has little to do with it," Tom said as everyone leaned in closer and gave him their attention. "Sean has been drinking vodka since we left the bar tonight. Staying drunk is his goal. It was inevitable that he would find a way." Tom sipped his coffee and chewed his strawberry toast. He was right. Sean was going to stay intoxicated no matter what. It was his solution to a good time, his solution to the energy brought about through confusion. And hadn't they seen Sean mix himself a screwdriver right here in Phil's at the counter after breakfast? Maybe they had, or maybe they had been too busy worrying about their own conscience, worrying about their own motives.

"Why would he want to stay drunk? He's easier to put up with when he's not." It was Sarah. They'd almost forgotten about her standing behind William and Vi, away from the counter, away from the food. Sarah could feel their thoughts on her even when their eyes weren't. She wanted to contribute to the discussion, to keep the attention on Sean and his deficiencies. She wanted to remain hidden even in the bright fluorescence of the diner. But she wasn't hidden, not in front of the giant mirror that reflected in the front window. They were eating now in silence, and Ray's laughter from the truck driver's comments reverberated in the small space.

They all looked away from her. They all wanted her to eat. It was obvious, everyone facing the counter, hovering over their plates of greasy slop, William sucking down his sugar and coffee. They were watching her, willing her to the food. Betty had served her a banana and some tea, and now she had served a cup of coffee that Sarah hadn't asked for and didn't want. And it disgusted her, all the fat and calories at three in the morning. She couldn't remember why she had thought of change, although she wished the feeling back for one moment when she wanted to fit in. All she had to do was ignore the coffee, live through the smell of the burnt grease, and then get home.

Sarah hated her life at home, but it was safe for her there. Her parents didn't care about anything, save a long look in the mirror. No one watched her eat, no one kept track of what she wanted, no one pressured her or made her feel guilt for her self-control, which was the one thing she had counted on for the past ten years. Sarah had no control of the people around her, no control of the men or her parents or her life, but she could control what she ate, what she looked like to the world. She felt fat in this place. She felt trapped. But inside with the food was better than outside with Sean. She could control her want for the food. She had stopped it a long time ago, but she couldn't control a drunk, horny, twenty-four-year-old Irish boy. So she stood and waited, hidden behind William and Vi, looking away from Betty and the trucker.

"Maybe it's his parents," Vi concluded.

"You don't get along with your parents?" Sarah asked.

"Of course I do." Vi crumpled her paper napkin and dropped it onto her unfinished plate of food. The runny eggs had swirled into the ketchup that Vi had poured over her hashed browns, and it was now soaking into the grainy white napkin. It looked like the artwork of a young child.

"There was a time when I didn't get along with my parents, you know the whole adolescent thing, but going away for college cured me of that. I love my parents and my sister. I guess I don't really understand the bad parent-child relationship after twenty-one."

"I hear ya, Vi. I think I was the same way. My dad got me a job laying bricks when I got out of high school. I didn't want it, of course. I didn't want his help, but I took the job and I busted my butt for the next four summers." William ate the half piece of toast that Tom offered.

"Then what?" Vi asked.

"I don't know. We became friends, I guess. I mean, one day I was trying to get out from under his shadow, and the next day I looked at him as a friend more than an enemy. I guess I realized he wasn't trying to manage my life. He had just been making suggestions, and I could take it or leave it. He didn't change, I did."

"How?" It was Sarah, standing, listening in the background. She thought for a minute that her parents might be perfect after all, and that she just couldn't find her way into their lives.

"I don't know," William was honest. "I just stepped back and took a good look at myself, I guess. I didn't have to prove anything anymore. I worked with him until he retired." William threw a couple of dollars on the counter for Betty and made his way around Ray and to the bathroom. "Finish up, you guys. I want to get going."

Sarah thought hard about what William had said. He was older and wiser and he loved his family, a sentiment Sarah was used to trying to prove rather than to feel. She had changed her view since moving back from college, but the need for acceptance had pushed her further into the woodwork, further into her mother's obscure view of the world. She was a child lured into the realm of perfection and then abandoned.

"What's the damage, Betty?" Vi called back to the kitchen. She had looked over at Tom for the first time since they had sat down together. He finished eating, and he was squinting, looking into a past that only he could see. Vi mirrored his expression and tried to find his thoughts, and although she could feel his mood shift, she could not begin to understand what ruled him.

Vi took her family for granted because she could. She had that opportunity. She supported them as they supported her. They were closely knit, but Vi could still understand someone who didn't have this. Her folk songs played out the depression and wrongdoings, the loves and the tragedies. It was she who had written the words, had made up the stories. Sometimes she forgot these stories weren't fiction for some people. They were part of their real lives, part of their memories, part of their pain.

Vi studied Tom again, but he was still there, stuck within himself. And then he lightened up, looked into Vi before she had a chance to look away. She didn't want to look away. She wanted to know what haunted him, but there would be time later to hear and to know and to reassure. Vi leaned into Tom who pushed back at her show of affection as Betty dropped the check and cleared the plates. William returned from the back and stopped at the counter to wish Betty a formal goodbye.

"I'd better go collect Sean before he breathes on the propane tanks and wipes this place off the map."

"It's not on the map," Ray yelled, not caring that William's comment were directed at Betty. The trucker laughed on cue as he had laughed at everything Ray said.

"You bring that boy back here, William. He's good company."

"What about me?" William asked, surprised.

"He smiles more than you, William. You need to work on that smile of yours." Betty winked and William blushed, trying to hold back the grin her words had pulled from him.

"See you next week?' William asked, already knowing the answer.

"Not if I win the jackpot tomorrow," Betty answered with a smile as she patted on the pocket of her apron where she had stowed her lottery tickets.

"Right," William answered. He had been waiting for the

same thing for a long time, the pattern of his weeks calling him back to the diner like a sinner to confession.

He huffed as he walked out of Phil's. The circling thought that he spent his time and money on the lottery each week and never really thought that he would win, drew up in him a hysterical laughter. Maybe it wasn't about the winning or the money, maybe it was about the time that he had left and how he intended to spend it.

———

The counter was clean and shiny, Betty's tip left folded underneath the saltshaker. Tom had taken his thoughts to the washroom leaving Vi and Sarah out front. Vi watched Sarah try on some sunglasses in the corner, her tiny fingers pulling the glasses from their beds and onto her face, Sarah modeling the plastic pieces in the window.

Vi was thinking about her plans to move to Nashville and her plans to record her music. Men she had dated had their own ambitions, but with Tom, she was his ambition, and he would follow her. That was wrong, Vi thought. He would go with her, next to her, he would share her dreams. He would take nothing away from Vi. He was adding another half, the piece that she had ignored for so long.

The end of this magical night was upon them. The ride home was all that separated these five new acquaintances from again becoming strangers. Vi anticipated the drive, her leg touching Tom's in the car, the sparks lighting up the pitch darkness of the countryside like the sun, blinding anyone strong enough to open their eyes. She flushed, remembering Tom's lips on hers, wanting him to pull her in and protect her like a child. Vi was a different person now. It was as though Tom gave her a chance at the present and the strength to look around and smell the flowers instead of forgetting that they were there. It was so simple. The somebody she longed to be was more accessible than ever. She was someone at the impending daybreak. She was Tom's.

Yet love seemed ridiculous to Vi. Six hours and it had turned her life around because of three words and a kiss? She was on a stool at Baker's Tap, seated on stage away from and above everyone else. She was judging the locals, judging Sarah and her boyfriend and all the other lovers. She was singing about relationships, heartaches, and life. But she was cynical, beaten in matters of the heart. They shut her into herself, having agreed that she would be single forever. And now she was a fool following her desire, taking the same chance she had sneered at others for taking. She was a different person in this place, on this night. It was as if she was on a vacation where no one knew her, somewhere she could be anyone she wanted to be because no one had any expectations of her, and in turn, she had none of herself. It was the same vacation that she had prompted Sarah to take. Vi held Tom's hand, closed her eyes, and jumped. And now she was tingling with expectation and her heart was free.

Tom returned from the back, followed by Betty. She was saying something to him behind the Pepsi cooler, something low and reassuring. He smiled brilliantly and then his face returned to its expressionless hideaway before Betty finished her thought. Tom looked at Vi and then walked toward the door where Sarah blocked him, her arms held out-stretched, her hair finishing its trip around after her model like spin.

Vi wanted to leap from her stool, to tangle her fingers

within his and move out into the moonlight. But she wouldn't because she didn't want to answer Sarah's questions, knowing that they would cause her to reevaluate the whole situation, giving her time to pull back in retreat. Now was no time to analyze, it was time to feel. Tom stood still and waited for Vi who tipped her head sideways. She would meet him outside.

"So," Sarah suggested as the door shut Tom outside. She didn't need to finish her thought. She sauntered over to the stool next to Vi's. Sarah's black skirt polished the burgundy leather seat cover as she slid on top, one leg mechanically crossed perfectly over the other. Sarah waited for Vi to see the 'I told you so' that was on her face. It was difficult for Sarah to be positive about anything. She was reaching for sincerity. In the bathroom of a convenience store, optimism had reared its head and then retreated.

Initially, Sarah had judged Vi, as she had learned to judge the lower classes. Later, out by the picnic table, she found humility, but she had lost her new forgiving quality as fast as she had learned it. Sarah might have lost Randy in Baker's Tap, but she knew that there were more men, better men, men who would give her what she wanted. She didn't have to be alone or to fix what wasn't broken. Sarah had been living this way successfully since adolescence.

Tonight, Sean wanted her, even after she had gorged herself with the banana. For a moment, Sarah understood the realness in life that Randy had been reaching for by going to the small bar and sitting among the small people. He had the understanding that Sarah lacked, and he had left her to take the trip on her own.

Tom might have wanted Vi, but Sarah knew that most

men would want Sarah. Her beauty developed from her own strength in discipline. No matter. Love was blind, and it was deaf and mute as well. Deaf as no spoken words could defeat it, mute as partners held back anything self-defeating. Sarah didn't need this lie, this magic trick that wore out its wonder as time discovered its secrets. It was like the inane drive they had taken. The tiresome feel of change in the air was choking her.

"You should take advantage, Sarah," Vi told Sarah.

Sarah questioned Vi with her eyes, not having any idea where the songwriter, the spinner of words, was leading.

"There's something to be said about the way strangers allow you room to change. No one is going to do it for you, and I think that tonight was a good start." Vi looked back toward the cigarette machine, toward the place Sarah had been sitting when she had eaten her midnight snack. Vi's smile was genuine and held in it the pride that Sarah should have been feeling. The pride she might have felt if she hadn't forced herself to throw up again.

18
RIPTIDE

William and Tom stood over Sean, the boy sound asleep on the picnic table, sprawled as if he had gotten stuck in the snow making an angel. William shook his head thinking that Tom would understand the smile on his face, not knowing that Tom would never understand this insane drunkenness or the need to party. William thought he might bring Sean back to Phil's, as Betty had suggested. Maybe William could be a good influence for Sean, make him realize that there's more to life.

William noticed for the first time how piercing Tom's eyes could be. Even in the semi-darkness of the parking lot, the green gems sparkled. Tom was concentrating on Sean's corpse-like figure, looking into the mess of the young man before him. William couldn't decide on the expression. Eyebrows pulled down low, forehead and jaw set in a scowl. He regarded it as a trance, Tom's mind taking him into a memory, maybe one as painful as William's own memory from years ago in the frat house. It amazed William that time could pass between memories, yet they remained present and vivid, hidden in the dark crevices of the human brain.

Of course Tom could relate to Sean's drunken state, and he could have related to William too, but not as William was thinking, that all boys had drunken themselves into becoming men. On the picnic table, spilled out and vulnerable, laid his father. Tom stood over-head, wanting to find something heavy for smashing. He needed a weapon within reach so he wouldn't walk away and lose his nerve, something that wouldn't break apart on impact, so that the old man wouldn't wake up and retaliate, so that the old man wouldn't wake up, ever. Tom stood there as a child, watching over his father in judgment, each time trying to work up the nerve to execute the same punishment he had received. Trying to find the forgiveness he had begged for when he was curled up and beaten and slumped into the floor.

The crashing of his will into his father's skull, the blood that would spray the surrounding furniture, covering the orange juice and vodka that his mother had failed to wipe away, these violent nightmares never bothered Tom. The aftermath would be filled with tears of rage and pleasure, the same warm pleasure that burned his father's belly, the clear poison eating into his humanity. Tom had contemplated the sticky redness that would cover his hands if he'd ever had the nerve to commit himself to his morbid fantasies. But he never did, never could. The body, the drunken lump that had pulverized Tom's hopes of a normal and loving childhood, it encased his father, the man that Tom was forced to acknowledge, and through hatred, was forced to love.

Tom stood across from William and leaned toward the table, leaned down to get a good look at the face that had laughed at a frightened and tortured boy. But it was Sean, his red hair haphazardly lining his features. Then Tom's father was gone as he had been for two years, his liver eaten away, his life's pleasure finally delivering him out of Tom's hell and into his own fiery eternity.

William was watching Tom, wondering what was going on in his head to invoke the demons on his face, and the eerie tingle in his spine told him he didn't want to know. William poked Sean hard in the stomach, and the boy shot up as if he had never passed out.

"You creatures ready to go?" he asked, pulling his long straight bangs over his head. Vi and Sarah were already sitting in the Towncar, Sarah taking the passenger seat, Vi waiting silently for Tom. Sean hopped off of the picnic table and followed Tom and William to the car. He tossed Vi the pack of smokes he had gotten for her, her expression of gratitude missing its mark because he forgot what he had wanted to prove to her when he stole them.

Tom sat behind William and the engine revved to life. They pulled out of the gravel lot to the flashing red light, leaving it behind for the acres of corn that lined the road. Sean was asleep before they were back to the stretch of road where he had relieved his bladder hours earlier.

Sarah turned around several times to inflict her judgment upon Vi and Tom. They were sitting quietly yet attentively, as if they were having a conversation of their own, no words passing between them. Sarah relaxed her arms and for the first time realized how she had been holding herself in a position of stress. She was folded up, her natural reaction to the chill she had felt through her blouse even though William had the heat on. Sarah fluffed her blouse a bit, tried to make herself feel pressed and proper, but time had left her wrinkled. She could feel her ribs beneath her blouse. She could see them in the mirror of her mind, the skin pulled away from the bone by her layers of fat. Sarah felt little pleasure when she remembered how fat she used to be, when she would wake up from a daydream and find herself bingeing. At least now she didn't do that, didn't eat as much and didn't have to throw up as much.

She breathed in and felt her torso expand, exhaling quickly at the sight in her mind. She couldn't stop the air like she could the food. Her body's natural reaction to choking was to breathe at all costs. Sarah had done this in front of the mirror, her size zero underwear hanging from her hips. She had exhaled and kept the air from entering, her frame pulled together tightly underneath the gray tinted skin. She stood there looking, judging herself for as long as she could before passing out. Losing consciousness was her body's weapon against her mind in its fight for oxygen.

Sarah turned again to Vi and Tom, two pairs of eyes peering back in the darkness. What did Vi know about Sarah's life? Vi didn't have to be pretty or perfect. Vi didn't have to show her mother how good she could be. She didn't have to show her mother how many people wanted her. Vi took advantage of this night. She took advantage of Tom's affections and the opportunity to change something that she wanted to, but Sarah didn't need four outsiders to tell her who to be. She was twenty-two and had spent her whole life becoming this person. No one was going to convince her in one night that she had been wrong about herself this whole time.

Sarah's stomach sank as her mind turned to her mother

and all the things that she expected. All this time, Sarah thought she had been retaliating. The men and trivial escapades, Sarah thought they were the tools she could use to get back at her mother. She now wondered why she wanted to. In all of her distancing herself, she had become that which she thought she had abhorred. The sitting up straight, the perfect make-up and clothes from the perfect money, made by the perfect man who had abandoned them for his work in order to take care of their needs. Sarah could see that he worked relentlessly for his own success.

The classes in manners and a college education, these had become items on Sarah's resume, the one presented to the gentlemen callers. In running away this night, in taking this side trip, Sarah had turned right into her mother's trap. But it wasn't that. If Sarah wanted to be like Vi and the other women she saw at Baker's Tap, if she wanted to be ordinary, if she wanted to change her ideals and her own expectations, she would have been with Randy now. She would have understood him instead of mocking him and sending him away.

No matter how Sarah tried, she could not understand how anyone else's life was more real than hers. So they were different. That's why they were each special, and that's why she was right about any decision she made for herself. Sarah didn't need to change, as Vi had suggested. She didn't need to break down and cry like she did at the picnic table when they first arrived at Phil's.

Sarah's head was pounding. She wrote her tears off as confusion and tried to sway her thoughts from herself. She wondered who Phil was, and why he had thought to put that stupid little diner, that vacuum for lost souls, out there in the Middle of Nowhere, Illinois.

———

William's eyes fought his brain each third mile. He would catch his eyelids giving in to gravity, then his mind racing awake, the car over the double yellow lines sometimes, and riding over the white at others. It was an exhausting night, and William was ready to crawl into bed long enough to wake up and call in sick. He couldn't bounce back like Sean would. He had fourteen years on the boy, and even his strong worker's frame was losing its battle with time.

"William," Vi tapped him on the shoulder. "Pull over and let me drive."

"I'm fine." He sighed heavily and tried to smile in the rearview, but Vi wasn't convinced.

"Come on, William. I feel like I'm on a boat here the way you're drifting all over the road. I won't smash your car, I promise." William drove on for two more miles before pulling over. He didn't like anyone else driving his prized possession, his expensive luxury, but it was that or the chance that he would crash it himself.

"Okay, Vi, fire drill." As the car stopped, Tom, Vi, and William got out of the car. Sarah was confused, but smart enough to follow suit. They made their ways in different doors, William taking his place in the center of the back seat next to Sean, Sarah pulling the door closed behind Vi.

"Don't crash," Sarah told Vi.

"Is that like break a leg?" Vi asked as the Towncar jumped back onto the two-lane road. Twenty minutes later they were near Spring Hill Mall and Santa's Village, Sarah and William both asleep next to Sean.

Vi enjoyed driving. She always loved the open road. It made her think of moving to Nashville, and how she longed to live on her own tour bus. She would drive from town to town, talking to strangers, finding herself amid the controlled chaos of life. Vi was never more herself than she was in this moment. On the road next to Tom, dreaming her dream, feeling warmth on her face as if the sun was shining down on her through the blackness of the countryside. She sighed and felt her soul smiling, hoping that this feeling could last after she saw Chicago again, after she returned to her days of paying her dues. Tom placed his hand on Vi's neck, and she could feel his electricity flowing down her neck, across her breasts, into her heart. It was a pure touch, this physical contact in a world of contamination and mistrust. His touch, which made Vi believe she could accomplish anything she decided to.

Vi thought how long it had been since a man had his hand there, caressing her sore muscles, seducing her with his fingertips. It had been ages since she had felt anything but the want to be left alone, left to her own goals. That seemed sad to her sister, and sometimes it seemed selfish to Vi, but she didn't want to count on anyone to get her through. She didn't want to let anyone into her castle, to trust anyone to stand on her wall like a sentry protecting her from the world. Tom's touch was different. It was protecting her and it was melting her heart. Tom wasn't destroying anything inside of Vi. He was merely in search of the other half of his love.

Vi was squinting at the road now, her thoughts deceiving her, playing out on her face. Tom caressed that tender part of her between her brain and her heart, her synapse sending messages between the two organs, the battle playing out. He knew that she would never turn away from him. Yesterday, Tom had been waiting for his death, the same activity he had been practicing since his childhood. It hadn't come for him. It hadn't taken him as Vi had. Tom didn't want to come between Vi and her music. He didn't want to slow her down. This was his chance to contribute to the life that she had breathed into him.

"We can go, Vi." His fingertips rolled around in her brown curls. "We can go to Tennessee." Vi's eyes left the road for a look into Tom's face. He had the stern look of a father, the loving stare of a mother, the unspoken knowing of a sibling.

"William might get a little pissed if he wakes up in his car eight hours from his house," she answered sarcastically, her weightlessness rolling out of the car as quickly as it had come. "I'm going, Tom. When it's time and I have the money, I'm going." She had wanted to say we're going. She had wanted to take his soul for her own, as she believed he was giving it.

"I have the money, Vi, so you tell me when it's time." Vi wanted to lose herself in Tom's eyes, but she needed to drive them home and question his intentions later. Tom knew that she would have her questions, and he knew that he would have to let her in and show her his scars. He would take his time and show her one day of his past life with each day of their future. She would wonder about the money, how he had saved thirty thousand dollars when, in fact, he had saved one tenth of that on his own.

Tom wondered if he would tell her it was from his

father's life insurance policy, his mother giving a share of it to him and his brother. To Tom, it had always been blood money. He thought he had willed the old man dead, that his thoughts alone had killed the old bastard. On the day of his father's funeral, Tom's mother had cried, actually shedding pieces of her heart for the man who had continuously beaten her and her children. Tom wondered about the man he would never get to know, the one underneath the layers of liquor and obscenities, the man his mother had loved and pardoned all those years. Tom could see it in his brother's wife, the way the light in her eyes was already dimming, her heart hanging on to the man she had met, the fire of her life slowly expiring. That was his own mother, and he felt shame for wanting dead the thing that had breathed her life in and choked her at the same time.

Tom never wanted the money. He could feel the evil clinging to it, tainting it. His mother insisted that he put it in the bank for a few years, and if he hadn't changed his mind, he could give it away, do with it whatever he pleased.

When she said, "Your father would have wanted you to have it," Tom almost laughed in her face. As if his father would have wanted anything for Tom in his life. And now it was his, and he wanted it. Tom wouldn't forget where it came from, his use for it becoming that much more impor- tant. He would use the money to start a new life wherever Vi wanted. He would use the money to save his soul. Vi was cleaning the money, she was laundering it, her soft voice willing the blood out of the green and white paper. She was recreating Tom as she had when she left her tears on his shirt in the parking lot at Phil's, as she had when she whispered to him in the darkness of the trees.

———

Forty minutes and they were back on the north side of Chicago, Sarah awake and telling Vi where to turn. They entered the town of Lake Forest, one of Chicago's wealthiest suburbs, which sat between Interstate 94 and Lake Michigan. The gated streets and long driveways announced to passersby that they could hardly afford to breathe in the rich air. Sarah's house was the fourth on the extended block, a strip of pavement that ran two times that of a city block. The gates within the gates were open, and Vi pulled up to the front circle. She put the car in park, and William and Sean opened their eyes as Sarah said her quick goodbyes. Eight ears heard her words, eight eyes stared in amazement at the monstrous white structure before them. No one noticed Randy getting out of his car that was parked in the driveway.

"Are we at the White House?" Sean burst.

Sarah was not willing to defend her family's wealth, but Vi couldn't help herself. "Yes, Sean, we are. She'd let you go in, but you know how the Secret Service can be."

Then Vi noticed Randy approaching, the sharp lights from the Towncar casting deep shadows across his face. Sean looked to pounce so Vi used the electronic locks for safety. But Sarah shook her head and opened her door, reassuring the new strangers that she would be okay. She closed the door and waved, and Vi and Tom waved back as Vi pulled around to exit.

Sarah was glad to see Randy. He was a bit of sanity at the end of an insane ride. She should have been angry with him. She should have slapped him and then stormed away to teach him a lesson. Maybe if it had been last night she would have, but it was a new day and she was different. Not different enough to accept change within herself, but something had changed. Sarah intended to stay beautiful, intended to control her food intake, intended to be the spoiled little rich girl her mother had trained her to be. She would remember this brief road trip, but she would not accept the change the night had offered.

The change in her was that she understood Randy better. He offered her something new, a bit of hope, perhaps the one thing she needed to begin her true journey. Sarah looked at Randy, and reflected on the passengers in the Towncar who were driving away, the red of the taillights to follow wherever they decided to go. She could see Vi's cynical mind in Randy as he tried to break free of his heritage, Sean's outrage and Tom's peace, and William's manners. Randy, the constant gentleman as he apologized to her, begged her for another chance. Randy, who had gone back to Baker's Tap and was frantic when she wasn't there. Randy, who covered her frame with his jacket just so she could reach her front door in warmth. Randy, who gently kissed Sarah goodnight at her door and closed the giant glass frame behind her. He would see Sarah again. They wouldn't start over, but this time, Sarah would give him a fighting chance.

———

The parking lot was empty, bits of trash still blowing along the two-story buildings and out onto Halsted Street. The apartment windows over the stores were dark. Nighttime workers scattered throughout Chicago waited for the clock to signal the end of another shift, and the rest of Chicago dreamt fantasies until the buzzer drew them back to the hustle and bustle. William took the keys from Vi as Tom removed her guitar from the trunk. Sean was at the wooden door of Baker's Tap, pounding away with both hands, begging someone to let him in. It was his last attempt at laughter, as he didn't want a drink. He didn't need one because he still had his flask tucked next to a pack of cigarettes in his pocket.

William stepped next to Sean and folded the note he had written to Ton. He folded the bartender's share of lottery tickets inside, hoping for their numbers to be the ones, to be the keys to the jackpot. William placed the paper under the door and tapped it with his hand, forcing it into the foyer of the bar. He tried to ignore Sean who complained that he didn't get to buy a lottery ticket. William offered to drive Sean to get tickets and then home, but Sean insisted he get his tickets from Betty like William had. William told Sean to be at Baker's next Tuesday, sober, if he wanted to go back out to Phil's. He hoped Betty was right, that the boy just needed a little influence in his life to make it into manhood. William wondered about the influences in his own life, his father and mother, his friends, his brother and three sisters. He thought that there might be hope for Sean after all, not intimating the life that Sean could make for himself, if he was done hiding from truth.

William walked to the car and offered a ride to Vi and Tom. Vi lived a few blocks down and would walk. Tom lived somewhere else but would walk with Vi. William didn't need to ask. He was human and he could see that they were at the start of something new. It was a new beginning, something that had to do with the same magic William felt about Phil's Breakfast and 7UP.

William noticed a green tint on his blue Towncar in the orange glow of the street lamps. He was used to riding in the large four-door vehicle alone. He spent time in his car, hours looking ahead and looking back. He knew his car, each inch of its shiny powder blue enamel coating, each crease of its leather interior. After tonight, it would never be the same. He knew this place so well, this car and the road its tires rubbed against. But as he sat inside alone, it had already become foreign to him. It was like returning to a place he lived in for years. The familiarity was ruined by time. He could see the same yet different streets, familiar yet unfamiliar landmarks, the home that was now someone else's home. William looked back and realized that not a minute of his time spent in this car before really mattered. The ride on this Tuesday night was different. He hoped he would see Vi and Tom again and that the camaraderie of their shared experience had bound them as friends.

The passenger door opened, startling William from his thoughts. Sean sat on the leather seat and then slid down so that he was properly slouching. The boy pulled on his cigarette, the cherry lighting his crooked nose as the sun did the moon. He threw the butt on the ground before closing the door, his exhaled smoke floating like a fog in the clean interior.

"Sean," William whined.

"Lighten up, old man. You stay like this and we're going to have to put you in a biosphere. Better yet, we'll cryogenically freeze you, and then you can wake up when the world is perfect. You'd better take some good reading and a nice blanket with you, though, because I don't see perfect in the future of this planet."

"We'll see." William pulled out of the lot, following Sean's direction. Six hours and the Irish boy hadn't changed, hadn't budged. He must have had his ears plugged and his eyes closed the entire night to not have been the least bit affected. Maybe the trip out to Phil's next week would do it.

———

The few trees on the block didn't rustle like the ones near the cornfields had. These trees were leafless, seemingly lifeless but for the wind which swayed their brittle sticks. Vi could see her breath falling out in front of her, announcing her life, but it didn't feel cold to Vi. She thought perhaps she was too tired to think, too lost to worry. She didn't want to discuss Tom's intentions as she had in the car. His motives didn't matter anymore. Motives would have suggested dissecting the night and speculating about the future. Although it would take some time, she wasn't afraid to give this man her heart. Vi knew that Tom held his own secrets, ones he would tell her over time, perhaps here or perhaps in Nashville.

Tom was carrying her guitar as they walked, keeping her pace. The moon was gone, but he could feel its gravity pulling at his blood. He knew its light was guiding him through this night, blind and still seeing, still feeling. The guitar case swung next to Tom, and he liked it rubbing against his leg as he walked. It was *her* guitar case; it held *her* guitar; it held *her* words and melodies. Tom wanted to tell Vi again that he loved her. He wanted to reassure her he had the time and the means to help her dreams come true. The sound of their soles mingling on the ground seemed to be enough to reinforce the fact that they were together and their destination was the same. The night had given Tom more than he would have dared ask for, yet there was one more thing that he wanted, one more thing he needed to know.

"Vi?" She didn't look at him, but he saw her smile brilliantly. He dared continue before his heart melted his insides beneath the power of her affection. "I don't know your name."

"It's Vi." She was teasing him, her eyebrows pulled up toward the angels, her smile pulled sideways to the devil. Tom nodded and waited for her to tell him what the 'Vi' really meant. They walked less than two more steps when Vi stopped to answer, her forwardness convincing Tom this would be the truth.

"I don't like to tell people. It's kind of corny." Vi looked at Tom and continued, her brown eyes piercing his green, pulling him in. "It doesn't really stand for anything. My parents were hippies, and the 'V' is for the peace sign." She held up her right hand, her thumb holding back her ring and pinky fingers, her forefinger and middle finger extended out as the symbol for peace. She showed her hand to Tom, then to herself.

Tom was looking down at the pavement now. He had believed her for a moment. He would have believed anything she might have said, any explanation she might have given. And then he had to ask. He had to challenge her. Tom knew these were the moments that kept Vi going. These were the moments that made her life wonderfully fun. "Really?"

Vi gave a half smile and laughed as she slipped her arm around Tom's waist and stepped into her future.

ALSO BY ANITA RENAGHAN

Silent Hearts

A grief-stricken mom. Two lost souls. A chance for all three to heal.

New York City. Liz Campbell is drowning in sorrow. Unable to find closure following the death of her son and pressured to start "living again" by her mother, the heartsick woman gets into her car and drives as far as it will take her. But when she runs out of gas while penniless in a tiny Illinois town, her only choice is to accept the kindness of two strangers.

Finding a job at the general store, Liz befriends the men who aided her—a haunted bachelor who won't keep time and a former soldier drunk on booze and survivor's guilt. And though she discovers their company soothes the ache in her soul, learning they also suffer from debilitating loss leaves her desiring to help them in return.

As Liz constructs a life worth living, can she bring peace to those who bear their own burdens?

With grace and empathy, Anita Renaghan weaves a tender story of three people lost in inexorable darkness climbing back to the light together. In a novel of unimaginable emotional pain and inspirational inner strength, she reminds us all of the need for true sympathy and the power of the human will.

Silent Hearts is a moving contemporary women's literature book. If you like rebuilding after adversity, personal growth, and sweet romance, then you'll love Anita Renaghan's touching tale.

Buy *Silent Hearts* to greet a new dawn today!

Ruby Island

Amy has been crushing on Matt for two years. When the impossible happens, will Matt finally notice Amy, or will he lose her to Bill Ruby forever?

Ruby Island is a sweet romantic comedy with a touch of the impossible.

The Suicide Man

A Chicago lawyer with a sad history is on the brink of suicide. Can Hazel save him from himself?

ABOUT THE AUTHOR

Anita Renaghan is the author of six books including literary fiction and a young adult trilogy. She loves a good character study and has been many characters herself including: an aircraft mechanic in the Air Force, a college graduate, a second degree blackbelt, lost, a waitress and bartender, a wife and mother, an account executive, found, and a constantly inventive singer-songwriter. Walter Mitty has nothing on Anita.

Growing up in the Chicago suburbs with her five siblings was a loud and adventurous time, and Anita was often found at the library reading her new favorite author or writing a poem or short story. Her high school English teacher presented the challenge of writing a novel, and that opened a door that would never close. Anita has written many novels in the past thirty years and she loves a good character study.

Anita can often be found zoning-out in a daydream in the Chicago suburbs where she lives with her husband and daughter. In the dark hours of the night, while her family sleeps, she is often perched in front of her laptop writing her next adventure.

Please go to www.anitarenaghan.com where you can find more titles and join the email list to receive a free ebook.

www.ingramcontent.com/pod-product-compliance
Lightning Source LLC
Chambersburg PA
CBHW070118120726
47909CB00002B/642